THE THUNDER HEAD

A NICK DRAKE NOVEL

DWIGHT HOLING

The Thunder Head
A Nick Drake Novel

Print Edition
Copyright 2025 by Dwight Holing

Published by Jackdaw Press
All Rights Reserved

ISBN: 979-8-9866978-8-8

For More Information, please visit dwightholing.com.

See how you can **Get a Free Book** at the end of this novel.

For Mary & Jaime

Pudge Warbler was the only patient in the hospital wearing a .45 on his hip and a gold star on his chest while chemo trickled through an IV needle stuck in his arm. The nurses had no more luck convincing the sheriff to unbuckle his holster than getting him to kick off his boots and doff his short-brim Stetson for the three hours he was on the drip.

For the past year, his daughter Gemma and I had been taking turns driving him to Bend for his monthly treatments. The flinty old lawman protested at first, grousing he could handle the two-hour trip from No Mountain on his own, but finally conceded the return was proving to be a bridge too far. Our vehicles were now equipped like planes with airsick bags.

I took him this time even though I'd done it the previous month. It was the waning days of fall and my wife and her veterinarian assistant, Nagah Will, had their hands full tending to livestock on Harney County's far-flung ranches. It wouldn't be long before Oregon's High Lonesome was covered in a thick white blanket that would make their work even more dangerous.

Storms had blown in a couple of times already. The windrows of plowed snow on the hospital's parking lot made me think of a skeleton when I returned to pick up Pudge after buying a camera with a telephoto lens that I needed for my job as a US Fish and Wildlife ranger.

A nurse who wore a flower-topped ballpoint pen on a chain around her neck and a don't-expect-me-to-sugarcoat-it expression told me "Old Sheriff Blood and Guts" was ready for discharge.

"Keep an eye on his infusion site for infection," she said. "He's been scratching at it in his sleep again."

"Have not," Pudge said as he rolled down his sleeve and buttoned the cuff.

"Well, somebody did. Don't tell me you got lucky last night?"

"Why? Jealous?"

"Honey, if I was to take you out for dinner and dancing, you'd never buckle that gun belt again. Now, go on, get out of here. I got another patient waiting for a fill-up. See you next month."

"Optimist," he said.

She didn't acknowledge his gallows humor nor did I offer him a hand as he crossed the newly waxed linoleum floor. Pudge had cancer coursing through his body, but it hadn't devoured his pride or courage any. The old leatherneck faced his latest enemy without blinking, the same way he had Tojo's army on Iwo Jima thirty-plus years ago and countless armed desperados since.

He made it safely across the icy parking lot without slipping too. As soon as he was settled in my pickup's front seat, I fired the ignition, threaded my way through Bend's busy intersections, and took Highway 20 east toward home.

Usually we made the drive in silence, but Pudge surprised me.

"Son, you know I'm at the end of the road, right? Only got a year left."

"You don't know that," I said quickly. "Chemo takes time. Remember what your doctor said. It's only one tool in the box. He's got others. Radiation. Combination of both. New types of treatment—"

He cut me off with a snort. "I wasn't talking about me dying. I meant me being sheriff. I'm three years into my term. The election's next year."

"Really? It seems like it was only yesterday you beat Bust'em. That was, what, ten years ago?"

"Seven," he said.

He'd been sheriff of Harney County for decades when his young deputy, Buster Burton, ran against him and won thanks to an ad campaign featuring a photograph of Pudge being wheeled out on a stretcher after having been shot in the line of duty. The tag line said he was too old and too slow. Burton even christened himself with a catchy nickname, "Bust'em."

Four years later, Pudge won his job back, but Burton got the last laugh. The state attorney general grouped Oregon's thirty-six county sheriff's departments into regions and appointed Burton to oversee the eastern part of the state, which included Harney County.

"You'll win easily," I said. "You haven't had an opponent since you beat Bust'em."

"But this time I do."

"Who?"

"Me," he said. "Well, the big C. I got a decision to make. What's best for the people of Harney County."

I let the drumming of the tires respond as we left Deschutes County and entered into a sea of sage scrub dotted with islands of black-capped buttes. We drove without speaking for another hour when the pickup's two-way chirped. I reached for the mike.

"Nick Drake. Over."

"Ranger Drake, it is Chief Deputy Orville Nelson. Over."

"Hey, Orville, how you doing?"

"I am well. Thank you for inquiring." The young lawman who once aspired to become an FBI agent until a backshooting cattle rustler sentenced him to a lifetime in a wheelchair cleared his throat. "Am I correct in presuming Sheriff Warbler is with you and you're on your way home from Bend?"

"He is and we are." I handed the mike to Pudge.

"What's up, Orville?"

"Sir, we have received a report of a suspicious death."

"Whose?"

"I did not take the call directly, but was informed of it via dispatch. I am currently in Crane investigating an armed robbery. Details were sketchy and the identity of the deceased was not provided."

"Which is where?"

"A ranch in Thunder Valley."

"Biggest spread up there is the Running R."

"Correct, sir. It is the site of the death and the source of the call."

"Who made it?"

"According to dispatch, a male who identified himself as Cass Railsback."

"Eldest son of the Railsback clan. His great-granddaddy Erdmann founded the Running R. Was it Cass didn't put a name to who's dead or wouldn't?"

"I do not know that. Nor can I confirm the death was a homicide. All I know is what you taught me, and that is securing the scene in a timely fashion is of utmost importance."

"Give yourself an A-plus."

The radio clicked and buzzed. "I am wrapping up here and

will leave for the scene shortly," Orville said. "If I am surmising correctly that you left Bend directly after your treatment and have been in transit for approximately sixty minutes, you could be at the Running R forty-one minutes before I am able to get there. That would give us an advantage. Is your health up to that? Over."

"The day I can't handle an investigation is the day I'll be looking up from the wrong side of the sage scrub."

"I meant no offense, sir, but both your daughter and November gave me strict instructions not to overload you with work, and I am more frightened of their wrath than yours."

"As you should be. I'll tell Gemma and that old Paiute medicine woman it was all my idea. Nick and I'll meet you there. You call Doc?"

"Affirmative. He is in the middle of a postmortem, but will leave Burns at its conclusion. By my calculation, that should put him at the Running R approximately two minutes after my arrival."

"I'm impressed."

"About what?"

"You doing all that calculating without being at your desk with your computing machine in front of you."

"It is precisely why I am developing a mobile prototype for in-the-field use. It will be a game changer for law enforcement."

"See you at the Running R," Pudge said and cradled the mike.

"Some things never change," I said. "Orville's still the boy wonder. Married, father, working a full shift and then some, and yet he always finds time to invent gadgets. He hasn't given up on what his hero Thomas Edison said about sleep being an unnecessary holdover from our caveman days."

The sheriff grunted. "How 'bout you put some lead in that

boot and see if we can't shave a few minutes off his calculating. Do Orville good to see even us old knuckle-draggers can move our asses when we have to."

2

———

The Thunder River burbled out of the southern flank of the Aldrich Mountains. It coursed through forests and canyons and picked up water from creeks, streams, rain, and snowmelt. After crossing the boundary between Grant and Harney Counties, the river flowed through Thunder Valley, a broad swath of hills and buttes, lush meadows, and miles of sage scrub. Stands of ponderosa pine, pinyon pine, and cottonwood provided shade in summer and a ready supply of firewood in winter.

A good chunk of the valley was owned by the Running R. The dirt road that led Pudge and me off the blacktop and onto the ranch took us over a cattleguard positioned between two tall timbers topped by a crossbeam. Hanging from it was a capital *R* made of steel. The feet of the letter's stem and tail were shaped like spurred boots.

"The Railsbacks breed horses with the speed to live up to the brand," Pudge said. "Always make it into the winner's circle at county fairs up and down the state."

"But their cattle look fat, not fast," I said, waving at the red Angus grazing on either side.

"Seeing them makes me wish I had my appetite back. Nothing beats a juicy ribeye. Your work ever bring you up here?"

"Never has even though I thought I'd visited every place there is between the Snake River and Klamath Basin." The two locations served as bookends to the half-dozen national wildlife refuges I patrolled.

"Is it called Thunder Valley because of the weather?" I said, glancing at the cumulonimbus clouds that were bunching up like the cattle were below.

Pudge's short-brim Stetson waggled. "I don't rightly know. It's always been called that since it was settled. I'm sure it has an Indian name like every place else in Oregon. November would know what it is in Numu."

He used the Northern Paiute word for what her people called themselves in their language. November's birth name translated to Girl Born in Snow, but the boarding school she'd been forced to attend renamed her as part of a government-sponsored program to destroy Native American culture.

"I take it you've been here before since you knew the Railsback name and ranch's history," I said.

"It's my business to know every single one of Harney County's seventy-five hundred residents."

"Especially those of voting age."

"No, especially the ones with bad tempers, bad intentions, and bad behaviors. They're the ones I get paid to know."

"That describe the Railsbacks?"

"Some, not all."

The dirt road ran straight for half a mile and then curved up the side of a low hill that resembled a bison's hump. I braked when we reached the top. Ahead rose a two-story ranch house made of stone and timber. Its wraparound front porch and big windows provided sweeping views of the river valley below and the mountains beyond. A barn, stable, corrals, and outbuildings flanked it.

"Pretty as a postcard," I said. "They sure built it to take advantage of the scenery."

"The high ground most likely. Old Erdmann was born in Germany, but was an American frontiersman through and through. Came over on his own when he was twelve and after years of soldiering, fur trapping, prospecting, and cowboying, staked himself a claim."

Pudge shifted in his seat. "Times being what they were, Erdmann picked a house site that he could defend from all comers. From up here, he could see people riding toward him and rain hellfire down on them if he had a mind to. There's a family graveyard behind the house complete with stone tombstones and a low iron fence around it, but it doesn't account for all the bodies buried here."

"What about his offspring?"

"His eldest son was a chip off the old block. Erdmann Junior. Had a reputation for doing whatever it took to acquire more land to expand the family's holdings, including shooting, shoveling, and shutting up about whoever stood in his way."

"More unmarked graves," I said. "And his children?"

"Erdmann Junior only had one son."

"Erdmann the Third?"

"You got it, but he went by the English translation, Adam. That wasn't the only difference he had with his daddy and granddaddy. The man had no desire to run the ranch, much less expand it. Left it the way it was when he inherited it and spent all his time hunting every wild beast he came across from here to Timbuktu."

"You're talking in the past tense."

"He clicked his cheek. "That's because Adam Railsback met his end at the wrong end of his favorite big game rifle a year ago.

His youngest son, Aiden, was holding the other end of it. Why I was here last time. I did the investigation and had to make a ruling."

"Which was?"

"Accidental death."

"The way you say it makes me think it wasn't so cut and dry."

"Fatal shootings rarely are, son."

Before I could ask him another question, two men and a woman stepped out of the house and waited on the front porch.

"Time to go to work," Pudge said.

I drove up to the house and pulled to a stop. The sheriff hung on to the pickup's door when he got out, taking a moment to find his sea legs after the long ride. He was gulping air and swallowing hard. It was his way of taming the nausea roiling his guts following a chemo treatment.

One of the men stepped forward. He looked to be about my age. His black hair had a slight curl in it and his beard and eyes were dark too. He stuck out his hand to the sheriff.

Pudge shook it. "Hello, Cass. This here is Nick Drake."

Cass Railsback took in the duck and fish emblem on the door of the pickup and my uniform and badge. "You're Fish and Wildlife, not county sheriff's."

"I was giving the sheriff a ride when his chief deputy radioed."

"Nick's my son-in-law," Pudge said.

"You're married to Gemma?"

"I am. You know her?"

"From when we were both rodeoing. She was winning blue ribbons for barrel racing and I was trying to for tie-down roping, but was always a split second too slow."

"You mean with women," the younger man called out. "But they didn't come all this way to hear about your trip down broken heart memory lane. We have a body on our property and the sooner we get it dealt with, the sooner we can get back to bringing this ranch into the twentieth century."

Cass hooked a thumb over his shoulder. "My little brother. Aiden fancies himself a big shot businessman and believes always being in a hurry and rude are tools of the trade."

Aiden was clean-shaven, fair-haired, and had a complexion to match. He started to say something, but the woman hushed him with a look. She had his coloring, but her hair showed more gray than blond and her face reflected a life spent outdoors. It made me think of how hillsides with folds in them were more beautiful and interesting than smooth ones because of the mysteries they held.

Walking straight to Pudge, she put her hand on his forearm and locked her blue-as-a-robin's-egg eyes on his. "I heard about your illness, Sheriff. It's a relief to see you looking so fit."

"That's kind of you to say, ma'am, even though we both know the diet I'm on no one wants." He patted his much-diminished paunch. "Wish I was here under different circumstances. Same as I did last time."

"And same as what I said then, I'll say now. Call me Jo."

"Be my pleasure, ma'am."

"Death is a poor reason for a visit from friends and neighbors," she said.

"Indeed it is. I'm ready to hear about what happened if you're ready to tell it."

"Let's go inside, shall we?"

"My chief deputy said it was a quote, unquote suspicious death. That being the case and time being of the—well, time's always been in short supply, hasn't it? I really should take a gander at the scene first."

"What you really mean is the stiff," Aiden said.

"Honey, show some respect," Jo said.

"Oh, Mother, you know Pillsbury doesn't deserve any. Been

a pain in our ass ever since he got here. The original doughboy. Imagine he's getting even pudgier swelling up out in that field."

She gave Pudge a frown. "You'll have to excuse my youngest. His manners have grown in short supply since Adam's death."

"You mean my patience," Aiden said. "That's because we don't have time to waste. Time's money and we have deadlines to meet."

Jo tossed her head like a horse balking at the bit. "The spot where Mr. Pillsbury was found is inaccessible by vehicle at present. It's on the other side of the river and high water from the recent storm washed out a split log bridge we normally use to reach those fields. There's a spot a short way downriver horses can ford."

"I'd be obliged if you lent Nick and me mounts along with someone to show us the way."

"Of course, but are you able to ... I mean, are you sure?"

"I'm sure I'm better off riding than walking any distance. My chief deputy is on his way along with the coroner. Might as well wait for them so we can do the scene investigation in one fell swoop and transport the body back to Burns."

"I'll have our head wrangler ready saddle horses as well as a packhorse. While he's doing that, we can go inside for refreshments."

Jo signaled to her eldest son with a smile. "Cass, tell KT what we need."

Aiden blew air. "What a bunch of horseshit! Doughboy slips and falls and suddenly it's an episode of *Gunsmoke* complete with an ailing Matt Dillon and a bugs and bunnies Festus." He stomped into the house.

The steps and floorboards of the porch were made of wide planks and the railing of slender lodgepole pines that had been stripped of bark and varnished. On the other side of the thick wooden front door was an entrance hall lit by an elk antler chandelier.

The living room featured a massive stone fireplace. Logs blazed in front of a pair of brown leather couches with hand-woven tribal blankets slung over their backs. I recognized them as Northern Paiute from their color and geometrical patterns. They resembled the ones at home that November had woven.

The glass eyes of mounted bighorn sheep, moose, and deer stared from the walls. A bearskin complete with head, paws, and claws lay on the floor along with a wolfskin, its mouth agape and teeth bared. It caught me by surprise. Wolves hadn't been seen in Oregon since the last one was hunted down and killed for a bounty thirty years ago as part of a government extermination program. Either this one was killed out of state or the taxidermist had done one heckuva job skinning and tanning the hide to make it look like it had been chasing down prey a week before.

"Have a seat," Jo said, waving at one of the couches. She sat in its twin and faced us over a coffee table hewn from oak.

"Tell me about the deceased," Pudge said. "Starting with his full name."

"Wilbur Pillsbury. I'll have to go back to the beginning, and I'd be grateful if you could keep some of what I tell you out of your report so it doesn't end up in the *Burns Herald*. The publisher and I have ... Well, you know how Bonnie LaRue is."

Pudge didn't say a word. Nor did he move a facial muscle. He and the fiery newspaperwoman had had an on-and-off relationship for years—most of it off.

Getting no response, Jo said, "I mean, keep out the parts that aren't relevant to his death and could hurt my family's standing in the ranching community."

"I'm only interested in how he died, Jo. If there's a why he died and a who that caused it, well, I'll have to take that into consideration with whatever goes along with it."

Jo drew a deep breath. "It all started before Adam's death. Despite all you see here—the acreage, the cattle, the horses, the stands of timber, the big house—everything, and I mean everything, is hanging by a thread.

"My husband may have been an expert hunter, but he was a lousy rancher and an even lousier businessman. He didn't care for it, nor care about what that meant to the ranch and everything that goes with it, the boys and me included."

She went on to describe how years of Adam's indifference along with declining beef prices, the loss of timber contracts to corporate logging companies, and a string of hard winters that required buying supplemental feed had forced them to take out bank loans during a time of sky-high interest rates.

"A ranch is a living, breathing organism the same as we are," she said. "It requires constant care and feeding whether you can afford it or not. Adam didn't see that despite having grown up here. Truth is, he refused to see it. All he cared about was bagging another trophy and the bragging rights that went with it."

"How's Wilbur Pillsbury fit into all that?" Pudge said.

Jo glanced at the living room's doorway. A young woman was carrying a tray with a fancy porcelain coffeepot and matching cups on it. She wore a white blouse and a handloomed red shawl. Her long black hair with a slight curl in it cascaded over her shoulders. Striped tattoos on her chin and cheeks gave her an expression that was both fierce and alluring. So did the inch-long sliver of polished ivory that pierced her septum.

Her footsteps made no sound as she glided toward us. Nor did the cups and saucers rattle when she set the tray on the coffee table.

"Thank you, Kagán," Jo said. "I'll take it from here."

The woman glided away as silently as she'd appeared.

"She doesn't look Paiute," I said.

"No, Kagán is Tlingit."

"She's a long way from her people's home on the Alaska Panhandle."

"Yes, she is. Would you like coffee?"

I nodded. Pudge shook his head.

"Something else I can get?" Jo asked him.

"No, I best not add any fuel to the fire. The chemo, you know."

"Oh, forgive me. I should've thought of that."

"It's my worry, not yours. Now, as you were saying about your late husband and the Running R's money hitches—"

"After Adam's death, an attorney paid us a visit. I thought it would be a meeting about Adam's last will and testament, his life insurance policy, that sort of thing, but it was akin to experiencing another death."

"How so?"

"He said we were facing foreclosure because of missed loan payments. It turns out that Adam had stopped making them and was using the money instead to pay for safari trips and, well, expenses of a personal nature."

"Mother means for his whore and bastards," Aiden said from the doorway.

"Aiden!" Jo said, jostling her cup and causing coffee to lap over the rim and splash the saucer.

"The sheriff's going to find out one way or the other." He walked to the fireplace and turned his back to the flames.

"The lawyer was actually doing us a favor by telling us the facts of life. The double life my father was living here and with his other family over there. We had two choices. One was sell the ranch to pay off the loans. Trouble was, once word got out about our debts, buyers would circle like vultures. We'd be lucky to get pennies on the dollar."

"And the second choice?" Pudge said.

"Get into bed with the devil," Jo replied.

"At least he's honest about who else he's sleeping with unlike dear old Dad," Aiden said.

Pudge didn't blink. "This devil got a name or is it really Lucifer?"

"Stuart Kinsey, managing partner of Thunder Valley Inc.," Aiden said.

"What's that?"

"Our lifeline. A company comprised of forward-thinking investors. They're helping us by turning a portion of our property into a destination resort and lifestyle community like Sunriver over in Bend. It'll be a place for mom and dad to bring the kids to vacation and grandma and grandpa to live out their golden years."

Pudge turned to Jo. "Why did you call him the devil?"

"Because the Running R has been the soul of this family for four generations and now we have to sell it to Stuart Kinsey and his ilk to survive."

"Oh, Mother. How many times do I have to explain it to you?" Aiden said. "We're not selling, we're partnering. The others are putting up millions of dollars to develop the project and all we're throwing in is a section or two of land. In return, we'll earn a hundred times the money we make running cattle on it every single year forever."

"Hell's forever too," she said.

Aiden threw up his hands. "This is the thanks I get for finding Stuart and bringing us the deal of a lifetime!"

"What's Cass think about all this?" Pudge said.

"My brother's still stuck in the past, but Mother and I outvoted him. He'll come around when the money's rolling in and realizes he doesn't have to go look for lost steers in a blizzard anymore. He can still play cowboy if he wants by taking guests on trail rides and show off his lassoing."

"And the other ranchers in the valley, what do they think?"

"They're none too happy about it," Jo said. "Especially our neighbor to the north, the Broken Wing. We've always had a challenging relationship with them."

"They're more stuck in the past than my dimwit brother," Aiden said. "They can cuss and holler all they want, but they're nowhere near as big as us and we're only going to get bigger thanks to Thunder Valley Inc. We'll buy them for peanuts and build custom homes on their precious land."

"I'm trying to recollect the Broken Wing," Pudge said. "That the Calhoun spread?"

"Yes. A backward bunch if there ever was one. Inbred hillbillies."

"Honey, please!" Jo said.

"How does Wilbur Pillsbury fit in with the development plan?" Pudge said.

"He was nothing more than a paper pusher," Aiden said. "A fat little man unable to see the big picture. He tripped over his two left feet and struck his head on a rock."

"Honey, stop. We don't know that," Jo said. "Let the sheriff do his job."

She put her coffee cup on the table. "As part of the development plans, lots of reports must be filed and approved by the State. Wilbur worked for a consulting firm Stuart Kinsey hired to conduct engineering and environmental studies. You know, is the dirt suitable for building on, what kind of animals live here, what's the source for water. All that sort of thing. He'd been at it for weeks."

Pudge asked if Pillsbury was staying at the ranch house or a motel in Burns.

"Neither. He rented a camper and was living and working out of it. Wilbur moved around the property depending on where he was conducting his field work."

"You ever talk to him?"

"A few times. He dropped by the house to fill up his water jugs, but I think it was really just an excuse to have a little human contact. It's pretty lonesome on the furthest reaches of the ranch."

"What did you talk about?"

"Weather. News. That sort of thing."

"Who found him?"

I recognized the way Pudge had been working up to that question all along. It was the same way he fished. Land a few casts far from the big trout he was really after and then drift a fly right in front of its nose.

"KT did. He's our head wrangler. He'd forded the river to check on a herd early this morning and spotted Wilbur's camper. Rode over to say hello and, well ..." She looked down at her cup.

"Was his body inside or outside of it?" Pudge asked.

"Outside. KT said he'd been dragged twenty yards or so away from it."

"Dragged? Why'd he think that?"

"Because of the marks he saw on the ground."

"I'll need to talk to KT."

"Of course. He's going to lead us across the river and show us the way."

Bootheels clacked in the entrance hall. Cass poked his head in. "Two vehicles driving up. One's got a star on the door, the other's a paneled rig."

"That'll be the meat wagon," Aiden said.

Pudge pushed himself up off the couch. "Time to saddle up and go have our look-see."

3

By the time we reached the front porch, Chief Deputy Orville Nelson had already swung out of his rig and into his custom-made wheelchair that resembled a dragster. The service revolver he wore in a shoulder holster wasn't his only weapon. A short-barreled riot gun rode in a scabbard on the back of the wheelchair's seat and a concealed 9mm automatic was attached on the right side that he could fire with the push of a button.

Cass's and KT's eyes were wide open as they watched Orville zoom toward us powered by biceps that had doubled in size after years of having to do the work of legs.

"How's he gonna ride that across the river?" the head wrangler said out of the side of his mouth.

"Maybe it floats like a boat," Cass said.

The still boyish-looking lawman skidded to a stop. "Who is the victim and where is he? Or is it a she?"

"A he, but we haven't seen him yet," Pudge said.

Doc joined us. The coroner had white hair, a ruddy face, and a dyspeptic temperament.

Pudge made quick introductions and explained the body was in a field on the other side of the river.

"The bridge is out so we have to cross by horse. You okay with that, Doc?"

"Why wouldn't I be? I was riding before you were born."

"We both know we're the same age."

Doc harumphed and hiked up his black suit trousers to show he was wearing a pair of embroidered calfskin cowboy boots.

"Then we're good to go," Pudge said.

KT coughed. He was as lean as a fence post and his legs were bowed from a lifetime on horseback. A holstered Colt six-shooter hung on his right side, a bone handle knife in a leather sheath on his left. Doffing his pinch front cowboy hat, he faced Jo Railsback.

"Pardon, ma'am. I saddled the horses your son asked fer 'long with one to pack Mr. Pillsbury out, but I'm afeared I weren't countin' on ... well, one to 'commodate the deputy here. Truth be told, I don' know nothin' 'bout what kinda riggin' that'd take."

"Nothing special at all," Orville said. "While a short-legged horse is always appreciated, as long as I can reach the saddle horn, I can swing myself up and hold on."

"Then I got just the mount fer you, Deputy. Biscuit's only fourteen hands but keeps up with the Runnin' R's fastest."

While KT returned to the stable, Pudge filled Orville and Doc in on what we'd learned about Wilbur Pillsbury, Stuart Kinsey, and Thunder Valley Inc.

Aiden joined us when KT returned with a string of saddle-horses. We mounted up. KT took the lead on a stallion that had the same coloring and black socks as my own buckskin back in No Mountain. Jo Railsback rode a beautiful bay mare.

As we rode away, I glanced at the ranch house. A flash of

white showed in an upstairs window. It wasn't a curtain billowing, but the Tlingit woman's blouse. Kagán was twirling something as she watched us go. I couldn't swear to it, but it resembled a tail like the one on the wolfskin down in the living room.

A trail took us to the river's edge. The water was dark green and moving fast as it sawed at the edges of the bank and broke against boulders. A flock of Canada geese using it as a guide was flying overhead, their bills pointed south. I knew they'd stop off at the Malheur to rest and refuel before continuing their annual journey to warmer climes.

We reached a dirt road that ended at water's edge.

"This here's where the bridge crossed," Cass said as he rode alongside me.

"Where's the road on the other side lead to?"

"Our north forty."

"Acres?"

"Square miles."

"How many acres is the Running R total?"

"Hundred fifty thou, give or take."

"Does the road continue on to the Broken Wing's property?"

"No, it stops short of the fence. Doesn't mean you couldn't drive a four-by across the Calhoun's property, but they'd shoot you for trespassing. Same as we'd do to anyone trying to come onto our spread. Could be rustlers, you know."

"There must be a bridge across the river at the Broken Wing."

"There is, but they'd never let us use it and we'd never ask."

"How come?"

"Bad blood. Goes back to my great-grandfather's time."

"What about a bridge to the south?"

"There isn't one on the Running R. You'd have to go a lot of miles before the first crossing."

"So you're stuck with fording."

He nodded. "We should've rebuilt this one long ago but it's one more expense we kept putting off."

"Your mother told me about Thunder Valley Inc.," I said as we continued following the trail to the ford.

He turned his head and spit. "They'll gobble us up acre by acre like a wolfpack does a herd cow by cow. Won't be nothing left when they're done but the brand, and even then it'll only be on matchbooks and brochures."

"Your mother called Stuart Kinsey the devil, but she still agreed to throw in with him."

"There's other words I'd use to describe him, but that one fits the bill, right down to the two Beelzebubs that never leave his side. Whatever he wants done, he just snaps his finger and they do it without a care of what gets broken or who gets hurt."

He sighed. "As for Mother agreeing to go along, I think the shock of Dad's death and finding out we were near bankrupt clouded her thinking."

"Along with finding out about him being unfaithful?"

"No, he never kept that a secret."

"Aiden made it sound like he fathered other children."

"If so, I wouldn't know them if they walked in the door. And they're never going to because I'll bar it."

I asked if he thought there was another way they could've paid off the loans.

"There's always another way. Just got to have the grit to find and do it. Railsbacks have never sold any land. Not a square inch. And especially not to a con man from back east."

"Why do you call him that?"

"You meet him, you'll know why."

"Do Kinsey and his group have plans to develop the Broken Wing too?"

"If they do, I haven't heard about it, and if they try, well, they'd be in for a tougher fight than Mother and Aiden put up."

"How's that?"

"Because the Calhouns are a rough bunch, maybe even rougher than Kinsey and his two goons."

He spurred his horse forward.

I pulled abreast of Orville Nelson. The chief deputy was clenching the saddle horn and reining one-handed.

"Pudge told me he was up here a year ago investigating the shooting of Adam Railsback. Were you with him?"

"Negative, though I prepared the report for him and filed it with Harney County Court per protocol."

"Anything unusual about the incident?"

"Why do you ask?"

"Aiden doesn't strike me as being particularly remorseful about it."

"Sheriff Warbler noted that in his notes, but he found no physical evidence to prove the shooting was either premeditated or done in a fit of anger. The two were alone on a bear hunting expedition. No eyewitnesses."

"Where?"

"On the side of the river where we are now headed."

"What happened?"

"The father handed his weapon butt first to Aiden so he could use his binoculars to search for the bear they were stalking. Aiden fumbled the transfer and the weapon discharged."

"It wasn't on safety?"

"Apparently the senior Railsback had a reputation for never using a safety. He said doing so once cost him a split second that prevented him from killing a huge lion that would have broken the world record."

"Where did the bullet strike?"

"Right in the heart."

"Bad luck for Mr. Railsback that the binoculars hanging from a strap around his neck didn't deflect it."

Before Orville could respond, KT held up his hand and reined to a stop. "This here's the ford. It's leg deep fer horses. I chose ones that all done it afore so shouldn' be no problem. Give 'em their head and they'll follow right along. They don' wanna go swimmin' no more than you do."

He led the way while Cass held back to see us all safely across. The current thrummed against my horse's legs and skimmed just beneath his barrel. I raised my knees while keeping my boots in the stirrups to try and keep them dry.

Pudge forded ahead of me. As far as I knew, he hadn't been on a horse since his cancer diagnosis, but he didn't look like he'd lost the know-how. He'd grown up on the ranch in No Mountain and learned to ride around the same time he learned to walk. It was a family tradition. Gemma had too. The same with our daughter, Hattie. When we adopted Johnny, our Saigon-born son, one of the first things we taught him was how to ride.

Everyone reached the other side with nothing more to show for it than splashed jeans. KT led us back upriver to where the bridge once crossed. We rode onto the dirt road and followed it through a field that was a patchwork of snow and tall grass.

A stand of cottonwoods grew between the field and river. A white pickup with a camper was parked near the trees. A single set of tire tracks led from the road we were on and across the field.

"Whoa!" Pudge said.

Everyone stopped and the horses nickered and shook their heads while the old sheriff's head looked like a periscope as it swung left then right and then zeroed in on the camper.

"Everyone stay here while Doc, Nick, and I go on foot and have our look-see. Orville, you ride behind us but stay well back of the camper and use your binoculars. You spot any tracks, give a shout so we don't walk on them."

"Hold on a second. This is my land," Aiden said. "You can't tell me where I can and can't go."

Pudge patted his chest. "I can and I will. This badge says so. Do I need to remind you about the dos and don'ts of a crime scene or did you forget that from a year ago?"

"That was an accident. You said it yourself."

"And maybe I'll rule this an accident too, but until I know that for sure, I need to treat it as a crime and you need to keep your butt planted in that saddle right here."

Aiden pointed at me. "Why's he get to go?"

"Because Nick's the best tracker I know. Sees sign before it's even been made. And not only wild animals. He earned his stripes and the medals that went with 'em leading long-range reconnaissance patrols in Vietnam tracking the enemy and finding lost soldiers while you were home playing with tin ones."

The sheriff dismounted. I could see him grimace, but he didn't let out a groan. He walked up to KT.

"You riding this horse when you came across Pillsbury?"

"Yep. Always ride him."

"Change his shoes since you were here?"

"Nope. No need to. I shoe him myself. They nailed on good 'n tight."

Pudge patted the buckskin, put his hand under his elbow, and clucked his tongue. The horse raised his hoof. Pudge studied the shoe, memorizing its pattern.

Letting go of the buckskin, he asked KT if he'd seen other tracks when he found Pillsbury. "Any fresh or old ones? Horseshoe, boot, or tire?"

"Nope, only them the camper made. Made afore the last storm 'cause still patched with snow. Any other tracks made after woulda showed and I wouldn'a missed 'em. I'm always on the lookout. Anyone trespassin' on the Runnin' R is after our beeves and horses and my job is to keep our stock alive and rustlers—"

"Not alive." Aiden snickered.

Pudge asked KT why he told Jo Railsback the body looked like it'd been dragged.

"Wasn't look like, t'were. Drag mark from the camper to where the poor fella was lyin'. Grass'd been flattened between patches of snow ain't melted yet."

"Was he face down or face up when you found him?"

"Face down. Still is far as I know."

"You didn't turn him over to see if you could help him?"

"Sheriff, t'weren't the first dead man I seen. I been cowboyin' all my life. Afore I signed onto the Runnin' R, I worked ranches from Wyomin' to Texas and back agin. You do this line of work, men die. Women too. It's a hard business. I knowed he were dead from ten feet away. Nothin' I could do fer him but ride back and tell Mrs. Railsback."

"You got any thoughts on how he died or why he was dragged?"

"First I thought he drug hisself." KT shrugged. "Weren't no tufts of grass pulled up a man woulda made pullin' hisself along. Somethin' pulled him."

"Something not someone?"

KT looked down at the ground and then back at Pudge. "Coulda been a someone, I s'pose, but weren't no boot prints, and, Sheriff, this here's Thunder Valley. We got bear. Big ones. We got cougar. They plenty big too. And"—he took a deep breath—"some say wolf even though they ain't s'posed to be round here no more."

Pudge hitched his gun belt and walked toward the camper by following the tracks its tires had made. He alternated between looking at the ground and doing the periscope thing again. Doc followed right behind. Orville rode while looking through his binoculars, making 180-degree sweeps of the ground. I began walking a zigzag search pattern. All I saw was a fresh set of hoofprints made by a shoed horse going in and coming out. KT's buckskin, no doubt.

When we were abreast of the camper, Pudge called out that he was going inside to search it and for Orville to bring him the crime scene kit stuffed in the chief deputy's saddlebag. He asked Doc to go with me and examine the body. Despite the cold weather acting like a natural meat locker, the coroner instinctively dipped two fingers in a jar of Mentholatum and stuck them in his nostrils.

4

K
T's observation that handfuls of grass hadn't been yanked up by a desperate man dragging himself across a field was accurate. Nor had any been kicked loose by that same man's feet pushing himself along.

As Doc took photographs of the drag mark and the face-down remains of Wilbur Pillsbury, I walked concentric circles looking for footprints, hoofprints, and paw prints of any kind.

I found none. Not from any two-legged and not from any four-legged either.

Looking up at the thunderheads gathering overhead, I toyed with the idea that maybe a giant eagle had flown down and dragged Pillsbury. But in all my patrols of wildlife refuges and studying of field guides, I'd yet to come across a winged creature big enough to tug a grown man.

"Let's roll him over," Doc said.

The coroner grabbed Pillsbury's leg as I put my hands on his shoulder. We tugged and tugged. Nothing.

"Blood must've frozen and glued him to the ground," Doc said. "I don't want to have to use a horse to pull him over. Too messy and it'd contaminate any laboratory findings. Let's try again."

"On three," I said. "One. Two. Heave."

We gave a tremendous pull. It sounded like a balloon popping as Pillsbury came unstuck.

"Heavens to Betsy," Doc groaned as we rolled him over. The coroner quickly averted his eyes.

I blinked mine, trying to erase the image even though I knew it would stick with me the same as the KIAs I'd seen in Vietnam.

Pillsbury's nose, lips, and ears were missing. The front of his blue nylon parka and khaki shirt had been ripped open. So had his chest cavity. He'd been disemboweled.

"Damn animals got to him," Doc said, holding a handkerchief over his already mentholated nostrils. "This is the worst-looking corpse I've come across in thirty years."

"You need to take pictures of this side of him too," I said.

Doc handed me the camera. "Here, you do it. I need to get out my thermometer and take his liver temperature to determine time of death."

"It doesn't look like he has one anymore."

Doc stared at the yawning mess of the man's midriff. "Damn. Now I have to do it the other way."

"What other way?"

"If you can't go through the front door, you have to go through the—"

"Yeah, I get it. Let me take the pictures while he's still face ... well, right side up before we need to roll him back over."

I started snapping, using the viewfinder as a way to distance myself from the dead man's condition.

Pudge joined us with Orville following on horseback.

"Don't look," I said, thinking how the sheriff's chemo-irritated stomach might do backflips at the sight of Pillsbury's lack of one.

It was too late. Pudge took a glance and then tugged his hat down even lower.

"Lord have mercy," he muttered. "Some critter's been gnawing on him. You're the wildlife expert. What kind was it?"

"Predators and scavengers always go for the soft tissue first, like lips, nose, ears, and stomach, but I think this was done by a who trying to make it look like a what."

"Come again?"

"His face? The parts were sliced off. Teeth and claws wouldn't have been so neat. Same with his chest. All the rips in his parka and shirt are slashes made by something straight and thin."

I put two sides of nylon fabric from his blue parka together to make my point.

"Cut like a pair of scissors do to a sheet of paper," he said.

"Something with a very sharp blade did all this," I said. "A well-honed knife or a straight razor."

I pointed at Pillsbury's head. "If a bear had bit him, the skull would be crushed. Same with a cougar. Besides, bears aren't known maneaters. They might kill a human if spooked or defending their cubs or territory, but they rarely devour. And a cougar? It'd still be here guarding the rest of its prey from scavengers. There's too much of him left for it to have been coyotes. The pack would've torn off his arms and legs and chewed into his sides by now."

"Maybe KT was onto something when he said wolf. A pack of them."

"They wouldn't have left anything but bones. If it was a lone wolf, it'd still be around to guard its next meal."

"Like a cougar," he said.

"And then there's the fact no wolves are left in Oregon. They got killed off for bounty decades ago."

"Could be one snuck in from Idaho."

"Anything's possible, but there'd be paw prints, and I don't see any."

"Maybe they melted with the snow."

"But there aren't any on the snow patches that are left. The odds they walked on everything but those are more than a hundred to one."

Pudge rubbed his jaw. "What do you think, Doc?"

"I don't think. I don't guess. I only know. It's all conjecture until I get him back on my table and run some tests. If an animal did this, then I'll be able to pick up traces of its saliva. If it was done by a human wielding a knife, then I'll need to examine the blade with blood still on it to make a conclusive finding. I'll also need to get the camper under my microscope. So to speak."

The sheriff looked back at the road where the others sat their horses.

"Wonder where that goes?"

"Cass told me it dead-ends at the edge of their property. The Broken Wing ranch is on the other side. He said it has a bridge we could use to drive the camper across, if that's what you're thinking, but the two families aren't on speaking terms."

"Meaning I'd probably have to get a court order to force them to let us on their land, but that'd take too much time. We'll leave the camper here for the time being and pack Mr. Pillsbury out."

He beckoned to Orville to ride closer. "Bring KT and that pack animal over here and tell the rest to go back to the house and wait for us there. Don't say nothing about what we're seeing here."

"Yes, sir."

Pudge looked down at the body. "If an animal did do this, then we need to find it or its den and check its innards or dung pile to see if we can find whatever might be left of Pillsbury to be sure. If it was done by a man to make it look like death by animal, then we still need to find the rest of Pillsbury for evidence to be able to make a case."

The coroner harumphed. "A man will be harder. He has hands, not paws. He could've tossed the body parts, er, the evidence, into the river or lit a fire and burned them or dug a hole and buried them deep."

"I know all that, Doc. That's why I'm deputizing Nick right here and now to do the looking. Whether man or beast, they still had to get here and get out. There have to be tracks of some kind, and if anyone can find them along with whatever may be left of what poor Pillsbury is missing, it's Nick."

The two old men trained their eyes on me.

I had just returned the day before after two weeks away patrolling distant refuges. When I got home, I found that Gemma had left that very morning to make rounds and would be gone for at least a couple of more days. Clouds passing in the night got closer than we'd been able to.

"Okay, I can give it a day or so," I finally said. "But no guarantees."

"Not asking for one. Only your best," Pudge said.

"Give me some room and let me finish," Doc said. "Pillsbury warms up any, it'll be a dinner bell for every turkey vulture around and that'll make even more of him for Nick to look for."

As the coroner got out his thermometer, swabs, and test tubes, I asked the old sheriff what he found in the camper.

"No signs of a struggle and I didn't see any blood splatter," Pudge said. "Pillsbury was very neat and tidy. A place for everything and everything in its place. Had the camper set up like an office, complete with typewriter, file cabinet, and a shelf for books and spiral notebooks the size you can stick in your back pocket."

"For taking field notes. I do the same. Did you find any

personal items that can give us an idea of who he was, what he liked to do, and what he might like to keep secret?"

"No. Clothes were all neatly folded in the camper's built-in cabinet. Nothing hidden beneath them, like dirty magazines or rolls of cash. Foodstuffs were canned goods and bags of rice and beans. No liquor bottles. Not even a can of beer."

"What about correspondence? Letters from a wife. Letters from a mistress. Letters from a blackmailer."

"Listen to you. A regular detective like on all those cop shows on TV and you don't even watch it."

Pudge hitched his gun belt again. Despite having added a couple of new holes to adjust for his weight loss, it was a constant battle to keep it from slipping down his hips.

"I know what you're doing, son. Testing to make sure I still got what it takes. Well, the big C hasn't gotten up here yet." He tapped the side of his head.

"I didn't mean it that way. Only thinking out loud."

"No need for apologies. I know your heart's in the right place. Truth is, I'm glad to have an extra pair of hands on this one. It's a puzzle, all right, a regular jigsaw kind where you got to find the pieces that fell off the table and got booted under the couch."

"I bet you've already boxed up everything in the camper you think is worth examining."

"Yep. A big ole cardboard one Pillsbury got at the grocery store when he bought all his groceries. Orville and I'll lug it back to the office and go through it. Might give us a lead on who he was and who his next of kin is."

"Stuart Kinsey will want to get his hands on Pillsbury's field notes and any reports he might have typed up. He'll say they're company property."

"Indeed he will, but wanting and getting are a country mile apart. Right now, all that is evidence, and until I see a court order demanding I hand 'em over, they're Harney County sheriff's property and will be guarded as such. And even if I get an order, well, you know the thing about paperwork. Newest always has a way of finding its way to the bottom of the pile."

"Any fingerprints?"

"I dusted, for what it's worth, which is less than a wooden nickel. Any don't match Pillsbury's are more than likely going to belong to the last person who rented the camper or someone who worked there. If it wasn't a critter who killed him, whoever crossed the river to get to him already had in mind they were gonna kill him and likely wore gloves."

"Orville will be able to sort out the prints quick enough using his computer."

"Indeed he will."

The chief deputy and the ranch's head wrangler rode up. KT was holding the lead to the packhorse.

"Cass is taking the others back to the house," Orville said. "Aiden put up a fuss, but Mrs. Railsback gave him the what-ho."

"She did, did she?" Pudge said it with more admiration than surprise in his voice.

KT was looking at Doc who was hunched over the body. When the coroner stood up, KT could see what was left of Pillsbury. His squint grew even tighter, but he didn't utter a sound.

"I need you to keep this to yourself," Pudge said to him. "We don't know what kind of animal did that and we also can't rule out it wasn't a man did it. Understood?"

"Uh-huh, but what I don' unnerstan' is what kinda man. That's pure evil right there. Plain and simple."

Pudge turned to the coroner. "You finished, Doc?"

"He's all yours."

KT dismounted and untied a canvas tarp lashed to the pack-horse. He carried it over to the body and unfurled it alongside him. I joined him and we lifted Pillsbury onto it and started to fold the ends over him

"Wait!" Pudge said. "Check his pockets."

"I'll do that back at my office when we strip him," Doc said.

Pudge shook his head "Gotta check now. Don't want to risk anything falling out when we cross the river."

"I'll do it," I said.

It wouldn't be my first time. I'd searched fallen GIs for half-written letters to home, good luck charms their parents had given them, and pictures of wives, girlfriends, and babies.

I started with the pockets of his parka. Nothing. I moved on to his shirt pockets. They were glued shut from blood. I patted them. Zilch. Pants were last. Back pockets first, front pockets last. There was a lump in the front right. I pulled out my jackknife.

"No, don't cut it," Doc said. "That'll only confuse things when I try to make sense of all the other rips and slices in his clothing. Use your fingers. Don't worry, I'll be able to rule out your prints on anything you find."

I held my breath, inserted my fingers, and fished around. "Got something."

I pulled the object out and held it up.

"What is it?" Doc said.

"A compass. A fancy one, but it looks broken. Here."

He took a quick look then placed it in a plastic evidence bag. KT and I wrapped Pillsbury up in the tarp. The wrangler whipped out his bone handle knife. The sharp blade made quick work of cutting lengths of rope. We tied up the tarped corpse like a Christmas package.

When we hoisted him up, the packhorse flared his nostrils, flattened his ears, and stomped a hoof.

"Easy boy, easy boy," KT cooed. He kept on cooing as we cinched the wrapped body to the pack saddle. "Where ya want me to take him, Sheriff?"

"Straight to Doc's rig. Keep him in the tarp and load him in the back. We'll get our horses and be right behind you."

Pudge motioned to the coroner. "Orville will escort you to the morgue. Log the body in as a John Doe."

"Why? We know his name."

"Without a face, how can we be sure it's really him?"

The coroner narrowed his eyes. "What's your real reason?"

"Time. I need to buy some so I can go through the field notes and reports I took from the camper before Stuart Kinsey and his lawyers come calling."

What Pudge had said earlier about time always being in short supply echoed. That made me even more determined to find Pillsbury's killer before it ran out for him.

5

We formed a cortège riding back across the field and fording Thunder River. No one spoke. Even the horses seemed to sense the solemnness of the occasion and kept their heads down and snorts and blows to a minimum.

Cass, Aiden, and Jo were standing on the front porch when we reached the ranch house. They watched in silence as KT and I dismounted, unlashed the canvas tarp, and placed the body in the rear of the coroner's rig. I glanced at the upstairs window. Kagán was watching too.

Orville moved from saddle to wheelchair to the front seat of his rig. He started the engine, issued a two-finger salute to the Railsbacks, and began driving away with Doc and what was left of Wilbur Pillsbury right on his tail.

Pudge eased himself out of the saddle and joined Jo and her sons.

"I know you have questions, but even if I had the answers, I'm not gonna give 'em because this is an open investigation. Man found dead in a field is always gonna give rise to rumors and stories, some of 'em half true, some of 'em all false. I'd be obliged if none came from any of you."

He sucked a tooth. "I've asked Nick to do some more poking around here. Given that sundown's on its way, he's gonna take me home, resupply, and be back at sunup. I'd also be obliged if you stayed out of the field until he says different. Also, if Nick winds up having to overnight—"

"We'll make him feel right at home," Jo said. Her pale blue eyes turned to me. "The front door's never locked. You'll find a guest room at the top of the stairs, third door on the right. If you're hungry, just ask Kagán. She'll prepare whatever you want."

"That's mighty kind of you," I said.

"It's the least we can do for poor Wilbur's sake."

Aiden gave an exasperated groan. "Is all this really necessary, Sheriff? Come on. We have a business to run."

"Nick won't get in the way of your ranching," Pudge said.

"I meant our development project. When investors see a delay, they see money burning—their money. I don't want our partners getting skittish."

"You need to understand something, son. I don't give a gol'-durn damn about their concerns. What I do give a gol'durn damn about is finding out how Wilbur Pillsbury died and who or what caused it. Now, if you're so worried about your money folks, then you best go hold their hands."

Aiden shot him a dark look, but Pudge ignored it and turned his attention back to Jo.

"I'm gonna need to notify Pillsbury's next of kin. You know who that might be, where he called home?"

Her blond-gray hair moved in a soft wave. "He never mentioned it, nor do I know the name of the consulting firm he worked for. Stuart Kinsey will. He hired him."

"Then I'll need his telephone number."

"I have it, but I want to speak to him first," Aiden said.

"Why?"

"Because it's better if I hold his hand, right?"

"You got one hour. I'll call him when I get to my office in Burns. Give me the number."

Aiden handed it over.

The old sheriff raised his chin at Cass. "You're awfully quiet. Does that mean you don't object to Nick poking around the ranch or me speaking to Kinsey?"

"No objections at all," he said. "Nobody likes secrets, least of all me. Nick needs a hand, all he has to do is ask. KT and me, we'll give him whatever he wants." He cocked his head at Aiden. "Little brother here? He'll do everything he can to get in his way."

"Screw you," Aiden said.

"Now, now, boys," Jo said.

"And screw you too, Mother."

KT was holding the reins to his buckskin, but a blind man could see his knuckles tightening beneath his leather riding gloves. Even the brim of his pinch crown hat couldn't conceal the flash of anger in his eyes.

Pudge stepped in first. "You're a piss-poor excuse for a man disrespecting your mother. I wish I had found evidence that would've put you in a cage where you belong."

He took a deep breath. And then another. Turning to Jo, he said, "Beg your pardon, ma'am. Something got the best of my manners. Nick and I'll be on our way now. You have my word I'll do everything to wrap this up as quick as possible. When I do, I'll come back and tell you myself."

"Thank you, Sheriff."

He strode toward my pickup.

"I'll be back at first light," I said. "I have my own horse and will park my rig and trailer so they'll be out of the way."

"Don't worry," she said. "You won't be any bother at all."

I didn't correct her because I had every intention of bothering whoever got in the way of me finding the killer.

Pudge had already climbed into the front seat and buckled up when I got in, turned us around, and drove away. We hadn't even reached the crossbeam with the spurred *R* dangling from it before his snores filled the cab.

The tires resumed their drumming when I turned south on Highway 395 and headed toward Burns. Deepening purple turned to black as dusk gave way to night. A few stars played peekaboo among the thunderheads.

As I drove, I revisited the afternoon's events and the folks at the Running R. A pioneering German who founded the ranch and handed down a legacy of not letting anyone get in the way of what he believed was his family's right. A philandering husband with a hole drilled in his heart courtesy of his hotheaded son. A scorned wife. Two brothers at odds. An investor who bought souls for lucre. A cowboy who wouldn't balk at dealing frontier justice to rustlers. A pudgy surveyor butchered in a field by who knows what and who knew why.

They all seemed to fit into a category with one exception. The Tlingit woman. Who was Kagán? Why did she move far from home to a remote ranch in Eastern Oregon? What was her relationship to the Railsbacks? Had she ever spoken with Wilbur Pillsbury? And was that really a wolf's tail she'd been twirling?

The sheriff's snoring had settled into a low rumble like distant thunder. Up ahead, the lights of Burns grew closer. Pudge wanted me to stop at his office so he could call Stuart Kinsey to get a line on Pillsbury's next of kin. I glanced at the speedometer.

For three decades, his pursuit of justice had been his lifeblood—it defined who he was and kept him going. As vital as it was to him, I decided that same blood could use another half hour of uninterrupted sleep. And so I bypassed Burns and drove straight to No Mountain and the ranch where he'd been born and lived all his life, except for the years he served in the US Marines, and where he expected to be buried next to his beloved and long-departed wife, Henrietta.

Rattling over the cattleguard at the entrance to the Warbler ranch finally roused him. He snorted, opened his eyes, and rubbed his face.

"You were supposed to take me to my office," he grumbled.

"Orville isn't the only one under strict orders not to overwork you," I said.

"I could give you a piece of my mind for disobeying my instructions, but it'd be a poor cousin to what you're about to get." He chinned at the front porch.

November, wrapped in a tribal blanket, was rocking in a chair. I could see the Paiute healer's breath in the cold and feel the burn of her eyes through the windshield.

"It's not like you're going to get off scot-free for coming home so late either," I said. "Bet you she'll force you to drink a double dose of her star lizard plant tea."

"Yep, and no telling what Gemma's gonna do to the both of us. Weren't you supposed to be in charge of supervising homework this afternoon?"

"I'll get to it as soon as we're inside. Besides, she's not flying back until tomorrow at the earliest."

"Think again." He cocked his head in the direction of the corral.

Beyond it was Gemma's single-engine plane parked on the dirt landing strip.

"Well, that's a surprise. A welcome one." I hesitated before unbuckling my seat belt. "Do me a favor, would you?"

"What?"

"Don't mention I'm turning around and going back to

Thunder Valley first thing in the morning. I want to tell her in my own way."

"Good luck with that, son, because we both know a man's excuse to a woman is a dog that don't hunt."

His laughter filled the cab even louder than his snores had, and hearing it made all the talking-tos I was about to get worth it.

6

November dogged us into the house while muttering about the sheriff being as stubborn as Bighorn Sheep who kept headbutting his reflection on a sheet of ice and I was no smarter than Ground Squirrel who went hunting for acorns with Bobcat.

She ordered us to sit at the table and brought Pudge a steaming mug of tea and me a bowl of stew and fry bread. Then she eagle-eyed him to make sure he drank every single drop of the home-brewed medicine.

Hattie and Johnny came galloping in and peppered us with questions about where we'd been and why we were so late.

"We were on our way home when we got a call about a situation up at Thunder Valley," I said. "That's north of here on a river that eventually joins the Silvies, which flows past Lyle Rides Alone's ranch." Hattie worked for the horse breeder as a stable girl during summers and Lyle gave Johnny his first horse.

Johnny didn't bite at the dodge. His command of English wasn't the only thing that had sharpened since we'd adopted him. "It had to have been a crime because they sent for you," he said to Pudge. "Was it a robbery or homicide?"

The sheriff waved his mug of tea. "A lawman never jumps to conclusions. He has to—"

"See where the evidence leads him," Hattie cut in quickly. She clapped when her grandpa winked at her and mouthed, "Atta girl."

"Then it was definitely a murder," Johnny said. "Whose?"

"It's under investigation," Pudge said.

"Aw, you're no fun. We want to guess whodunit."

Gemma walked in and said, "Last time I checked, it's still a school night."

"We got our homework done," Hattie said.

"We *finished* our homework," she said.

Hattie rolled her eyes. She was at the age where she thought she knew it all. The fact was, she usually did.

Pudge once told me Gemma had been the same way. "I was so busy losing myself in work after Henrietta died, I never tried to rein her in," he explained. "Some might think that's an excuse for poor parenting, but look how she turned out. Got a veterinarian degree, opened her own practice, and convinced all the ranchers she could treat a sick cow or lame horse as good, if not better, than any man."

The horse doctor now touched the corner of her eyelid at me. I got the message, sopped up the last of the stew, and pushed away from the table.

"Come on, you two, time for bed. I'll tell you a story about how Thunder Valley got its name." I abruptly tipped back my chair so it crashed to the floor and roared, "Boom!"

Hattie shrieked and Johnny tried to pretend like he hadn't been startled, but he was the first to race down the hall.

After they were tucked in, I joined Gemma in our room. She was sitting up in bed making notes in a medical file. A stack of manila folders with tabs bearing the names of ranches towered on her nightstand.

I showered, opened the window, and slid into bed next to her.

"I'm glad you came home early," I said.

She looked up from her paperwork. "Me too."

"I owe you an explanation about today."

"Pudge already told me while you were putting the kids to bed. What did you think of the Railsbacks?"

"The mother and older brother were neighborly enough, considering the circumstances. Cass said you two used to rodeo together."

"That was a long time ago. And Aiden?"

"Comes off like he has something to prove. Did Pudge tell you he's working with a group of investors to turn the ranch into a big resort?"

"Ranching's a tough enough business, but what he's trying to do sounds even riskier."

"I know what you're thinking. Taking Pudge there straight from chemo was risky too. Riding a horse across Thunder River and walking through a half-frozen field was even more so. But, babe, you should've seen him. It was like he forgot he has cancer."

"But it hasn't forgotten it's got him." She drew a deep breath. "Cancer killed my mother and now it's trying to kill my father. I ... I don't want to lose him too."

Gemma shivered and I drew her closer.

"Nor do I or the kids. But Pudge taking a little holiday from it sure seemed like good medicine. He was in his element. Being a lawman. Looking for evidence. Questioning people. Dealing with a dead body. Dealing with a possible homicide."

"Possible? Come on, hotshot. You're not talking to the children here. I've known Pudge all my life and I'm married to you. That sudden giddyap in his step? You with that steely look in your eyes? We all know it was a murder and you two aren't going to rest until you solve it, cancer be damned."

She pointed her pen at me. "What time are you leaving in the morning for the Running R?"

"Who said I am?"

"Your little trick of opening the window during a freeze to get me to cuddle up next to you all night long."

"Caught that, did you?"

"Not my first rodeo."

"You've been known to open the window on occasion too."

"Maybe you and I need to take a break from thinking about cancer too," she said and closed the folder and turned off the light.

As we gathered one another in our arms and said how much we loved each other, a coyote began yip-howling on a hill behind the ranch. I tried to drown its calls by pulling Gemma even closer and kissing her while listening to our hearts pound harder and breathing grow faster. But even as all those efforts reached their much-desired and even more-needed crescendo, the image of a howling wolf and not a coyote haunted me.

A few hours later, I slipped out of bed, dressed, and tiptoed to the kitchen. Closing the swinging door behind me, I switched on the light. November was sitting on a stool beside the stove.

"Pudge told me about the Tlingit," she said.

"Good morning to you too, Girl Born in Snow," I said and put water on to boil for coffee. "What did he say?"

"Only her name and what she looks like. Face tattoos have many meanings. Kagán means 'Light' in her tongue. Like the light of the sun in the morning or the light of the moon at night. Light always brings a change. Perhaps Kagán does also."

"You speak Tlingit?"

"A few words." She elbowed me out of the way and put a cast-iron skillet on a burner and gave it flame. "I danced at a powwow in Seattle a long time ago. Tlingit from Canada and Alaska danced also. They call themselves People of the Tides and believe the Northern Lights that shine above them are the spirits of departed warriors."

"Talk about a fish out of water. I wonder how Kagán ended up in the High Lonesome?"

"She is not the first of her people to find her way here, according to legend."

"To the Running R?"

"To Thunder Valley."

As she added bacon to the heated skillet and started making fry bread in another, she told me how elders from her mother's clan had passed on the legend they'd heard from their elders.

"A band of People of the Tides left their home where the sea breaks its back in large wooden canoes adorned with paintings of spirit animals," she said. "Their journey took them down the coast and then up the Columbia River, what the Chinook call the Wimahl."

"Why'd they leave home?"

"You will need to ask Kagán that when you see her today. It is why you are up so early."

"Right as usual, but I'd still like to hear what you know."

November cracked two eggs into the skillet and began frying them alongside the bacon. "The ancients then paddled up what White men now call the John Day River. The journey grew even more difficult as that river is smaller and rockier.

"One day, a storm sunk their canoes. Some of the ancients drowned; others were injured and left behind. Those who could, continued on foot. Mile after mile, month after month. More died. Many times they had to hide from other tribes who called the river and lands on either side their home. The Tenino, Umatilla, and Cayuse."

She flipped the bacon and eggs with a wooden spatula as she

described how the ancient Tlingit lived off the fish in the river and the animals that came down to drink. There were places they could've made their new home, but still they walked.

"Some say they left their mark by dipping their hands in blood and pressing them against rocks and carved signs in them with knives made of ivory."

"They could've been trail markers for those who were left behind to follow or as directionals to lead them back home," I said. "The John Day canyon has plenty of petroglyphs and petrographs of unknown origin."

The water boiled and I threw in a handful of coffee grounds and added cold water to sink them.

As I poured myself a mug, November continued. "The ancients followed the river until they reached the mountains. They had to climb up them and then down the other side. They followed a stream that became a river that finally led them to a valley."

"Thunder Valley," I said.

"But it did not have that name then because it was not home to any other people."

"So the wandering Tlingit made it theirs."

"Yes."

"But why there after all that time and after so much hardship? Was it really so different than any of the other places they'd paddled past or walked through?"

"You will have to ask Kagán."

She put the eggs and bacon along with a piece of fry bread onto a plate. I asked her what finally happened to the Tlingit ancients.

"They built a great wikiup, not with slender willow branches like we Numu do, but out of big trees they cut down. The posts that held up the roof were carved to tell the stories of their journey and that of their people's history.

"They chopped down the tallest tree in the forest, cut off its limbs, and skinned its bark. Then they carved animals into it stacked one on top of the other. Beaver, bear, raven, eagle, and killer whale. On top of this great pole they carved a giant beaked bird with outspread wings. Thunderbird."

"I thought that was a Navajo spirit that delivers rain and warns of danger."

November tsked. "My Diné brothers and sisters are not the only people watched over by Thunderbird. Zuni, Ojibwe, Cherokee, and many others are also."

"If the totem pole and big clan house were still there, people would know about it. It'd be one of the greatest attractions in Oregon. But I never heard about it. Does the legend say what happened to it and the ancient ones?"

"The legend had many endings depending on who was telling it and when. The people journeyed home to the place where the sea breaks its back. They all died. The forest grew so thick it swallowed the totem pole and the big wikiup with them inside it. They climbed on Thunderbird's back and flew away."

"But you know what really happened to them."

"It is not for me to tell you."

"But Kagán is."

"If you ask and if she wishes."

November handed me a parcel wrapped in cloth and tied with a string.

"What is it?"

"Food. You will need it to keep your strength up."

"Thanks, but I don't plan on being gone that long."

"That will be up to Kagán."

"Not Thunderbird?"

November harumphed. "You still have much to learn, my son."

7

———

The first rays of the sun encircled the hanging Running R. I gave the halo a nod, hoping it was a good sign and not a warning. An out-of-the-way spot in the lee of the stable beckoned. I parked and led Wovoka out of the trailer. He snorted his pleasure, but then quickly laid back his ears and tossed his head as a couple of stallions started squealing warnings and stamping their hooves from a nearby corral.

"It's only the ranch's welcoming party," I said and stroked his muzzle. "We'll soon leave them in the dust."

The big buckskin shook his black mane as if shaking off the other horses and relaxed. I saddled him, slung on saddlebags, and tied my oilskin duster behind the cantle. I was switching out his lead for reins when KT ambled over. He was pinching a hand-rolled cigarette in one hand and holding a mug of coffee in the other.

"Pot of joe warmin' in the bunkhouse, you wanna cup."

"Thanks anyway. I drained a thermos on the way up from No Mountain."

"Then you'll be drainin' soon enough." He took a drag from

the hand-rolled and said as he exhaled, "Good-lookin' cuttin' horse. Could be brother to my buckskin."

"I noticed that yesterday. They both have matching black socks."

"What d'ya call yours?"

"Wovoka."

"Like the Paiute holy man from back in the day, the one started all that ghost dancin' stuff?"

"Named after him, but not by me. You know your Native history. Most people think the Ghost Dance religion was started by the Lakota when they wore ghost shirts at Wounded Knee. Didn't save them from being massacred."

"Well, you been cowboyin' long as me, you hear stuff. Most is bullshit, but some's got more truth than lie in it. Your horse, he named Wovoka 'cause he's got a lot of spirit?"

"He's got plenty of that, but the man who bred him is Paiute. Lyle Rides Alone. He named him that because the holy man was a woodcutter and that's what it translates to in Numu. Wovoka."

"That's a good one. Cutter for a cuttin' horse."

He watched as I finished with the reins and slid my Winchester into the saddle scabbard.

"Can't beat lever action when you're shootin' on the gallop. What I ride with. You always carried it?"

"Since I signed on as a wildlife ranger. Goes with the job."

"And afore?"

"M16 or whatever was close at hand."

"That's right. You served. Sheriff said so."

"You?"

"Too many busted bones for humpin' a pack all day. If the army let me ride instead of walk, well ..."

"You from Oregon?"

"Nope, I'm saddle tramp born and bred. If I weren't cowboyin' I were rodeoin'."

"How long you been with the Running R?"

He took another hit from his hand-rolled and chased the nicotine with caffeine. "Goin' on four year."

"Then you knew Mr. Railsback. Adam."

"I seen him when he were here, though t'weren't regular like."

"Doesn't sound like you thought much of him."

"He were a sorry sumbitch. Didn't give two shits about ranchin'. Cared even less for his wife and sons. Jo didn't deserve that. I mean, Mrs. Railsback."

"Cass told me he had another family. That they aren't welcome here."

KT shrugged. "Pie only got so many slices in it. Start handin' 'em out to people who claim to be kin but maybe ain't, well ..." He puffed his cigarette.

"Sheriff Warbler didn't recognize you from when he was here investigating Adam Railsback's death."

"No reason he woulda. Me and some of the boys was takin' beeves o'er to Pendleton. Gone when Aiden shot his old man. Still gone when the sheriff came up and gave him a pass."

"You don't agree it was an accident?"

"I'm a cowhand, not a lawman. Not my place to say one or the other. Don' matter no ways. He's still dead."

"What about Kagán?"

"What about her?"

"How long has she worked at the Running R?"

KT took another drag, holding the smoke in longer this time before exhaling it straight at me. I didn't wave the cloud away.

"That what pokin' round means, askin' lotta questions?"

"Part of it."

"Well, Cass told me to give you a hand and he's the boss. Kagán, she showed up goin' on a year now."

"Filling a job or asking for one?"

"Neither. Said she were passin' through and heard a story or some such about her kind havin' lived here. She were curious about it. You know, who her kinfolk mighta been."

"You mean other Tlingit?"

"That's her kind. But no one here knew nothin' 'bout 'em. Mrs. Railsback felt sorry for her and told her to spend the night, it gettin' late. One day led to the next and she's still here. You know, workin' for her bread 'n butter."

"You talk to her much?"

"A howdy or you need a hand with that, but, truth is, she don' come outta the big house much and I don' go in. I see her, it's usually her standin' up there in that window like she's lookin' for somethin' or waitin' on someone."

He finished the cigarette, pinched the lit end until it was out, and put the butt in his front shirt pocket. It reminded me of all the men in my squad who smoked. It wasn't so much they didn't want to leave a butt on the ground for Charlie to find and track us, but more about waste not, want not.

"Look like you're fixin' to ford the river. Show you the way agin, you need."

"That's okay, I can find it. One last thing. This deal Aiden is working on. Have you met Stuart Kinsey or any of the other investors?"

"You mean, what do I think about the whole kit 'n caboodle?" He turned his head and hawked, the spit as dark as coffee and cigarette tar.

"I see."

"Aiden kilt his daddy and now he's hellbent on killin' the Runnin' R. Bring the two-lane up here and all the cars comin' and goin' scare the beeves to skin 'n bones. Turn good pasture into a golf course?" He spit again. "Can't eat no golf ball."

"Mrs. Railsback made it sound like the family doesn't have a choice."

"Mebbe so, but one thin's for sure. It'll break her heart clean in two. Jo loves this place."

Jo, again, I thought. "She called Kinsey the devil. Cass said he was an East Coast con man."

"Well, I ain't never been east of Texas, but I come acrost his kind ever'place I ever cowboyed. Always lookin' fer a fast buck and don' care who they gotta hurt to git it."

He hawked. "Kinsey might be workin' it at a higher level, but he's no different than some dude hustlin' eight ball in a two-bit saloon."

"Appreciate your take on all this. I better get moving if I'm going to make the most of daylight."

I swung into the saddle. Before I could urge Wovoka forward, KT grabbed my stirrup.

"It ain't Kinsey you gotta keep your eye on. It's his two shit-kickers. He talks you into playin' eight ball with him, they be the ones gonna come up behind you while you're linin' up your shot and bust a cue cross your head then shove it up where the sun don' shine."

"I'll keep that in mind."

"Better you keep your hand on that pistol you're strappin'. You're gonna need it."

He let go of the stirrup and I clucked at Wovoka to step lively. We headed back down the trail to the Thunder River. I didn't need to turn around to see if Kagán was watching from the upstairs window. I could feel her eyes on the back of my head and hear a wolf tail swishing.

Wovoka didn't balk as I steered him into the ford. He'd crossed rivers plenty of times—in spring, summer, fall, and winter. He kept his eyes trained on the far bank and so did I as the sound of the water swirling around his legs and rushing below his barrel played a sweet song of freedom.

We climbed onto dry land and I gave him his head and he

broke into a lope to dry off. The water sheeting off him sparkled like dewdrops. I slowed him when we reached the dirt road that had a gap in it where the bridge once stood. We followed it through the fields to the stand of cottonwoods and the white camper.

Pudge had already inspected the inside but I needed to take a look-see too. Weak daylight shone through the windows and illuminated black smudges on the table and cabinet knobs where the sheriff had dusted for fingerprints.

The layout was just as Pudge had described. Everything was neat and tidy, down to the sheets and blankets on the bed that were tucked in tight. I flashed on how my father who was career-military would conduct white glove inspections on his rare visits home. If he could bounce a quarter off my bed, it was mine to keep. If it sunk into the folds, it went back into his pocket while I gave him twenty pushups. It was a tradition I didn't carry on with Hattie and Johnny.

I opened cabinets and drawers, peeled up carpet and pried off paneling, but found nothing that could shed light on Pillsbury and, more importantly, who'd killed him and why. After an hour of searching, I got out and closed the door behind me.

Maybe I was shooting way wide of the mark. Maybe he had been killed by a wild animal. Scenarios reeled through my mind like 8mm home movies. It was nighttime and he had to take a leak. Being the fastidious person that he obviously was, he opted to step outside rather than use a honey bucket. Wham! A cougar pounced on him. Or he turned the corner and came face-to-face with a bear that had been lured by the smell of whatever he'd cooked for dinner. Bam! Pillsbury became dinner.

I spent the next hour searching the ground around the camper, but didn't find so much as a boot print, much less one made by a paw.

What was missing? What was I missing? A voice from the

past started calling, faint at first and then growing louder. It belonged to the squad leader I eventually replaced who'd showed me the ropes on how to track. "You gotta look for what's missing as closely as what's there," he always said.

Pudge and I had focused on what was in the camper, but that wasn't the only part of the rig. I walked around to the cab and tried the driver's side door. It was unlocked, the same as the camper shell's door had been. The cab was immaculate except for the floor mat. A puddle pooled beneath the pedals. Whoever had driven it last had done so with snow on their boots and it had melted. I checked the ignition. No key.

I looked around. It hadn't been tucked above the visor for safekeeping. It wasn't in the ashtray or the glove box. Under the seat was also a big fat empty zero. Not even a gum wrapper or peanut shell.

When I first moved to Harney County, it'd taken me a while to get in the habit of not locking anything. No one in No Mountain did. Not the front doors and windows to their houses and not their vehicles either. They even left the keys in the ignition because they didn't want to slow anyone down who might need to borrow it in an emergency.

It was a safe bet Wilbur Pillsbury wasn't from Harney County. If he had been the last to drive the camper, he would've pocketed the key out of habit, even when parking alone in a field far from anyone. But there weren't any keys when I'd searched him, only a fancy broken compass.

Someone else was the last to drive his rented camper and it sure wasn't a bear or cougar.

8

Ever since Girl Born in Snow was a little girl—even before the boarding school teachers renamed her November and tried to kill the Indian in her by beating her when she spoke Numu and locking her in a covered pit when she tried to run away—she'd been able to see things that needed to be seen, find things that needed to be found, and understand things that needed to be understood.

She did that in what she called dreamworld, a place where her mind's eye was free to soar like an eagle over deserts, rivers, mountains, and time, and see into people's hearts and minds. Because she'd been born outdoors in a blizzard protected only by her mother's arms, she was unfettered like other people who believed most things were impossible. Her feet didn't always have to touch the ground. She could talk with anyone and anything, including the Nuwuddu—what the Numu called the first people, animals; Numu were the second people—and the wind, the rain, the rocks, the trees, the moon, and the stars.

I often wished I could free myself to experience dreamworld, but wishing wasn't the same as needing. And right then in a field of grass patched with snow alongside cottonwoods growing beside the banks of the Thunder River, I needed to see how Wilbur Pillsbury's killer had dragged him from the camper, tortured and gutted him, and escaped without leaving a trace.

Being able to see all that was the first step in figuring out who did it and why. It could also lead to knowing if anyone else was involved.

Since I couldn't soar, I could at least gain a new perspective. Grabbing my binoculars, I climbed on top of the camper and mimicked Pudge's periscope maneuver. The voice of the squad leader I'd replaced echoed. Look for patterns: jungle vines that have been shoved aside from the same direction and plant stems that are broken on the same side. Then—and even more importantly—look for the single vine or broken stem pointing in the opposite direction, the one puddle on a trail where the splash mark goes a different way.

I began by making sweeps with my binoculars. Five feet out. Ten feet. Fifteen. Twenty. A pattern began to emerge in the patches of snow and grass. Was it one of the twelve patterns found in nature? Spots, stripes, spirals, cracks, flows, meanders, bubbles, chaos? Was it a checkerboard, a chessboard? A paisley blouse? A gridded window? Was it a pattern on one of November's blankets?

I focused on where we'd rolled Wilbur Pillsbury over, lowered the binoculars, closed my eyes, and tried November's trick of seeing beyond what was right in front of me.

The patches of grass and snow slowly began to move. One patch forward, two to the right. One patch back. One to the left. Two more forward. Something started humming in my head. It was me. I was humming a song. Humming like I did when Gemma and I slow danced alone in the stable, two-stepped at a neighbor's hoedown.

It was a dance pattern.

I opened my eyes and could see it. The killer holding a sack filled with Pillsbury's body parts and dancing with a tree branch, skipping from one snow patch to the next, twirling as he brushed away his footprints, and then continued dancing his way toward the stand of cottonwoods.

A whistle and a jump and Wovoka and I were already in the woods when I realized I was holding the reins in one hand and my Smith & Wesson in the other.

It didn't take long to find where the killer had stopped trying to cover his tracks. Footprints showed in the snow. A broken branch had been cast aside. I dismounted and pulled the camera I'd bought in Bend from the saddlebag. The snow had melted during the day and then froze again at night, making it hard to calculate the shoe size and width of the prints. There were no discernible sole or tread marks to make out either. Still, I snapped away and took pictures of the makeshift broom as well.

The tracks wound their way between the trees in the direction of the river. I exchanged the camera for my Winchester and followed on foot with Wovoka trailing behind.

The sound of rapids grew louder and I could hear Doc's voice in them: If the killer was human, he'd chuck whatever he cut off Wilbur Pillsbury into the river. I reached the fast-moving water's edge and stared into reality. Any evidence thrown in there was on its way to Malheur Lake over a hundred miles away.

I turned around to reach for Wovoka's reins. The big buckskin had turned sideways to me with his head pointed upriver. He hadn't done it to make himself easier to mount; he did it instinctively to position himself on a trail. I hadn't noticed it until then. Most likely it'd been made by deer coming down to drink, but Wovoka wouldn't be the first horse to use it.

The camera came out again and I snapped pictures of hoofprints on the trail. They'd been made by more than one and I couldn't tell how new or old they were. No matter. They were sign, and so I climbed aboard Wovoka. Thirty minutes later the trail drew right alongside a narrow spot in the river.

The opposite bank appeared as close as it was where I'd crossed a few hours before. A bed of gravel and rocks being washed downstream had piled up in front of a chain of boulders and formed another ford. The higher, faster water would make it more sporty to cross, but it looked doable for a horse as strong and tall as Wovoka. I turned my attention back to the trail. There were hoofprints coming and going.

I decided to stay on the trail. It wound back through the trees and into an open field patched with snow and littered with cow pies. Bisecting it was the dirt road I'd left a couple of miles back. I followed it for half a mile where it ended in front of a barbwire fence strung on poles made from the thick limbs of cottonwood trees. It was the boundary with the Broken Wing.

I could've turned around and ridden back to the ford, but I'd learned long ago that coulda, woulda, shoulda's were cancers of the soul that can eat a man alive. I steered Wovoka toward a sag in the fence and asked him to jump.

"Attaboy," I said when we landed.

The Broken Wing's side was identical to the Running R's only without the dirt road. Its share of the field was similarly dotted with patches of snow and cow pies. I scanned the horizon for a ranch house or buildings of any kind, but saw none. Wondering if the riverside trail I'd been riding on picked back up down by the water, I clicked my cheek and Wovoka broke into a trot toward the trees.

After five minutes of threading through the cottonwoods, the roar of rapids grew closer. But then came an even closer noise— the familiar cha-ching ping of a lever action jacking a cartridge into a Winchester followed by a heavier metal-on-metal click-clank of a rifle bolt being thrown.

"Stop right there and put your hands up where I can see 'em," a voice on the right called.

"Try for your irons and I'll drop you where you sit," a nearly identical voice on the left said.

9

The technical term written on the basic training chalkboard was "interlocking fire." Drill sergeants called it "crossfire" during maneuvers. Different terms were used in Vietnam depending on the makeup of the squad, but no matter the slang, it all boiled down to the same message: shoot the shit out of whoever's in the middle.

Seeing it was me between the two rifles, I whoaed Wovoka and reached for the sky. "Don't shoot. I'm here for a good reason."

"We didn't give you no permission and we don't need none to shoot you," the voice with the Winchester on my right said. He didn't show himself from behind the tree he was using as cover.

"That and then some," said the voice with the rifle on the left. He stayed behind his tree too.

"I'm not after your stock."

"Bullshit," said Winchester.

"Double bullshit," said Rifle.

"I'm a US Fish and Wildlife ranger and—"

"Meaning you're a rustler with a badge," Winchester said.

"And I've been deputized by the sheriff of Harney County to investigate a killing on the Running R."

A moment of silence made me think either my words had bought me a pass or they were taking better aim before squeezing their triggers.

Instead, I got whoops of laughter in stereo.

"You're the most donkey dumb man in Oregon," Winchester said from behind his tree.

"Make that the world," Rifle said from behind his.

"I'm telling the truth," I said.

"Maybe, but donkey dumb still sticks. How do you know we ain't the killers?"

"Because if you were, I'd already be dead."

That brought another round of silence.

"Fair point," Winchester finally said. "Was it a Railsback got killed?"

"Does it matter?"

"Depends on the Railsback. Cass, he's a square shooter. Aiden, he's a snotnosed punk. Now the mother, you get on her uppity side, you find out lickety-split she ain't all sweet tea and honey biscuits."

"It wasn't a family member."

"Wasn't KT, was it? We had us our differences, but he's cowboy through and through. Whatever he does, he does 'cause he's getting paid to do it."

"Not KT either. A man hired by the outfit developing a part of their ranch."

"Well, we won't shed no tears for him. That outfit's bad to the bone," Winchester said.

"Double bad," Rifle said.

"Have you had run-ins with them?"

"And run-offs," Winchester said. "That's what we do every time they try coming on our land. Run 'em off."

"Can I put my hands down? Get off my horse so we can talk out here in the open?"

They mulled it over. Winchester finally said, "Okay, but leave your rifle in the scabbard and drop your holster. Try it a different way and you'd wish you hadn't, but you won't have no time to wish. Follow?"

Once off Wovoka, I unbuckled my holster and took a couple of steps away from it.

I was right about the make of the lever-action. It was a Winchester the man was cradling as he stepped out from behind the tree. He wore a black slouch hat and sported a Civil War-era beard recently brought back in fashion by ZZ Top. Rifle moved away from his tree shouldering a .30-06 Springfield aimed at my heart. He looked exactly like Winchester, from the top of his slouch hat right down to the tip of his beard that brushed the bottom of his sternum.

"Name's Nick Drake," I said. "I live on a ranch in No Mountain. Are you Calhouns?"

"Yep," Winchester said. "I'm Zeb, he's Jeb."

"Twins?"

"We shared a womb."

They both chuckled at what was obviously an oft-told joke.

"Pleased to meet you. I heard this ranch has been in your family for quite some time."

"It has," Zeb said. "Our great-grandpappy came up from Fort Smith, Arkansas in the eighteen oughts and claimed the Broken Wing."

Jeb nodded and lowered the .30-06. "We been fighting Rails-backs over the line between our spreads ever since."

"You sound like you're fighting the developers too."

Zeb Calhoun's eyes were close-set, but they managed to narrow even further. "They're no better than carpetbaggers. What our kin used to say back home."

"Double damn right we're fighting 'em," Jeb said.

"Did they offer you a deal like they did the Railsbacks?"

"Tried but we made it clear we'll never sell." Zeb shook his Winchester. "Why we run 'em off when they keep on trying."

"You must've met Stuart Kinsey."

The two ZZ Top beards bobbed in unison.

"He's the slickest carpetbagger ever born," Zeb said. "Drives a fancy rig and wears fancy clothes, but he ain't no Fancy Dan. You can see his real self in his eyes."

"Slit your throat as soon as shake your hand," Jeb said.

"What did he say when you told him you didn't want to sell?"

"Smiled and said that's your answer today but it won't be tomorrow," Zeb said.

"Like I said, slit your throat as soon as shake your hand," his twin said.

"Does that mean you saw a knife on him?"

"Pshaw," Jeb said. "He's got one, for sure, but you won't see it till it's sticking outta your craw."

"He come to your place on his own?"

Jeb pshawed again. "He's got a man drives him. Skinny guy with a closed-lip smile, but he ain't laughing. Got another man. Big fella. You reach up to scratch your beard, he'd snatch your fingers before they got there and break 'em all. Why when we see 'em now, we fire a few over their heads. Don't wanna tangle with 'em up close."

Zeb's slouch hat tilted as he scrunched his face at me. "How did this fella on the Running R die?"

"Somone took a knife to him. Carved him up to make it look like a wild animal did it."

Neither guilt nor horror nor fear crossed their faces, at least the parts I could see that weren't covered with facial hair.

"Where's the poor fella now?" Zeb said.

"At the Harney County morgue. The coroner took him back."

"And why are you here and not the sheriff?"

"He returned to Burns to take a different angle on the investigation."

Zeb turned to his twin. "I told you things were gonna get a whole lot worse before they got better with that big-city gang showing up and spreading their money round trying to buy us all out."

"Double worse, brother. Why we gotta be double on our toes."

"Have they approached other ranches in Thunder Valley?" I said.

"All of 'em, I reckon," Zeb said. "We heard from a couple who got the knock on the door. They're pretty small compared to us. Don't have the hands to fight anyone off when it comes to that."

"Is that what you think will happen?"

"As sure as Sunday. Men like Stuart Kinsey, they don't need to say out loud what they're gonna do if they don't get their way. It's understood."

His eyes studied me from beneath the brim of his slouch hat. "All this still don't explain why you decided to jump our fence? You got reason to believe the man who carved up Kinsey's man came this way?"

"The body was three miles back. I followed the killer's tracks into the woods and down to the river. He might've left a horse there and rode it upriver to a ford. There's tracks going in both directions and I couldn't tell if he crossed or not. I continued riding this way to see if I could pick up fresh ones."

"If he took the ford, it'd put him back on the side where the Railsbacks all live. Makes me think he's one of them."

"Could be, but no one there is going anywhere and so I decided to see if he might've gone a different way."

"So, you're the kind takes a trail you don't know instead of the one you do," Zeb said.

"One's easy, one's hard. Double hard," Jeb said.

"I had to take a look-see, but your field is a muddle of cow pies, snow patches, and all sorts of hoofprints. Left me two choices. Go back the way I came or keep riding on this side and see if he cut down to a trail along the river."

I looked in the direction of the sound of rapids. "I assume there is one."

"There is."

"Any objection if I ride down to it and see if I can find any sign?"

"That'd be a trick, seeing it gets lots of traffic," Zeb said. "Beeves and horses and cowhands going twixt the bunkhouse, barn, and corrals. Million prints in both directions. The big house where Jeb and me and our wives and children live is also down there."

"All on this side of the river?"

The twin slouch hats bobbed.

"Then your bridge must be pretty big."

"Big enough to drive a semi and cow carrier across."

"Double big," Jeb said.

"The Railsbacks' bridge over to this side of the river got washed out. The man who got killed drove his camper over it before it did. It's still there. The sheriff wants to take it back to Burns."

"You want to drive it onto our land and cross our bridge?" Zeb said.

"The sheriff would consider it a favor. Could have evidence in it that might get us closer to identifying the killer."

The two brothers looked at each other. Silent words passed between them.

Zeb finally spoke up. "We want to know what's in it for us if we let him."

"What would you want?"

"Help when we need it, and we're gonna need it sooner than later. That Kinsey fella? He won't stop coming after our land till he gets it or we stop him for good. We figure he's got plenty more men like the two riding with him now. Jeb and me, we're gonna need some more fellas ourselves."

"I'll see what I can do."

"Fair enough. We'll take you down to the river and show you the trail. Stop by the house and have a cup of coffee. Something stronger if you like. We still it ourselves." He winked. "Then you can test our bridge yourself and take the easy path to the Running R and maybe find out who the real killer is."

10

———

Thunder rumbled and the drops of what started off as a light rain grew heavier as I neared the Railsback compound. The beads rolling down my oilskin duster gathered speed and I urged Wovoka to do the same.

As the big buckskin cantered, I fished out my flashlight and aimed the beam over his head to light the trail ahead. It paled in comparison to the sheets of lightning starting to flash. I tried not to think about the bit in his mouth, the metal D rings and buckles on the tack, and the steel revolver strapped to my hip.

Wovoka and I were old hands when it came to being outside in a storm, but coronas glowing from the ranch house windows were definitely a welcome sight. I was heading straight to my rig so I could trailer him out of the rain when the sliding door to the stable screeched open.

"Bring him on in," KT hollered over the growing din. "He'll be needin' a rubdown and dry place to stand. Bag of oats too."

"Much obliged," I said and rode inside. "Glad you happened to be opening the door just now."

"Heard his hoofs poundin' from back a spell." He slid the door closed. "Got a sense fer it."

"A sixth sense," I said as I dismounted.

I gave Wovoka a pat on the neck. "Sure-footed as always."

When I threw up the stirrup to unfasten his cinch, KT said, "I'll git that fer you. Git him all squared away and bedded down in an empty stall o'er there. You'll wanna git on o'er to the big house. They fixin' to have supper."

"You sure you don't need a hand?"

"This what I do. You're the guest and Mrs. Railsback wouldn' want it no other way. 'Sides, you might be interested in the company they keepin'."

"Who's that?"

"Mr. Stuart Kinsey and a couple of his money men."

"That a fact."

"Aiden, he ask 'em over for a business meetin', but really a way to tell 'em 'bout Mr. Pillsbury bein' dead 'n all."

"You're right. That's a conversation I wouldn't want to miss."

"You find what you lookin' for on the other side?"

"Found more questions than answers, but I did meet Zeb and Jeb Calhoun. They said to say howdy."

"Them ole boys, they good ole boys, but I sure don' wanna see what's livin' in them beards."

I took the grin with me as I strode to my pickup, grabbed my duffle bag, and hustled over to the house. The front door was unlocked as Jo Railsback had promised it always would be. I hung my oilskin on a hook made of an upturned deer foot and made for the stairway. Jo stepped in from the living room.

"Oh thank God, you're back. I was worried about you being out in this storm. You'll join us for supper, won't you?"

"As soon as I change."

"Perfect. I'll ask Kagán to set a place."

A white Hudson Bay blanket with its trademark green, red, yellow, and black stripes covered the bed in the guest room upstairs. A matching pitcher and basin set on a stand beckoned.

I stripped off my clothes, washed up, and sat on the edge of the bed. If it weren't for the promise of meeting the notorious head of Thunder Valley Inc., I would've fallen backward and slept until daylight.

After putting on a fresh pair of clothes and dry socks, I looked at my boots standing in the corner. They were a dripping wet reminder I should've brought a second pair in case of an invitation to a fancy meal.

"*Best laid plans of mice and men,*" I muttered, quoting my favorite line from Robert Burns.

At least I had a backup. I pulled out a pair of ankle-high deerskin moccasins that November had made me and laced them up.

"For walking through the house or across the desert when you do not want anyone or anything to hear you," she'd said when she gave them to me.

"Except for you," I'd replied. "Nothing gets past your ears."

"Who says they are the only things I listen with?" she tsked.

With no bootheels clacking on the treads, no one heard me walking down the stairs. Or so I thought. I'd barely stepped onto the entrance hall's polished floor when the Tlingit woman appeared out of nowhere.

Oystershells dangled from a pair of silver hoop earrings and caught the light from the elk antler chandelier. It made the shells gleam like opals. Obsidian eyes staring over the polished piece of ivory piercing her septum met mine. Her face tattoos were no less fierce and alluring, but they didn't crease when she whispered, "Careful." Her moccasins were more silent than mine when she glided away.

I tried not to dwell on her warning when I entered the living room. Jo Railsback sat on one of the leather couches bookended by her sons. Three men sat on the one across from them. Glasses of amber liquid were set on coasters in front of them. I made the one in the middle as Stuart Kinsey. He wore a custom-tailored suit and open collared shirt. His wavy dark hair was stylishly long in the back and on the sides, but not too long.

Aiden jumped up when he saw me enter. "Gentlemen, this is Nick Drake. He's a ranger with the US Fish and Wildlife Service."

The three men stood and looked me up and down. Their eyes stopped at the Paiute moccasins.

"You don't look Indian like the housekeeper," Kinsey said.

"A gift from a friend. My boots are soaked from being out in the field all day. You must be Stuart Kinsey."

He gave a mock bow. "My reputation precedes me."

His gold wristwatch flashed as we shook hands and his manicured nails were as polished as a fancy new car.

"And these gentlemen are also members of Thunder Valley Inc.," Aiden said quickly.

"Burt Symes," the one who'd been sitting closest to the fire said. He was flushed and sweaty, more likely from having an extra sixty, seventy pounds on his short frame rather than his proximity to the fireplace.

"Jeffrey Parker," the third man said in a Texas drawl. He was the tallest of the three, wore a string tie and alligator boots. His grip was firm and his palm calloused. I made him for a wealthy rancher.

Neither of the two fit the description of the bodyguards that KT, Cass, and the Calhoun twins had painted. I wondered where they were? The kitchen, maybe. Kagán's warning echoed.

"What brings you to the Running R?" Kinsey asked.

"Your man, Wilbur Pillsbury. Harney County Sheriff Pudge Warbler deputized me to help find out how he died."

"That makes sense, given your line of work with Fish and Wildlife. Did you find what kind of wild creature was responsible."

"What makes you think an animal did?"

"It's my business to know everything and everyone in the place where I'm investing my money."

"Sheriff Warbler already cautioned the Railsbacks from speculating on Mr. Pillsbury's death since the cause hasn't been confirmed by the coroner yet or made public. I'm sure he'd advise you to do the same."

"I don't speculate, Ranger Drake. And certainly not in business or anything related to it. The information I have on Pillsbury death comes directly from law enforcement officials themselves."

"Not from Pudge or anybody in his department," I said. "Or the Harney County coroner either."

He smiled. It was the kind that made you want to pat your pockets and check your fingers and wrist to make sure you still had everything you'd come with.

"In my world, it pays to converse with those who operate at a higher level than an aged constable in the fifth-least populated county in Oregon. In this particular case, I spoke personally with Warbler's supervisor at the behest of my good friend, the state attorney general. I'm speaking of Regional County Sheriff Buster Burton."

Kinsey's smile didn't leave. "I understand you knew Sheriff Burton when he had your father-in-law's position before the attorney general promoted him."

I didn't blink. Not because he already knew who I was before Aiden had introduced me, but because I didn't want to give him the satisfaction of seeing me react to a name from the past that was sure to roil the old sheriff's guts more than a dose of chemo.

"You're not from around here, are you?" I said.

"What makes you say that?" Kinsey said.

"Because if you were, you'd know Bust'em has a reputation

for being so eager to kiss ass he puckers his lips before he gets all the facts straight."

Cass laughed and even Jo couldn't stifle a giggle.

"I'll keep that in mind, ranger. By the way, does your boss Liz Bloom know your father-in-law deputized you? The US Fish and Wildlife director is an old friend too. I'm sure he wouldn't be pleased if he knew she was allowing her direct reports to moonlight."

Jo stood abruptly. "Gentlemen, please, this way to the dining room."

I stayed back to cool my temper as they filed out. So did Cass.

"This Bust'em fellow may be an ass kisser, but Kinsey's a complete asshole," he said.

"And then some," I said. "Was he surprised to learn about Pillsbury's death?"

"Not at all. It was like he already knew. Hearing him now, it's obvious that he did. But he still let Aiden tell him."

"To test him."

He nodded. "My little brother is in way over his head. As usual."

I asked Cass if he'd met Symes and Parker before.

"Only once, and it was early on. They were part of a group of potential investors that toured the property. Burt Symes is with a bank of some sort. Not like the kind where you keep your savings account or cash your paycheck. He called it a private investment bank for wealthy clients. Jeffrey Parker? He made a bundle in oil when he was drilling for water on his cattle ranch out in the middle of Texas and hit a gusher by accident."

"Where are Kinsey's two sidekicks? The Beelzebubs you called them."

"Sitting in the kitchen. Mother asked Kagán to rustle up

something for them to eat while they wait for Kinsey to finish dining with us."

"They're not going to spend the night? It's pretty stormy out there."

"No, they drove up in a four-wheel-drive. It's parked in the barn to keep warm. Kinsey stays at the Double Ought when he's here. That's a ranch down the highway." Cass shook his head. "The owner's an old-timer. You ever see that movie *The Godfather* came out a few years back? Kinsey must've made him an offer he couldn't refuse."

I chinned in the direction of the dining room. "Shall we?"

"Sure, but did you find anything today that could help figure out how Pillsbury died?"

"Nothing to speak of," I said. "But in here just now, yeah, I found out something, all right."

11

———

The wine had already been poured when Cass and I joined the others. Jo was seated at the head of the table and waved me into the empty chair next to her. Kinsey sat across from me.

He cast his eyes around the table before raising his glass. "I'd like to propose a toast. Please join me in saluting our lovely and ever-beautiful hostess."

All the glasses went up and saluted Jo, but before anyone could take a sip, Kinsey continued.

"Burt, Jeffrey, and I are honored that you've elected to partner with us in this bold and remarkable venture to chart a new future for Thunder Valley. What we're doing will benefit generations to come. Not only for us as investors, but for the people who will find well-paying jobs here and the families who come to live and play. The memories they create will be our true and lasting legacy."

"Here, here," the pudgy banker said and downed half a glass in a swallow.

Kinsey turned his gaze on me as I lowered my still-full wineglass. "You're not drinking? That's considered bad luck."

"More unlucky for all of us if I did," I said.

He smiled slyly. "Ah, that's right. You're an addict. My friend in charge of Fish and Wildlife shared some of the darker chapters in your history."

"You mean my heroin addiction before I signed up with the wildlife service's program for hiring Vietnam War vets. Yeah, that was a dark time for me, but it was even darker for the men I served with who didn't make it home. It's still very dark for the loved ones they left behind. Parents, wives, children."

Jo's hand shot out and patted my wrist. "You poor thing."

"No one needs to feel sorry for me. I made it back. I was able to kick it."

"How?"

I didn't tell her about the months I'd spent at Walter Reed, going cold turkey, the counseling I received there, the days and nights during the first few years I lived in No Mountain where I'd put a pebble in a can to mark every day I went without using. How when the need grew hard to resist, I'd rattle the can as long as it took. How when the devil's knock became so loud it drowned out the rattling pebbles, I'd kickstart my motorcycle and tear across the desert at full speed so he couldn't catch me.

"Short version is, I got wounded, got hooked, but even if I hadn't taken a bullet, I probably still would've used." I pointed at my head. "It used to be called shell shock, then battle fatigue, and now combat fatigue. No doubt they'll come up with a new term one of these days."

"But something must've cured you."

"An addict's never cured, but now I have a wife, two kids, a good job, and all the people in Harney County reminding me every single day that life's worth living."

She patted my wrist again. "There's nothing like children to keep you thinking about something besides yourself. I keep telling Cass and Aiden that. Meet a girl, get married, have kids. Have lots of kids."

"Touching story," Kinsey said, but even the sip of wine that followed couldn't drown the cynicism.

I raised my water glass. "I'd like to make a toast too. Something that was overlooked in the first one. To Wilbur Pillsbury. May he rest in peace. To his family, condolences for your loss."

"To Pillsbury," Cass chimed in loudly.

"Of course," Jo said. "The poor, poor man."

I downed my water while staring at Stuart Kinsey. War had taught me a lot about enemies. Never underestimate them. Never stop learning all you can about them. And never, ever take your eyes off them. The way Kinsey returned my stare told me he'd learned the same lesson.

Kagán appeared bearing a large platter with a prime rib roast on it. She set it in front of Jo. Close behind came two men carrying serving dishes. Both wore dark suits with black turtlenecks instead of collared shirts. One was thin with a fixed closed-mouth smile and long chin. The other was even heavier-set than the banker and had a black toothbrush mustache. The Beelzebubs, Cass had called them. Shitkickers was the word KT used. Despite their menacing air, I pictured Laurel and Hardy.

Laurel set a bowl of roasted potatoes down and Hardy followed suit with one filled with cooked peas. They both stepped back and stood behind Kinsey. Kagán waited beside Jo.

"It all looks perfect, dear," Jo said to her. "Thank you, I'll carve."

As Jo picked up a large knife and sliced the roast as masterfully as a trained butcher, the Tlingit backed away toward the open door. Her head turned toward Kinsey and her nostrils flared as if to show that the polished ivory piercing her septum was the tip of a harpoon aimed at him.

Jo placed thick slabs of rare roast beef on plates. They were passed down the table along with the serving bowls of potatoes and peas. Aiden and Kinsey engaged in a question-and-answer session about the project as they ate. What was the status of the building permits? Was the architect ready to unveil his blueprint for the main lodge? Had a contractor been selected to clear the forest on a particular section of the ranch? How would the onset of winter affect construction? When would phase one of the custom homes be ready to market?

As Kinsey answered, he abruptly stopped cutting a piece of meat and pointed his knife at me.

"I didn't forget about Wilbur Pillsbury. And I sure haven't forgotten about all the field notes he took and the reports he typed up. Your wife's father is about to learn how much trouble he's in for refusing to turn them over to their rightful owner when my attorney requested he do so today. I have a binding contract with the engineering firm that employed Pillsbury that states any work product he produces is legally mine."

He jabbed his knife for emphasis. "Regional Sheriff Burton is on his way to Burns to teach Warbler about living in the real world. Though from what his doctor in Bend says, he's not destined to be doing that much longer anyway."

Kinsey went back to conversing with Aiden, but Laurel and Hardy's attentions were swiftly focused on me. As soon as their boss cleared his plate, Laurel spun and departed. The sound of the front door opening and closing quickly followed. Kinsey stood even though his fellow investors were still chewing.

"Jo, that was a delicious meal. And while I'd enjoy basking in the warmth of your delightful company and most inviting fire-place, the storm outside sounds unabating. We have a very early morning and best leave while the ranch road is still open."

The banker and rancher pushed away from the table and the trio filed out with Hardy shooting me a final glare over his tooth-brush mustache before following. Aiden scurried after them. I could hear the heavy door opening and the idling engine of a powerful vehicle out front. The door slammed shut and the youngest Railsback stomped back into the dining room.

"Who the hell do you think you are, insulting our partners like that?" he shouted at me. "You picked the wrong people to piss off. You'll see."

"Aiden!" Jo said. "Nick is our guest and will be treated as such."

"Some guest. Can't you see he wants to scuttle our project. He must like animals better than people. But guess what? Animals aren't going to save us. Stuart Kinsey will."

"Don't be so sure of that, little brother," Cass said.

"What do you know?"

"I know that Wilbur Pillsbury wound up dead and now Kinsey is doing everything he can to get ahold of whatever he wrote up in his field notes. That means it must be something bad, something that could blow up the whole project. Maybe our so-called savior believes in shooting the messenger."

"You think you know everything, but you're still a dumbshit," Aiden said. "Pillsbury wasn't shot."

"How do you know?" Cass said.

"Uh, because of what Stuart said. An animal attacked him. A cougar or a bear."

For the third time that day, my former squad leader's voice echoed, this time when he was testing me on spotting sign: "'Uh.' Did you just say 'uh' when I asked you if that broken leaf stem was sign? Sergeant, this is war! There's no time for doubt, none for hesitation. It either is or it isn't. Uhs cost lives. Yours and your men's."

It was the second-to-last lesson he taught me. The final was when he was walking point one day and turned around to mouth "Halt" instead of raising a clenched fist. He missed spotting the trip wire that triggered an empty artillery shell packed with pieces of metal and gunpowder that turned him into red mist.

Aiden glared at his brother. "Why are you so against Stuart? What has he ever done but handed us the opportunity of a lifetime. Do you really want to lose the ranch? Because that's what'll happen if we put up any roadblocks. He'll go partner with one of our neighbors and we'll lose the Running R to the bank. If not the bank, then to someone like the Calhouns. Worse, to dear old Dad's whore and his bastards."

Jo slammed her palm on the table. "That's quite enough, Aiden. You know you're never to mention that woman in my presence. Never."

"Oh, Mother. Spare me the you're-so-delicate act. I heard you cussing out Dad plenty of times and calling her worse."

12

———

Gemma answered the phone on the third ring.

"Is this that there female animal doctor?" I drawled.

"This is she."

"Got me a big emergency."

"What's wrong?"

"Sick horse."

"What kind of sick?"

"Lovesick."

"Take two aspirin and call me in the morning."

"Wait, don't hang up. It's me."

"As if I didn't know. You sounded like a drowning bullfrog."

"Can't get anything past you."

"Oh, I can think of one thing you get past just fine." She let it hang and then laughed. It was the best laugh in the whole world.

I asked her how Pudge and the kids were.

"Everyone's asleep. How come you're not?"

"Had to wait until everyone here at the Running R was so I could sneak downstairs and use the phone."

"Now you're going to tell me you're really calling for Pudge."

"Matter of fact, I do need to pass a message on to him, but I was hoping I could give it to you to deliver to him in the morning. That is, after we talk a while."

I gave it a beat. "Remember before kids when we were both away on work trips. We'd call and—"

"Of course I remember." Her tone turned a little huskier. "I also remember the time you called me on your radio. We were both so lonesome, we forgot anyone could've been listening to that channel until—"

"Until we did remember. That made the conversation go a lot—"

"Faster," she said. "You know what I also remember?"

"What?"

"When you used to call back then, you didn't ask to speak to my father."

"Ouch," I said.

"Age," she said. "What's the message?"

I told her about meeting Stuart Kinsey, that his big shot connections got him hooked up with Buster Burton, how Bust'em along with some high-priced lawyers were coming after Pudge for the field notes he took from the camper.

"I'll tell him, but I doubt he'll be surprised by any of it. Since his illness, he seems to have become even more attuned to everything going on around him. Things that he can't see, things that haven't even happened yet."

"Like November and her dreamworld."

"You took the words right out of my mouth. I mentioned it to her and she said it's common for people in Pudge's condition. It's like they're able to tune out all the distractions and focus on what's really important. November says we all have the ability to do it any time we want, but we're so busy with day-to-day stuff, we can't hear it, see it, feel it."

"Whatever *it* is."

"The world around us. The people around us. Beauty, love, music, art—"

"Birds, animals, stars, clouds. A river's babble. Wind through the trees."

"Exactly," she said.

"I've come across people at a wildlife refuge standing there admiring the view. A herd of pronghorn racing across the scrub at Hart Mountain. The patchwork quilt of meadows and fields at Malheur. The sky black with waterfowl winging over Klamath Lake."

"I can see all those things right now."

"The people notice my uniform and tell me how lucky I am to work there. I can see they're moved by the view, but as soon as they drive away, the feeling they had will likely pass the same as wind blowing across the High Lonesome."

"I like to think it's still there inside them and they can feel it when they need it most."

"Maybe so."

We let the silence sit between us as we thought about the times and places where we'd been moved by the real world—the natural one, not the make-believe world of TV and movies. We didn't need to say it, but we both believed we'd become that feeling when our time on earth was up. I hoped Pudge believed that too.

Gemma's sigh carried across the telephone line. "It was storming here earlier, but now it's quiet. I can see stars outside our bedroom window. I wish it were open and you were here in bed keeping me warm."

"Don't we both."

We let that sit, the silence between us nice and easy, and then bid each other sweet dreams.

I continued sitting in the Railsback's living room as the

once-blazing logs turned to embers. The storm had also let up over Thunder Valley and some stars and a glimpse of the moon shone as clouds slipped by. The lunar light illuminated the new blanket of snow that had collected during the evening and made me think of Wilbur Pillsbury lying face down in an old patch.

Could Cass be right that Stuart Kinsey had killed the messenger because he didn't want whatever Pillsbury had discovered to become public? If so, why hadn't he taken his field notes and any reports he'd typed up?

Something else didn't fit. While Kinsey definitely struck me as someone who would do anything to get what he felt he was entitled to, he was too shrewd to kill Pillsbury himself. Order it done, yes. Do it, no.

That left Laurel and Hardy. No doubt they'd do whatever their boss asked, and probably even enjoy torturing a man by cutting off pieces to get him to talk, but neither looked capable of dancing their way from snow patch to snow patch covering their tracks with a makeshift broom, much less saddling a horse and riding back across the river.

Even if they had done all that, why did they take the camper's key and leave Pillsbury's paperwork behind?

The snow outside shimmered as the reflection of stars danced on it while dancing in the sky above. I marveled how they could be in two places at once.

And then it struck me.

Maybe Pillsbury's field notes and reports had been left behind on purpose. Maybe Kinsey making a big fuss over trying to get the ones Pudge took was nothing more than a feint to keep anyone from questioning if there was another, more important document that had been taken.

"Your spirit's restless," Kagán said softly as she stepped into the sliver of moonlight now shining through the window.

"Because a man was murdered," I said. "I meant died. Cause hasn't been confirmed yet."

"You and the sheriff both know it was murder. He wouldn't have deputized you otherwise."

I shrugged. "Protocol."

"Mm. And why do you care so much that it unsettles you about a man you didn't know, a man you never met?"

"Because he matters to someone. Because the truth about how he died and why matters. Because justice matters."

"Justice," she said.

"You say it like you don't believe in it."

"I believe there's injustice. I've seen it too often to think otherwise."

"Among your people?"

"Among many peoples."

The ivory piercing her septum was the same color as the moonlight. I wondered if it was from the tusk of a walrus or a tusk from one of the woolly mammoths that were walking the frozen north only thirteen thousand years ago.

Kagán realized I was staring at her, but didn't blink or turn away. "Is it justice or vengeance you seek?"

"Why do you ask?"

"Because the two don't always stay apart."

She was right. I had seen it in war when the lines between waging a just battle and revenge quickly blurred once men you were fighting beside fell.

"You speak from experience," I said.

"Mm."

She moved closer to the window and looked out. Her black hair with the slight curl reflected the glimmer of the stars. Now they were dancing in three places.

November's story about the ancient Tlingit echoed. It was a

seed the old healer had planted; she never said anything that couldn't be used later.

"Is your experience from having heard about the ancient Tlingit who paddled up the Columbia and John Day Rivers and settled in Thunder Valley?"

"Who told you about them?"

"A Numu healer and dancer whose name translates to Girl Born in Snow. She only told me part of the story. Whether or not she knows it all, I can't say. What I do know is, she wanted me to hear it from you."

"Her medicine is strong."

"Very," I said. "I get the sense yours is too."

"That's for someone else to decide."

"KT told me when you first arrived here, you said you were looking for your people who'd come before. Were you talking about the old ones or someone who was here more recently?"

Kagán turned away from the window and drew two fingers across my cheeks as if tracing a tattoo.

"Your medicine is also strong for you to think that."

"That is for someone else to decide."

She smiled at that, and when she did, her tattoos spread like an eagle's wings.

"Will you tell me the story about the ancients?" I said.

"Mm."

"And will you also tell me why you really came here?"

"We'll see."

She began at the beginning.

The Tlingit were created by the trickster Raven—Yéil in their language—who brought light to the world by stealing the sun, the moon, and the stars. Using her hands to draw descending columns, Kagán explained how the People of the Tides orga-nized themselves into lineage groups, known as moieties. Each moiety was named after a powerful animal spirit: Raven, Eagle,

Wolf, Killer Whale, Thunderbird, Frog, Hummingbird, and Butterfly. The moieties were further divided into clans and each clan was subdivided into houses.

"My moiety is Wolf—<u>G</u>ooch naa," she said. "And my clan is Thunderbird—Shangukeidí."

"Thunderbird. Is that how the valley here got its name?"

Her eyes reflected the embers glowing in the fireplace, but she continued explaining how the name of each clan revealed their own origin story and they self-identified with a specific crest—a crest that could be carved into a totem, on the wall of a cedar plank house, on the top of a wooden helmet, and woven into a blanket or painted on a yaak, their word for canoe.

Clan allegiance, Kagán explained, was matrilineal, and couples had to come from opposite moieties and clans in order to marry. Violating that was taboo.

"Women were in charge and kept the house and raised the children while the men hunted, fished, and warred," she said.

I asked if the wars were between moieties and clans or with outsiders.

Again, the embers reflected in her eyes. "Some men fight with strangers. Others with those whose blood they share. And then there are those who fight with their own self."

"The ancients who came to Oregon, what did they fight over?"

"Fishing grounds at first. And then over the secret marriage of a girl from one clan and a boy from another."

Kagán described a time when the weather grew harsh and the bounty of the sea became sparse. Two clans from the same moiety began quarreling over a once-bountiful inlet that had sustained both for generations. The argument took a dark turn when it was discovered the daughter chosen to assume her mother's position as the head of one of the clans and the favored son of the other had broken taboo.

I could hear music from *West Side Story* playing. It was the Tlingit version of the Jets and the Sharks, the Montagues and Capulets.

"The girl's clan became so angry that they sent a war party to the boy's clan and demanded that he and all the people abandon their houses and move far away or there would be war. Fighting broke out and people on both sides were killed, including the favored son.

"After the girl's clan returned to their side of the inlet, the dead boy's mother and father demanded justice. Their clan organized a war party, but the girl's clan got wind of it, packed their belongings into their yaaks, and fled."

Kagán described how the dead boy's clan boarded their yaaks and chased the other clan down the jagged coastline and past the broken islands, dodging killer whales and the undersea grizzly bear that threatened to capsize them. They could never quite close the gap.

One day a thick fog blanketed the water. Even though the members of the boy's clan could no longer see their enemy ahead of them, they continued paddling. The fog clung for days, and days turned into weeks, but finally it lifted.

The dead boy's clan found themselves at the mouth of a great river beyond the world they knew. Despite their fear, they paddled up it, convinced their enemy was right around the next bend. When they spotted a raven flying up a tributary, they took it as a sign and followed.

The tributary flowed through a narrow canyon. The weather grew stormy. Driving wind and pelting rain capsized all the yaaks. Some of the people drowned. Others were severely injured. The dead boy's parents refused to turn back and convinced the survivors to continue on foot. Eventually, they climbed over a mountain and reached a valley.

"Thunder Valley," I said.

Kagán's seashell earrings shimmered as she nodded.

Injured, exhausted, and hungry, the people decided to rest. They built a plank house as a fortress and raised a totem pole with Thunderbird on top to warn them of danger, so sure they were that the girl's clan would double back and attack them.

"Days passed, then weeks, then months. Years did too," she said. "The mother and father of the dead boy grew old. As death neared, they told each other that victory had been theirs, for as much as their clan had suffered from having left their beloved home behind, so too had the girl's clan.

"That's when Thunderbird appeared and told them the truth. Many years before, when the clan was paddling their yaaks through the great fog, the girl's clan had used it as cover to turn around and paddle back home where they had the inlet all to themselves and enough fish to sustain them forever.

"'Why did you not tell us this before?' they asked Thunderbird. The great spirit replied, 'Because you would not have believed me. You had become blinded by seeking vengeance rather than enlightened by asking for justice.'"

The last of the embers sizzled and popped and their glow grew gray and then turned as black as Kagán's eyes and hair.

"A lesson worth remembering," I said, thinking how long and how many lives it had taken for the US to learn it in Vietnam. "Have you told that story to anyone else here at the Running R?"

"Not to any of the Railsbacks. They wouldn't understand."

"What about Wilbur Pillsbury?"

She was quiet for a while. "I only spoke with him a couple of times. He would come to the house for water or to wash his clothes. He was gentle, but curious. When Wilbur asked me about my people, I told him the story I told you."

"What did he say afterward?"

"He said he would look for signs of them while doing his work."

"And did he ever find any?"

"If he did, he didn't say. And now he is dead."

"Tell me the real reason you came to Thunder Valley."

"Another time," she said. "It's late."

Kagán drifted out of the room as silently as she'd entered, taking the moonlight with her.

13

———

An explosion shook the house, rattled the windows, and had me throwing off the covers and jerking open the door before I was fully awake.

"What the hell!" Cass yelled as he bolted out of his bedroom.

I looked past him. The window in his room faced the river. Though the sun hadn't cleared the horizon, a flame was shooting up beyond the cottonwoods illuminating a funnel of smoke darker than the dawn.

"Pillsbury's camper," I said. "Someone blew it up."

"First they shoot the messenger and now they shoot the envelope too," he said.

Jo stepped into the hallway, knotting the cloth belt of a flannel robe over her nightgown. "Is everyone all right?"

"Someone set fire to Pillsbury's camper," Cass said.

"Why on earth—"

I returned to my room, pulled on my clothes, and grabbed my holster.

Aiden was coming up the stairs as I started down. He was wearing a heavy jacket and his boots were wet.

"Where have you been?" I said.

"It's none of your damn business," he said.

I grabbed his shirtfront. "Pillsbury's camper is in flames. Did you do that?"

He tried yanking my hand away. "Get out of my way. Get out of my house."

"Only when I find out who killed Pillsbury, and right now, you're looking pretty good for it."

I pushed past him and ran outside. KT was coming out of the bunkhouse as fast as his bowed legs could carry him. He was carrying the gun belt that held his holstered six-shooter and sheathed bone handle knife.

"Fire burnin' acrost the river," he said. "No lightnin' so ain't from a strike."

"It's Pillsbury's camper," I said. "Someone's worried about leaving evidence behind."

"Fer Pete sakes, there's beeves over there. Fire surely spooked 'em. Gonna be spread from here to hell 'n back. I get my hands on the sumbitch done it—"

"He'll be long gone by the time you get there."

"Me? You ain't goin' ride over 'n check it out?"

"No, I'm heading straight to the Double Ought."

"How come?"

"Stuart Kinsey overnighted there. I want to see if he and his men smell like smoke."

His pinch crown hat cocked. "You wantin' to talk to 'em right now makes me think you heard sumpin' at supper last night didn' strike you as Jake."

"Maybe. I'll let you know."

"Mebbe I better go with you. Watch your back."

"I don't plan on turning it to them. Right now, Jo needs you to round up her cattle. When you're across the river and if you see anything about the camper you think Sheriff Warbler ought to know about, give him a call."

"You got it, podner. Keep your eyes open fer pool cues."

I unhitched the horse trailer from my rig and sped down the snow-covered dirt road. The two-lane hadn't been touched by a snowplow, but late-night logging trucks and big rigs had done a pretty good job carving tracks that I could use to keep my speed up without tobogganing off the pavement.

A few minutes later a wooden sign with two *O*'s branded into it marked the turnoff to the ranch. Someone had driven down the dirt road after the snow stopped falling last night. The tracks came from a cluster of ranch buildings. The house wasn't as grand as the Running R's, nor were the barn, stable, and corrals as big.

A light blue Ford pickup with a busted taillight was parked in front of the house. I pulled to a stop beside it and counted to ten. No one fired a shot, either at me or as a warning. I got out and knocked on the front door.

Getting no answer, I tried the knob with my left hand while keeping my right on the butt of my pistol.

"Anybody home?" I said as I opened the door a crack while stepping to the side.

The response I got was like hearing Zeb and Jeb behind the trees all over again—this time the metal-on-metal sound was a shotgun being racked.

"Push that door any wider, stranger, and you're gonna get a face full of splinters and double-ought."

The voice was an old man's, but I didn't doubt he had the will and strength to pull the trigger.

"Fair enough. Man's home is his castle. Name's Nick Drake. I understand Stuart Kinsey is staying here. Why I came. I'd like a word with him."

"You missed him. He and his two business partners left before sunup."

"Where'd they go?"

"Burns. Kinsey said they had a meeting there today."

"He say with who?"

"Sonny, I'm a rancher, not a secretary."

"But he's staying here."

The voice behind the door hooted. "Because he's paying me good money. Fool not to take it, and Momma didn't raise no fool."

"Is he buying your property too?"

"I wish, but he don't want it. Says it's on the wrong side of the two-lane. Only wants riverfront acreage. Like what the Running R and Broken Wing got."

"What about the other two he travels with, the skinny one drives him and the—"

"Fat one. What about 'em?"

"Did they go to Burns too?"

"'Course they did. Kinsey don't go nowhere without them, probably not even to the john." He hooted again.

"What kind of rig do they drive?"

"Black Suburban. A rental."

"Can I ask you another question?"

"This shotgun's heavy and I'm getting plum tuckered holding it, so make it your last."

"How long has Kinsey been staying here?"

"On and off a few weeks. Comes and goes as he pleases. That's what he's paying me for. Treats it like it's his house not a motel. Told him he could own the whole shebang but he only wants to rent it."

"What about the last few days?"

"Coming and going, like I said. He was here then gone a couple days, then back again last night with his two partners. Now he's gone again. Won't know when he's coming back till he's back."

"Thanks for your time."

"Time I got, it's money I need. Cattle prices are for shit. How about you pay me for what I told you?"

"Sure, how's twenty dollars sound?"

"Sounds square. Push it under the door."

I took two tens from my wallet and slipped one under.

"Hey, that's only a sawbuck."

"And you'll get its twin if you answer another question."

"Ah, for crying out loud."

"Did you ever meet the man Kinsey hired to survey the Running R, name of Wilbur Pillsbury, or hear Kinsey talking about him?"

"Nope."

"All right, here you go." I pushed the other ten dollar bill under the door.

"Man of your word. For that, I'll give you a freebie. Kinsey never mentioned Pillsbury, but his two hired men did."

"They did?"

"Yep. Heard 'em the other morning. Voices coming through the wall. Fat one was saying how they didn't need to worry about old Pillsbury spilling his guts no more. And the skinny one who's always smiling but never laughing, well, he finally laughed. Sounded like a damn coyote with his paw caught in a trap. Made the fillings in my back teeth ache."

14

The sheriff's office was a drab two-story pink building next to the Harney County Courthouse in downtown Burns. Pudge Warbler's pickup was parked around the corner. Right next to it was Chief Deputy Orville Nelson's rig. Their dented bumpers, scratched paint jobs, and spiderwebbed windshields were akin to scars on old warriors.

In contrast was the brand-spanking-new rig with a shiny seven-point gold star and Regional County Sheriff painted beneath it parked right in front of the office's entrance. Even the vehicle's wheels and side panels looked freshly washed despite the dirty snow melting on the city streets.

Knowing who it belonged to soured my gut but didn't stop me. The lobby in the sheriff's building was smaller than a dentist's waiting room with no room for chairs or a table heaped with old magazines. Pudge's private office was right off it, but the door was uncharacteristically closed.

I walked down the hall to find Orville Nelson. When he first joined the sheriff's department as a college intern, he'd been relegated to the file room. Despite the cramped quarters, the FBI-wannabe proved himself indispensable with his fearlessness about new technology, ceaseless curiosity, and limitless energy. His skill at linking evidence to suspects led to a record number of arrests and convictions.

Pudge acknowledged Orville's track record by assigning him a larger patch of real estate. He promptly assembled three long tables into an electronics-strewn U-shaped desk that he christened "the Bridge." It was a tip of the hat to *Star Trek*, his favorite TV show.

Orville became even more indispensable after his paralysis, proving his talents and doggedness time after time. With his dream of going to Quantico crushed, Pudge hired him as a deputy. A few years later he didn't hesitate to name him his chief deputy when the position became open.

The young lawman was seated at the helm of the Bridge wearing a telephone operator's headset and staring at two TV set-like terminals set on top of metal boxes he'd wired with who-knows-what kind of gizmos. His boyish grin flashed when he looked up and waved me in.

"Ranger Drake, I am glad you are here. I have been speaking with a contact at the FBI about Mr. Stuart Kinsey. He had some very interesting things to say and is sending me several relevant public records."

"What his take on him?"

"Kinsey has been on the Bureau's watch list for a couple of years now. He originally came to their attention as a suspect in a Ponzi scheme involving the sale of the equivalent of Florida swampland. Now they have reason to believe his operation has grown more sophisticated. My contact hinted the FBI's organized crime unit is looking into a possible link between Kinsey and the underworld."

"They really think the mob's come to Harney County?"

Orville's fingers tapped a keyboard while we spoke. He didn't look at the terminal to check his spelling.

"The connection is speculative at present, but, nonetheless, Kinsey's prior activities strongly suggest he is not above skirting the law if there is profit in it."

"Does your contact have an explanation of why Kinsey is targeting Harney County?"

"Changing demographics. Oregon is experiencing an influx of people moving here from California and the East Coast. Not everyone is happy about their impact on the job market, real estate prices, and traffic congestion. I hear in some towns locals are sporting bumper stickers that say 'Don't Californicate Oregon.'"

"The FBI thinks Kinsey is pulling the equivalent of a Willie Sutton?"

"Precisely." Orville grinned. "I always appreciated his simple explanation of why he robbed banks. 'It's where the money is.'"

"Rolling in here with two goons who look straight out of central casting and arm-twisting ranchers into selling their land isn't exactly trying to stay under the law's radar," I said. "Kinsey's even enlisting the help of government folks to try and stop Pudge and me from investigating Pillsbury's death."

"You mean, convincing Sheriff Burton to come here today."

"Actually, he got to Bust'em by talking to the attorney general first. Kinsey also told me he was going to tell my boss about me moonlighting as Pudge's personal tracker."

"Stuart Kinsey knows Miss Bloom?"

"No, he got Liz's name by personally calling the director of US Fish and Wildlife. Or so he says."

Orville's forehead scrunched. "Both the director and attorney general are very high up in government. It is difficult to believe either would be complicit in a criminal enterprise."

"I know, but we did see crooks operating at the very top level of government just a few years ago."

"Yes, but the Nixon administration was a statistical anomaly.

It is highly unlikely we will ever experience that level of corruption again in our lifetime. Mathematically speaking, of course. I could devise a hypothesis and test it on my computer to get the precise odds."

"What I'd rather know is what's the Bureau going to do about Kinsey and Thunder Valley Inc.?"

"My contact advised me that, lacking any substantive evidence of wrongdoing, there is not much they can do beyond assisting local law enforcement authorities."

"A man in Kinsey's employ who was carved up like a Sunday roast isn't enough wrongdoing for them?"

"They need irrefutable evidence that a federal crime was committed before they can act."

"Evidence just got a lot harder to find. Someone torched Pillsbury's camper this morning."

"Oh my. Were you able to determine what kind of propellant was used to start the blaze?"

"I didn't check it out. I went to look for who might've started it, namely Kinsey and his thugs. They were spending the night at a nearby ranch, but they were gone when I got there."

"To come here."

"You mean here, here?"

"Kinsey, at least. He arrived with Regional Sheriff Burton. They are meeting with Sheriff Warbler right now."

"What about the other two?"

"All I know is they are not in the office. Perhaps they are waiting outside for Kinsey to finish up in here."

"No, I would've seen them and their rig. A black Suburban."

"Perhaps they are running errands."

"More likely dropping off two investors at the Burns Airfield. One's a banker. The other's a rich Texan who probably has his own plane. If they're smart enough to look the other way, then they're smart enough to get out of Dodge when bodies start dropping."

"Give me the four men's names and I can run a search."

"Burt Symes is the banker and Jeffrey Parker the rich Texan. I call Kinsey's goons Laurel and Hardy."

"Do their physiques match their namesakes?" I nodded. He smiled and his fingers were a flurry as he typed. "Fingerprints would be helpful."

"Maybe they left a set at the Running R or Double Ought. I'll dust for them next time I'm there."

"You are going back?"

"Until we find out who killed Wilbur Pillsbury. I take it you already started a search on him and the firm he worked for."

"I did. I shall have the results shortly."

"How long has Bust'em and Kinsey been in Pudge's office?"

"Nearly an hour. Sheriff Burton closed the door as soon as they went in. I have been debating whether or not I should create an excuse to go in there."

"I'll go. Bust'em can't fire me."

"But he could provoke you into taking a swing at him again. This time he'll certainly arrest you."

It happened when I was a relative newcomer and he was the newly elected sheriff. Burton wasn't content with having taken Pudge's job; he set his sights on Gemma too. When he wouldn't take her no for an answer, he roared up to my place and accused me of being the reason why. Then he called her a slut.

I didn't bother rattling a can of pebbles to drown the voice of my counselor reminding me that moral outrage was a trigger for me using. I planted my fist right above Burton's carefully groomed brush mustache. He didn't file charges because he didn't want voters to think that if he couldn't block a punch, he sure as hell wasn't going to be able to block one thrown at them.

Shortly after Burton left my place, Gemma stormed over.

She told me in no uncertain terms that she neither needed nor was looking for a self-appointed knight in shining armor, that she could fight her own battles just fine. We had a stare-off and then she stormed out. Later, we told each other we both knew right then and there what the future held for us.

"Don't worry, Orville. I'll play nice," I said. "I'll even keep my hands in my pockets. Let me know what you find out about Stuart Kinsey and the others."

"Affirmative."

I gave the door to Pudge's office a quick rap while twisting the knob. I didn't wait to be invited in or ordered to keep out. The old sheriff was sitting behind his desk and Burton and Kinsey were across from him.

"Sheriff, got news about Pillsbury's camper at the Running R you'll want to hear. Someone blew it up this morning. It was still burning when I left."

"You come straight here after investigating it?" Pudge said.

"No, I went to the Double Ought to tell Mr. Kinsey."

I turned to him. "I figured you'd want to know since you said everything that Pillsbury had is yours, and that must include the camper. You know, in case you want to alert your insurance agent."

Kinsey's glare wasn't as hot as the one Gemma had shot me all those years ago, but I could feel the anger burning behind it.

Burton ran the tip of his finger across the bottom of his carefully clipped mustache. It was a nervous tic I remembered from when he lived in Burns; he did it every time he was about to face the public or a reporter.

"This is exactly what I was talking about, Warbler," he said. " Deputizing a civilian to do your legwork. Well, I won't stand for it."

"I've been asking you to increase my budget for years so I can hire another deputy," Pudge said. "Until you do that, don't tell me how to do my job."

"And if you'd ever showed more respect for my position and authority, then I would've gotten you a bigger budget. Now, I'll just wait until you're replaced, and from what doctors tell me, that won't be too long."

"You've always thought mighty high of yourself, haven't you, Bust'em? But thinking you know more than the man upstairs? He's the one who's gonna make the call on how long I got, not you. And seeing I'll be there before you, I'll be happy to remind him when you come knocking on heaven's door how you believed you had divine power."

Stuart Kinsey stood abruptly. "We appear to be at the end of our conversation. Warbler, I trust you've reached the conclusion that you're on the wrong side of the law when it comes to ignoring my attorney's request to hand over documents that are legally mine."

"That's Sheriff Warbler, Mr. Kinsey. I earned this badge and the title that goes with it. Show some respect, you hear?"

"All right, Sheriff. You leave me no choice but to turn the matter over to the state attorney general. I've already ordered my attorneys to file a civil claim against you for willfully hindering my rights to pursue a lawful business. A project of this size, the damages will amount to millions of dollars. I'll win that suit. I always win."

Kinsey's lip curled. "You? You'll have to sell your ranch to pay me. And, oh yes, the lawsuit will include a provision to enjoin your heirs. Your daughter, Gemma, and your grandchildren, Hattie and Johnny, will never see a cent. Everything will go to me and I'll personally be there to watch them evicted."

He turned his sneer on me. "As for you, I have a call scheduled with the director of the US Fish and Wildlife Service in thirty minutes. Not only am I going to ask him to dismiss you immediately, but also file charges against your supervisor for the misuse of public funds."

"Good luck with that," I said.

"Luck has nothing to do with it. The president of the United States does. The director of Fish and Wildlife is a presidential appointment. I was a major campaign contributor to his election and I know he'll be counting on me again for his reelection."

I shrugged. "Fired or not, I'm not going to stop looking for who gutted Wilbur Pillsbury like a hunter does a buck to lighten the load when he has to carry the meat back to camp."

"A wild animal, you mean. That's what killed him."

"You're right. The killer was an animal. But it seems you ditched science class the day the teacher taught taxonomy. We're all members of the kingdom Animalia in this room, the same as wolves and cougars."

I gave him and Burton a hard eye. "Skunks and rats too."

Burton started to protest, but my attention remained focused on Kinsey. "That includes your driver and your other man. By the way, I'm looking for them. See if they smell like gasoline and smoke from this morning's fire."

"Careful what you ask for," Kinsey said. "You might not like the answer."

"You won't either if you even so much as whisper my wife and children by name again. I'll give you another science lesson about animal behavior."

"Touched a nerve, did I? Cute little Hattie a daddy's girl? Johnny more than a souvenir you picked up in Saigon? Maybe daddy's own little half-breed?"

Both fists balled, but before I could swing them, Pudge barked. "Don't do it, son. He wants you to. Kinsey's that type. A chickenshit hides behind lawyers."

"Go on, hit me," Kinsey taunted. "I might get a bruise, but

you'll get prison stripes. By the time you're out, I'll all own everything you got."

"Don't listen to him, Nick," Pudge warned again. "Be smart."

"Who's the chickenshit now, little Hattie's daddy?"

Once again, metal on metal clicked. It was the hammer on Pudge's World War II-issued .45, the gun he still strapped, preferring it over the standard sheriff's sidearm because it had saved him in the Pacific more times than he could count.

"Mr. Kinsey, you know I'm an old man with cancer," Pudge said. "I may be aiming my gun at my son-in-law to prevent him from slugging you, but you're awful close. If I'm forced to take a shot, there's a good chance I shake and the bullet strikes you dead. Then in my panic, I go and drop the gun. Dang if it doesn't fire again and hit Bust'em."

The old sheriff clicked his cheek. "They put me on trial, it's Nick's and my word against ... well, I was gonna say you two, but you won't be able to talk because you'll both be stone dead. Even if the jury finds me guilty of manslaughter, it's unlikely I'll still be living come time for the appeal to get decided."

I hadn't taken my eyes off Kinsey's. He didn't blink and neither did I. But then he huffed, brushed past me, and walked out. Burton hurried after him without taking the time to tell Pudge he was going to file a disciplinary action against him.

15

———

I could make the drive from Burns to No Mountain in twenty minutes—summer, fall, winter, and spring, in the dead of night, dead tired, and half dead. But I was pushing the speed limit even harder this time because I wanted to get to my office and call Liz Bloom before Stuart Kinsey could.

The US Fish and Wildlife field office was an old lineman's shack that I'd lived in for years after I was hired as a ranger. It was only one room with a woodstove in the middle, a single bunk in the corner, and a rickety table and chair beside a kitchen sink, but it seemed like a palace after sleeping in tents and foxholes for three years.

When Gemma and I got married, I moved to the Warbler ranch. Once Hattie was born, I never considered living anywhere else, and then doubled down on that notion when we adopted Johnny. But I was still partial to the shack with its cock-eyed stovepipe and uninterrupted view of the High Lonesome. Not only did it work out well as a quiet place for doing paperwork, but as a refuge late at night where I could crank up the music to drown out the occasional demon that came howling from the past without freaking out my family.

I was going over what I'd say to Liz while picturing the heavy black telephone I'd call her on when a much larger black object caught my eye. It was a shiny Suburban parked in front of Blackpowder Smith's, the combination saloon and dry goods store on No Mountain's block-long Main Street.

I put calling Liz on hold and hit the brakes.

Laurel and Hardy were standing on one side of the bar and Blackpowder Smith on the other. The old codger tipped his black cowboy hat with its rattlesnake skin band at me.

"Well, look what the cat drug in," he said. "Why, howdy there, young fella."

"Hey, Blackpowder. Don't know if these two told you who they are, but I just came from a meeting with their boss. He's planning to build a resort and housing development in Thunder Valley."

"What the big fella here just told me. The other don't talk. Not sure he knows how. They want to buy me out."

"No Mountain's a long way from Thunder Valley."

"That it is," Blackpowder said and stroked his white billy goat beard. "Someone up there needs a quart of milk, be a whole lot quicker to shop in Burns than drive all the way down to my little emporium. I been trying to tell the big fella that, but he don't seem to understand."

I could tell from his tone what he thought of the pair. They weren't just city slickers wearing black suits; they were back-shooting claim jumpers.

"I don't know your names because Kinsey didn't introduce you last night," I said to them. "They are?"

Laurel's fixed smile didn't move. Hardy's toothbrush mustache twitched. "All you need to know is we work for Mr. Kinsey. He wants to buy this dump. If the geezer don't want to sell it, then we got a problem."

"What kind of problem?"

"Kind needs fixing."

I glanced at Blackpowder. "Did they give you a price?"

"Not yet, but it don't matter how many zeros they put on the end of it. This place ain't for sale. Not now. Not ever. When I kick the bucket, it gets passed on to my heirs lock, stock, and barrel."

Blackpowder didn't have any. He was engaged to be married a long time ago, but a bank robber killed his fiancée and broke his heart forever.

Hardy said, "You mean, you was to die, no matter the cause, some relative gets all this?" He waved his pudgy hand.

"That's right."

"Then we'll talk to them." He made a kissing sound. "After you're dead, that is."

"Be my guest," Blackpowder said. "But you should know, I put a codicil on the will says they can't sell it and gotta keep this place as is. Right down to the furnishings and paintings on the wall. Got 'em when some Hollywood folks turned it into a movie set. Collector items, each and every one. They try to break the will, they forfeit it."

He sipped from a mug that wasn't filled with coffee. "Then the city of No Mountain gets it and has to maintain it as a historical monument. On account of the collector items and me being the proprietor, city mayor, and head of the volunteer fire department too. The saloon stays open so they can make money to pay for the upkeep. Don't want taxpayers to have to foot the bill."

Hardy's little mustache stopped twitching. "You're making a mistake, old-timer. Passing up a big payday. Take the money and retire. Go on a vacation somewheres nice. Hire a sweet young thing to be your nurse." He made the kissing sound again.

"And where would I go?" Blackpowder said. "I got everything I want right here."

"Anywheres is nicer than here. Outside looks like a giant cat litter box. All that sand and them hills that look like cat dump."

"It's a fact, No Mountain's got plenty of sand," Blackpowder said as he put the mug down. "But so do I." And he quickly brought up a sawed-off double barrel he kept under the bar. "Now get the hell outta here!"

Laurel looked like he was trying to scratch his armpit, but I had the .357 out and aimed at his grin. "Uh-uh," I said.

His eyes narrowed but he lowered his gun hand.

Hardy glowered at me. "You already made one mistake last night. This makes two."

"Your boss made a bigger one this morning. Now you made a second. That makes us even."

They took their time walking toward the door. I followed right behind and made sure they drove away. When I turned around, Blackpowder had laid the shotgun down and plucked a bottle of whiskey from behind the bar. He filled his mug and then raised the bottle at me. "I know you don't drink nothing but coffee and water, but—"

I shook my head. "I was on my way to call Liz Bloom and let her know that pair's boss is calling her boss to get us both fired."

He took a long swallow. "Been a while since I raised a loaded gun at a man." He took another swallow. "Felt pretty damn good."

"Why do they want to buy your place? As you said, it's a long way from Thunder Valley."

"Cuz I got something they want. No, something they need."

"What's that?"

"Big fella didn't own up to it, but it's my liquor license they're after. There's only so many to go around. You know how it is in Oregon. You're thirsty; you can only buy beer and wine at a grocery store or by the glass at a tavern. You want anything stronger"—he raised the bottle again—"you gotta buy it from a state-run liquor store or at a licensed saloon like yours truly's."

"They need one for the resort they're going to build."

"Yep. You know, buying my license way back when was the smartest investment I ever made. Paid off better than selling canned goods. Paid off a lot better than the stock market too."

"Can it be transferred?"

"With the right lawyering and fee paying, I s'pose. But I hear there's a waiting list about as long as Thunder River."

"You know they're going to keep after you for it. Their boss is that way. Doesn't take no for an answer."

I gave him a quick rundown on Pillsbury's murder, Kinsey siccing Buster Burton on Pudge, and Orville's conversation with the FBI.

The snakeskin band on Blackpowder's hat all but rattled as he shook his head. "Been a long time since a bunch this shady rode into town."

"We need to keep our eyes and ears open," I said. "I'll let Pudge know about Laurel and Hardy's visit."

Blackpowder guffawed. "Those are good monikers you got for 'em, but them two yahoos, they're not in it for laughs. I can tell they like hurting people. Especially the one who don't talk. He's got that smile plastered on his puss but his eyes are dead as a mackerel's."

"You okay here? I need to shove off and call Liz."

"Better than okay. They got my dander up and that's always good for whatever ails you. I'll let people around here know about them via my grapevine. If they're trying to strong-arm anybody else, I'll let you know."

I got back in my pickup and drove the short distance to the lineman's shack. Like everyplace else in No Mountain, the front door was unlocked. I put water on to boil, checked the answering machine, and then filled a mug of strong black coffee. I was going to need it as I dialed the Fish and Wildlife's office in Portland and asked to speak to the regional director.

Liz Bloom had only been with the service a couple of years,

but she was a fast climber. Energetic, headstrong, and impatient, she was out to change the way the outfit had always operated since it began as the US Commission of Fish and Fisheries in 1871. Liz was never secret about her goal: protect all the nation's wild animals and the places where they lived.

The first time we worked together was on a whitewater raft trip down a raging river during flood stage. Escaping death bonded us in more ways than one. Though we rarely spent time in the field together after that, we maintained a close friendship cemented by mutual admiration and respect despite our differences in job title.

"Imagine my surprise getting a personal call from the director in Washington and then you all within the span of five minutes," is how she answered the phone.

"Good to hear your voice too, Regional Director Bloom," I said.

"Cut the sugarcoating crap, Nick. It doesn't suit you. And remember, I've seen you wearing only your birthday suit."

Liz followed that with a laugh and I didn't bother to remind her what the actual circumstances were that led to us being naked after a capsizing in a freezing river and in a hot spring later.

"Did he tell you why I'm helping out Pudge?"

"He didn't care about the why, only the fact I've been letting you double-dip and he'll get the blame if reporters get wind of it."

"Give me a minute and I'll explain."

"Sure, Nick, love to hear it, but you do know I trust you a lot more than him."

I gave her an even shorter version of what was going on than I had Blackpowder. Liz didn't interrupt or ask questions until I finished.

"I understand why you feel obligated to help your father-in-law since he's ill. What's his prognosis?"

"The doctor talks about a five-year survival rate, but Pudge's only got one down and four to go."

"It's a tough battle. My grandfather didn't even make it a year after his diagnosis. Give him my best, and Gemma and the kids too. Now, about nailing whoever killed—what was his name again?"

"Wilbur Pillsbury."

"Here's what I'm going to do. I'll sign off on the request you submitted last week for taking some personal time without pay. It only now made its way to my desk. You know how it is with paperwork." The wink she was giving me came across the phone line loud and clear.

"Thanks, Liz."

"I'm also going to ask your partner to cover for you. Loq owes me considering how understanding I've been with his even more than usual absenteeism." She paused. "I'm assuming he's still seeing that tribal cop on the Umatilla Reservation and is spending a considerable portion of his time driving back and forth between her place and his in Chiloquin."

"I really can't say."

"Can't or won't?"

"Truth is, since he and I agreed he'd focused on the Klamath Basin refuges because of what happened last year and I'd take the others, there hasn't been a pressing need for us to work together."

"I'm not keen on that arrangement. When you two work together, you're force multipliers. I'll see about changing that, but not right now. I'll give Loq a call and you do what you need to do."

"Thanks, but Stuart Kinsey told me he was going to have the director fire you. Said he could do it because he has a lot of clout with the president due to all the money he gave to his campaign."

Liz laughed. "The thing I love about you is you're brave and tough, but so damn innocent about the way the world really works. Kinsey may think he's got clout because he wrote a big check, but I know secrets about the director that he doesn't want made public, so he doesn't dare fire me. Got to go. Late for a meeting. Keep me posted."

The line clicked and the dial tone returned. I hung up the heavy black handset and thought about Liz. She'd matured considerably since taking the job as regional director. In the process, she learned what it really took to save animals, and that was becoming a political animal herself. Instincts, connections, favors, and secrets were Liz Bloom's claws and fangs, and she kept them sharp and wasn't afraid to use them.

16

Nagah Will was walking out of the house when I clattered across the cattleguard and pulled to a stop. He'd moved into an apartment Pudge and I built for him out back when his grandfather Tuhudda Will died a few years ago. Gemma hired him as her assistant while encouraging him to go to college and veterinary school. She also taught him how to fly and he piloted her plane more often than naught.

Now, on the verge of leaving his teenage years behind, he wore his hair long in the traditional manner with a folded red bandana tied low across his forehead as his grandfather always had. The headband wasn't the only thing he'd inherited from Tuhudda. Nagah adopted the old man's belief in the power of the spirit world and was on his way to becoming as knowledgeable about Paiute history and traditional healing methods as many of the tribal elders.

"Greetings, Nick," he said as I got out of my pickup.

"When I come home after being away, I half expect you to say what your grandfather always said to me."

"'Nick Drake. I knew you were coming before you left. This is so.'" Nagah's imitation of Tuhudda's slow way of speaking was pitch-perfect.

I put my hands on his shoulders. "Hearing that makes me miss him even more."

"As do I, but Grandfather became your spirit guide as he did mine when he went to live with his ancestors. His wisdom is always there whenever you need it."

"I know, it's just that I haven't had a reason to ask for it since last year."

"From what Girl Born in Snow tells me, you may have one very soon."

"The murder in Thunder Valley."

"Evil isn't bound by geography."

"So I learned when I stopped off at Blackpowder Smith's." I told him about Kinsey sending Laurel and Hardy to buy the saloon's liquor license.

"Then we'll meet this danger like we always have."

"'With honor and spears from all sides,'" I said, quoting his grandfather.

Nagah waved his hand in front of him. "I don't see when this danger will strike."

"The men Pudge and I are dealing with are the kind who do their dirty work under the cover of darkness."

"Then I will be back by nightfall to stand guard. Gemma got a call about a sick herd. We're going to fly there now."

"Well, I'm glad you'll be home by dark."

I started to head toward the house, but he stopped me.

"Girl Born in Snow says there's a Tlingit woman living in Thunder Valley. What's she like?"

I'd never heard Nagah ask about a woman before. When he wasn't working with Gemma, he had his head buried in a book or was listening to November's teachings.

"Her name is Kagán." I described her face tattoos, ivory

piercing, and earrings. "She's a powerful storyteller, but mysterious. I asked her why she left Alaska and came to Thunder Valley, but she hasn't told me why yet."

"She is from the north and her name means 'Light' in her language," he said more to himself than to me.

"That's right," I said.

"Do you remember how I got my name?"

"Of course. Tuhudda gave it to you when you were a little boy taking care of your family's sheep alone in Catlow Valley and protected them from coyotes for three nights. Because you showed such courage, he renamed you after a brave mountain sheep called Nagah who was turned into the North Star by Shinoh of the sky people so travelers would always be able to find their way in the dark."

"This is so," he said, using his grandfather's voice.

Hm, I thought. Nagah, the North Star. Kagán, Light from the north.

"I can introduce you to her," I said.

"I would like that, but now I must go and preflight the plane."

I went inside. The house was quieter than usual, and then I remembered it was a school day. November was nowhere to be seen. I found Gemma in our bedroom. She was packing an overnight bag.

"Nagah says you're off to tend to a sick herd. Looks like you think you're going to be pulling an all-nighter."

"It's the same as taking an umbrella," she said.

"Then pack two suitcases because I want to make sure you get back before dark. There's a chance the trouble in Thunder Valley might spill over down here."

"You won't be here?"

"I have to go back to the Running R. The sooner we can ID

the killer, the sooner we can put Stuart Kinsey and his gang behind us."

"You don't believe that, do you?"

"He's got his sights set on Thunder Valley and his claws in deep. He's already got Bust'em Burton in his pocket and maybe the attorney general too. Even if I'm able to uncover damning evidence, Kinsey will have a ready-made alibi and proof he had nothing to do with it along with an army of lawyers ready to defend him."

"Then do what you have to do, but don't worry about us. Nagah and I'll be home by nightfall and Pudge and November will be here too. We can handle things. We always have."

"I was with Pudge this morning. Bust'em was there in all his brown-nosing glory. He'd brought Stuart Kinsey with him to try and scare Pudge into giving him the documents he took from the dead man's camper."

"It's not hard to imagine how that went."

I didn't mention Kinsey's not-so-subtle threat. Gemma wasn't a mother hen when it came to Hattie and Johnny; she was a mama bear. And a grizzly at that.

"Where's November?" I said. "She's not in the kitchen or sitting in her rocker on the front porch."

"She's been out of sorts all morning. Last I checked, she was in her room with the door closed. I think Pudge's cancer has finally gotten to her. She's always believed her medicine would work, but now ..."

The weight of the unspoken settled over us like a cloud heavy with rain.

I shook it off as best I could and tried to change the subject. "Guess what? I spoke to Nagah when I pulled up. November told him about the Tlingit woman living at the Running R. He asked a lot of questions about her."

"What kind of questions?"

"The kind men ask about a woman when they're interested in getting to know her."

"Nagah's not a little boy anymore so we shouldn't be surprised. In the old days, he would've been married by now, even a father. Who is she and what's she like?"

I described her and told her the connection Nagah made about their names.

"Maybe it's destiny she came to Harney County," Gemma said.

"You don't believe that kind of stuff, do you?"

"Look at us. Of the two hundred forty-five national wildlife refuges in the US, you ended up here."

"You mean it wasn't just dumb luck?" I deadpanned.

Her smile told me what she thought about that.

"As for Nagah and Kagán, it's up to you now," she said.

"To do what?"

"Convince the Railsbacks they need a visit from a veterinarian. Tell them about the new testing we're doing for Johne's disease. Nagah and I'll fly up. A ranch that size is sure to have an airstrip."

"It does, but isn't that a little unethical?"

Gemma laughed the same way Liz had when she told me how naive I was about the way the real world worked.

I grabbed the overnight bag and walked her to the plane. As we passed by the corral, Gemma's sorrel mare nickered.

"Sarah misses Wovoka," she said. "Why'd you leave him at the Running R?"

"I was in a bit of a hurry this morning."

"To come see me because of our phone call last night?"

"That too, but someone torched the dead man's camper. I wanted to see if Kinsey's two, uh, assistants knew anything about it."

"Assistants, huh? That's a good one."

"Why do you say it like that? You haven't met them."

"I don't need to, hotshot. I can hear what you think in the tone of your voice. How dangerous are they?"

"Lighting that camper on fire was a mistake. Now, they've overplayed their hand."

"But what if they didn't do it? What if you're looking so hard at them, you're not seeing anyone else, either someone you think couldn't've done it or someone you haven't even identified yet?"

"Target fixation," I muttered.

"What's that?" she said.

"Something I learned the hard way in country. It's when you become so focused on a target, you increase your risk of running straight into it."

"Sounds like tunnel vision. Then you'd better open your eyes a little wider."

"That's something your father would say. Pudge ever hangs up his star, you'd be a shoo-in as sheriff."

"Sometimes you say the dumbest things."

"Do I?"

We reached the landing strip. Nagah had already removed the plane's tie-downs and wheel blocks and was behind the stick. Gemma took the overnight bag from me and pitched it into the open passenger door.

"See you later," she said.

I grabbed her and planted a kiss. When we broke off she gave me a smile. "Give me a call tonight and maybe we can relive our old radio show."

She was laughing when she boarded and closed the door behind her. Nagah readied for takeoff and soon the single-engine plane was roaring down the runway. As it gained altitude, the wings waggled. I knew Gemma asked Nagah to do that for me, but I couldn't tell if she was saying yes to a late-night phone call or yes that I was right about sheriffing being in her blood.

Back inside, I peered into Pudge's office that doubled as a sheriff's substation. He was stretched out on the couch with his eyes closed. The police band radio was on and the chatter of incoming calls and dispatches droned like angry bees.

I debated saying anything in case he was asleep, but his built-in radar sensed me before I could walk away.

"What did your boss say when you told her to expect a call from her boss?"

"Liz said don't worry about it, that the director has more secrets in his closet than suits and she knows every one of them."

He chuckled. "I liked her from the git-go when she first showed up here."

I told him about Laurel and Hardy trying to strongarm Blackpowder into selling his liquor license to Stuart Kinsey.

"Oh Lord. Don't tell me Black pulled a gun on 'em," the old sheriff said.

"He did and ran them off, but you know they won't stay gone."

"I expect not. Speaking of, new intel's come in. Pull up a chair."

I rolled the oak captain's chair over from his desk.

Pudge started talking. "Doc issued his preliminary finding on Pillsbury. Homicide. Time of death was the evening before we got to Pillsbury. Weapon? Blade of unknown origin. Victim died from blood loss and removal of vital organs. No trace of animal contact."

"Were there any signs of being tied up or beat?"

"No rope burns on his wrists or ankles and no broken bones or fractured skull, but Doc couldn't tell if he'd been hit in the nose or stomach since both are missing."

"Any luck with the fingerprints from inside the camper?"

"Orville sent 'em to the state police lab in Salem for ID'ing. Another day or two before we get anything definitive on 'em. 'Course, they'll be able to match Pillsbury's fast enough as Doc sent over a set from the autopsy."

"Why didn't they send them to the FBI?"

"Protocol. Goes to Salem first unless some kind of federal law was broke."

"Does that mean the Bureau isn't going to lend a hand identifying Laurel and Hardy?"

"That they'll do because they'd already been looking at Stuart Kinsey and it's pretty obvious those two crossed state lines to get to Harney County. But they need more than a physical description to go on."

"I'll try and get some prints when I go back to the Running R. They spent time in the kitchen. Also might be some at the Double Ought where they overnighted."

"That could work, but I figure it'll be a whole lot easier to red-light their rig and ask for their driver's licenses. Why I gave my deputies a standing order to do just that if they see 'em, speeding or not."

"How about the two money men who were at dinner last night? I gave Orville their names."

"He's already run backgrounds on 'em. Both are who they say they are. Clean records. Not even parking tickets."

"Have you had time to read the field notes and reports from the camper?"

"Titles mainly. Orville's going through 'em now. We got the name of the outfit Pillsbury worked for. Engineering consulting firm out of Seattle. He was a licensed geotechnical engineer with natural and biological resources being his specialty. Forests, rivers, critters, and so on."

"Hope Orville's making copies of Pillsbury's notes before Kinsey's lawyers storm your office."

"They can try, but we can pull up the drawbridge pretty damn quick and hold 'em off until Orville goes through 'em. It's like he took one of those speed reading classes."

"That it?"

"I also asked Orville to take a look-see into the Railsbacks. All of 'em."

"Even Jo?"

"She's one of 'em."

"What did he come up with?"

"The story about the family being in debt up to their Stetsons is true, all right. And, of course, Aiden generated the biggest paper trail because of my investigation into his daddy's death last year. But other than that, there's nothing to speak of. Cass, he had a drunk and disorderly and an assault charge stemming from a bar brawl that was later dropped. But all that took place back when he was rodeoing, and name me a bronc rider or roper who didn't end up on the wrong side of the bottle and law on at least one occasion."

Pudge's eyelids drooped, but he forced them back up. "A couple of somethings in Orville's searching did come up. The cowboy, KT? He did a stretch in a Texas federal pen."

"What for?"

"Manslaughter. Killed a guy with a knife."

"Any other details?"

"Still waiting on 'em to come through."

"You said a couple of things."

"The Indian woman served us coffee?"

"Kagán. That's her name. I talked to her last night."

"That a fact? Anything I need to know."

"She gave me a more detailed version of the legend of the

People of the Tides coming to Thunder Valley that November had told me earlier."

"And?"

"That's it. My gut tells me she's at the Running R for a different reason than searching for a connection to her long-lost ancestors, but she went mum when I asked her."

"That goes along with her having no record at all. Orville ran her through all the ... what d'ya call 'em, databases? And when I mean no record, I mean no birth certificate, no driver's license, no member enrollment form in the Tlingit Nation, no nada. It's like she's a ghost."

"But even ghosts have a past," I said.

17

I stuffed some clean clothes in a bag and checked the kitchen for any leftovers I could eat on the road. The door to November's room creaked open and the old healer stuck out her hand.

"Take this," she said.

"What is it?"

"Medicine."

The small leather pouch was made of soft deerskin and the mouth closed by a leather drawstring.

"Am I supposed to wear it, burn what's inside, or make tea with it?"

November tsked. "It is not for you. It is for Kagán. She will know what it is and what to do with it."

"Is she in danger?"

"Kagán is an Indian woman living in the White man's world. Her history, traditions, and culture are always in danger of being stolen. If she were to lose them, she would be cast into the whirl-wind. How would she ever be able to put her feet back on Mother Earth to walk in harmony? How would she learn how to make the journey to the spirit world to sit with her ancestors?"

The door started to close.

"Wait. I'm going back to Thunder Valley and will give it to her. But the men she's in danger from are likely the same who are trying to get Pudge and me to stop investigating a murder by threatening to harm Gemma and the kids. We need your help. Can you keep your eyes open for strangers in dreamworld and let us know before they get here?"

"And if I do this, what will you do?"

"Stop them."

"How?"

"With whatever it takes for however long it takes."

"Good. If I see them with my own eyes, I will tell you."

As I sped north, I glanced at the side mirror and saw the ranch grow smaller, but quickly returned my focus to the road ahead. Gemma's point about tunnel vision and being blind to other possible suspects rang in my ears. Was I falling victim to target fixation all over again?

Had I learned nothing after having led my squad straight into a target we'd been chasing, my blindness costing all of them their lives?

While I was focusing on Stuart Kinsey and Laurel and Hardy, who was I blind to? Aiden and Jo Railsback? Both had plenty at stake riding on the development deal and wouldn't want a damaging report to come out that could delay or stop it. The same for the two money men, Burt Symes and Jeffrey Parker.

But maybe I was looking at it the wrong way altogether. Maybe it wasn't a negative report that was taken from Pillsbury, but a positive one. Something that would've erased any doubts about the project and greenlighted all the required permits.

Top of the list of people who'd want such a report to disappear was Cass Railsback. KT had also made it no secret what he thought about building a resort and houses on the ranch. And then there was the fact he'd used a knife to kill someone before.

Zeb and Jeb Calhoun were also against developing Thunder Valley, but would they kill for it? Maybe their decision not to kill me when I was in their sights was just a ploy to get me to believe they were innocent of murdering Pillsbury.

And then there was Kagán. What was her stake in all of this? Did she even care about the Running R and a deal that would bring hundreds if not thousands of people to Thunder Valley, a place made sacred by her ancestors who'd lived and died there?

So many possibilities left me gasping. I reached for the radio mike and was patched through to Orville Nelson.

"Ever hear of target fixation?" I said.

"Of course," the earnest chief deputy quickly replied. "The FBI conducts special training sessions on it for surveillance work, counterintelligence, and sting operations."

"I'm going through it right now. Pudge too. We need to open our eyes to the possibility there is someone other than Stuart Kinsey and his gang who killed Pillsbury."

"Like the Railsbacks or another landowner who stands to benefit from the deal?"

"Yes, but also those who are opposed to it. Pillsbury might've been killed for a positive report that would've led government officials to approve the project."

Orville uttered an uncharacteristic groan. "I had not thought of that. It seems that I have fallen victim to target fixation as well."

"I still think Kinsey and his goons are the most likely to have killed him, but see what else you can find out about the Calhouns who own the Broken Wing. Ditto with the Double Ought where Kinsey's been staying. I don't know the owner's name, but he told me he was willing to sell but Kinsey didn't want to buy. Maybe the owner wanted to give Kinsey a reason to give his property a closer look."

"I will add them to the list," Orville said.

I was about to sign off when sunlight broke through the clouds and the rays glinted off the windshield, making me squint. Losing sight of the highway, I quickly pulled down the pickup's visor to block the glare. Attached to the underside was a snapshot of Gemma, Hattie, and Johnny. Something clicked.

"Wait!" I said.

"What?" Orville said.

"The family. All of them. Not just Jo, Cass, and Aiden, but Adam Railsback's other family. They may have a stake in this too. Cass said he never kept them a secret. Aiden called them his father's whore and bastards. Jo forbid anyone to mention them in her presence."

"What do you know about them?"

"Nothing. I don't have their names or where they live or anything. We'll have to find that out so we can rule them in or out."

"I will need something to go on if I am to conduct background checks."

"Yeah, and the only way for me to get that is to ask."

"Who?"

"Whichever Railsback is willing to talk."

The turnoff to the Double Ought came up before the Running R's and I took it. The road was all but cleared of snow. Someone had driven up and down it since I had. Maybe more than one somebody.

The old rancher's light blue Ford pickup with the busted taillight was gone. I gave it a ten count before getting out and knocking on the front door. No one answered by voice or shotgun. I turned the knob and toed the door open.

"I got another twenty bucks if you got time to talk," I said.

Getting no response, I stepped inside. The air was chilly. The woodstove used for heating was cool to the touch. The kitchen was empty. So was the dining room and pantry. A hallway led to a main bedroom and a pair of guest rooms. I checked those two first. No suitcases were in them, nor were there any shaving kits in the guest bathroom.

I searched the main bedroom last. The closet was filled with clothes. The bathroom had a toothbrush in a glass next to the sink and bottles of prescription drugs were in the medicine cabinet. The patient's name was Nils Sandberg.

Back outside, I went and checked the bunkhouse. Two of the bunks looked like they'd been hastily made. I figured Laurel and Hardy had slept there while Kinsey and the two money men had used the guest rooms in the main house. All had packed up and left that morning for Burns and beyond.

But someone had arrived and then left since I had.

The additional tracks on the road coming and stopping in front of the ranch house and then going back down the road proved it. I examined them more closely. One set was wide like a big Suburban's. My gut told me Nils Sandberg hadn't driven away on his own or gone willingly.

I snapped a few photographs of the tracks with my new camera before leaving. As soon as I hit the highway I radioed Orville again.

"I have the name of the Double Ought rancher. It's Nils Sandberg. Find out his license plate number too." I described the light blue pickup. "My advice? Add it to the black Suburban that Pudge ordered his deputies to pull over."

"Why is that?"

"Sandberg and the pickup are missing and I don't believe he went shopping for a quart of milk."

"Excuse me?"

"Something Blackpowder Smith said."

"If you believe there has been foul play, I should get a warrant to search the premises."

"Good idea. When you get to the Double Ought, dust for fingerprints in the bunkhouse. Laurel and Hardy slept in there. You'll know which bunks they used. You couldn't bounce a quarter off them."

"I will get right on it."

Unlike the deathly quiet at the Double Ought, the road to the Running R was bustling. Cowboys were herding cattle up it while calling out, "Clop, clop. Git, git. Hi on." The cows mooed and bellowed back while horses snorted. Someone cussed. A stock whip cracked.

I pulled to a stop behind the herd. KT spotted me and rode over.

"Gimme a sec and I'll git the boys to move the beeves off the road," he said.

"Don't bother. Cattle come first."

"Could be half hour or so afore they clear."

"I can wait."

"As long as you're sure." KT didn't seem to be in a hurry either. He pulled a cloth bag of tobacco from his shirt pocket and rolled a smoke. "Keepin' yourself busy?"

"I paid a visit to the Double Ought on my way down to Burns and then went on to No Mountain."

"What's shakin' down there?"

"Stuart Kinsey was at the sheriff's office trying to get him fired. The two men I call Laurel and Hardy were in No Mountain trying to buy a liquor license from a friend of mine."

"He gonna sell it?"

"No."

"Doubt they liked that."

"They didn't."

"Them two? They don' look like they take no for an answer. What's your friend gonna do?"

"Protect what's his."

"He can handle himself all right?"

"Always has. Had two navy ships torpedoed out from under him. Fought off claim jumpers when he was a prospector and later put down some bank robbers."

KT gave an approving look and took a drag. "How'd it go between Kinsey and Sheriff Warbler?"

"Pudge has worn the star a long time. He's met a lot of Kinseys in his day and he's still wearing it."

"But now you're back here."

"I still need to find out who killed Wilbur Pillsbury."

"Who not what, huh? It's official now, t'weren't no wild animal?"

"Doc made it so. Death by knife."

"Thought as much, the way he looked and all."

"I won't BS you, KT. It's come out about your time in a Texas penitentiary for killing a man with a knife."

"I were waitin' on that boot to drop."

He took a long drag and blew the smoke out through both nostrils. It mimicked what the beeves were doing as they trudged through the cold air.

"Orville didn't have any details in the report he got from Texas beyond it was manslaughter and you served seven years."

"Yep, I paid my dues on what I done that night. T'weren't premeditatored or accidentallied done neither. Jury couldn't rule self-defense seein' I were defendin' somebody else. Purty young thing I met in a saloon and I were purty young myself. Couple local boys didn' like the idea of a saddle tramp talkin' her up."

He took another hit off the hand-rolled. "One grabbed her and the other grabbed me and afore long boots was kickin' and fists was flyin' and then the boy got hold of me pulls a pig sticker and it winds up hilt deep in his heart not mine."

"So, it wasn't your knife."

"Hell no. I were purty young but not so young I didn' know better not to be strappin' goin' to a local saloon."

"You're carrying a knife now," I said.

"Uh-huh. Soon as I got out of the pen I bought this from an ole Apache who made it hisself. Wear it to remind myself what it could cost me if I used it on a man. You know the sayin', gun's the devil's right hand? So's a blade."

"Did you get across the river this morning to look for cattle?" I said.

"These here are them. By the time we got on to 'em, they was way downriver. We drove 'em back acrost and up a trail runs 'long side the highway. Puttin' 'em in a pasture up here so's to keep an eye on 'em."

"When you were over there, did you get a chance to check on Pillsbury's camper?"

"Yep, but flames was out by then and not much left but a smokin' heap of burnt metal and tires melted into black puddles. Smell worse than cowshit."

"Could you tell how the fire started?"

"I ain't no scientist, but I reckon all it took were twist open the gas cap, stuff a rag down, and strike a match. Gas tank's same as a bomb."

"That'd do it all right."

He finished the smoke, twisted the lit end off, and stuck the butt in his pocket. "Jus' in case you're wonderin', you don' need to keep what I done a secret from nobody up here. Mrs. Railsback, she knows about Texas. So do all the boys."

"What about Adam Railsback's other family?"

"Do they know what I done? Don' rightly know."

"What I mean is, what about them? What's the other woman's name and her kids and where do they all live?"

KT squinted at me. "You need to ask Jo or Cass or Aiden that. It ain't my place to know 'bout it, much less say nothin' 'bout it."

"Understood," I said.

He touched the brim of his pinch crown hat, clicked his cheek, and the big buckskin broke into a lope to catch up with the herd.

18

When the road cleared of cattle, I headed for the stable to check on Wovoka. He was in the corral and had made friends with the other horses. I reached over the top rail and held out my hand. He pushed his muzzle up against it and the half a carrot quickly disappeared.

"Attaboy," I said.

"He's a beautiful stallion," Jo Railsback said as she joined me. "Is he fast?"

"When I need him to be."

"I didn't know rangering called for chases on horseback."

"There's been an occasion or two."

"The Running R has a reputation for breeding top cutting horses. We've won more than our fair share of ribbons."

"So Pudge told me. Do you think you'll be able to keep your breeding business going once there's a resort, golf course, and houses all around?"

"I can't allow myself to imagine otherwise. It's one of the reasons I agreed to partner with Thunder Valley Inc. We've had to sell some of our best mares and stallions already just to make ends meet."

"Stuart Kinsey doesn't strike me as being much of a horseman."

"He's not. But he's smart enough to know that our reputation for cutting horses and prime red Angus will be a key attraction for guests looking for a real western experience."

"And you're okay with sharing your land with all the people, traffic, and noise that comes with it?"

"Is it my ideal? No. But is it the reality my sons and I are faced with? Yes. You have to understand how much I love this place. How it's my everything. My world."

I asked Jo if she'd grown up in Thunder Valley.

"No, I'm originally from Willamette Valley. We lived outside of Albany. My dad worked at the paper mill there." She wrinkled her nose. "I can still smell the sickly sweet stink. Here? The air is so fresh and clean. The scent of sage and pine and rain and sun and— Sorry, I sound like a greeting card."

"How did you meet your husband?"

"Chance. Fate. A new hairdo." A rueful smile tugged her lips. "I was eighteen, fresh out of high school, and waitressing at a truck stop. Adam stopped in for lunch on his way back here. He asked me out for dinner and I said yes. I said yes again when he asked me to marry him. I never went back to Albany. This is my home and always will be."

"Cass says Kinsey's going to gobble up the Running R acre by acre until he has it all."

"I'm well aware of what my eldest thinks. I'm also well aware of what kind of man Stuart is. What he isn't aware of is what kind of woman I am."

"I saw Kinsey in Burns earlier today. He's trying to force Pudge into backing off. It won't work, by the way."

"Back off from what?"

"Finding who murdered Wilbur Pillsbury. It's official now. Doc released his finding."

"It wasn't a wild animal?"

"A two-legged one wielding a knife to try to make it look like a four-legged did it."

"Why would anyone want to kill Wilbur? He was so, uh ... I can't even think of the word I'm looking for. Harmless? Ordinary? Unremarkable, I suppose."

"He must've found something on the ranch. Something someone wanted bad enough to kill him for it."

"What, gold? A buried treasure? A buried body? There's plenty of those in the family cemetery."

"Don't know for sure, but my guess is it has something to do with the development project."

"I can't imagine what that would be."

Wovoka came back for the rest of the carrot. I handed it over and gave him another attaboy.

Jo asked again what someone would've killed Pillsbury for, but my answer was only a shrug.

"Okay, then what's Pudge doing about it," she said.

"Looking at different things from his office while he has me back up here looking at other things."

She puffed her cheeks and blew in exasperation. "Things don't murder people, Nick. People do. Who does Pudge suspect? Me? My sons? Stuart? Who?"

"Everyone."

"That's ridiculous."

"Everyone until he rules them out. That's the way a murder investigation works."

As Jo chewed on that, I pulled a Pudge and put the fly right where I wanted it to land all along.

"He also wants to talk to your husband's other family. It'd be a lot easier if he knew their names and where they live."

"So, that's what this is all about! You want me to tell you."

I nodded.

"Dead a year and my husband is still able to break my heart every single day." I could feel the pain in her sigh. "We weren't married long before I realized Adam was unfaithful. I thought it was me, that I'd done something wrong. I thought having children would stop him, but it didn't.

"His entire life was nothing but unfaithfulness. Unfaithful to his grandfather and father for not keeping the ranch going. Unfaithful to his sons for always being away and not raising them. Unfaithful to me for sleeping with other women. And, yes, unfaithful to them for getting them pregnant and not helping raise their children."

"Does that mean there's more than one other family?"

"I don't know. Maybe. All I know for sure is the one in Sun Valley. She called here once asking for him. Hysterical. Threatening to kill herself. Adam spent a lot of time over there. It's how he met her."

Jo brushed back a lock of hair that had fallen across her cheek. She explained how her husband went to Idaho supposedly to hunt elk and bighorn sheep, but what he was really doing was stalking Ernest Hemingway.

"Adam was fixated on him. He saw himself in Hemingway. Tried to act like him. Grew a beard. Dressed like him. You know, the big game hunter, big game fisherman, big drinker, big womanizer, big everything. Well, not the writing part."

"Did they meet, become friends?" I said.

"According to Adam they were, but who knows if that was real or not. He always stayed at Sun Valley Lodge like Hemingway did. One time while he was there, he met a girl. She was a waitress. Just like me. He got her pregnant. Just like me. She had two kids. Just like me. Only hers were a boy and a girl."

She reached through the rails and Wovoka nosed her hand. "The day Hemingway committed suicide, Adam came home and never went back. It was like something died in him too."

"That was, what, seventeen, eighteen years ago."

She nodded. "Were you a big fan too?"

"I've read him."

What I didn't add was when I was at Walter Reed, one of the shrinks told me about the effect constant gunfire and explosions had on the brain. The same with concussions; I'd had more than one. He used Ernest Hemingway as an example, how it was possible the untreated concussions he'd suffered from being in car wrecks, two airplane crashes, boxing, and playing football led to severe depression that drove him to end his life. The shrink told me what I was going through wasn't my fault. I wasn't crazy, he said, only injured, the same as if I'd been shot.

"If your husband didn't return to Sun Valley, does that mean he stayed home?" I said.

"Hardly. He started going on even more hunting trips. Africa. Canada. Back to Alaska. He loved it there and had gone many times before."

"What's the woman in Sun Valley's name? The children's too."

"I never wanted to know it. I didn't want to know anything about them."

"But Adam told you, didn't he? To make himself feel big. Big like Hemingway and all the other women he had when he was married."

"Yes."

"What are their names?"

"The mother is Connie. Connie Long. The children are Ernest and Pauline."

"He named them after Hemingway and the woman he left his first wife for?"

"I told you, Adam continues to break my heart every day."

"Are the children's last name Long or Railsback?"

"He was married to me, not her. I always assumed it was the

same as their mother, but I've never met any of them. I was never curious about them and I'm still not."

Jo started to walk away.

"One more thing. When the attorney went over your husband's will with you, was there any provision for them?"

"What?"

"Did your husband leave the Longs any money, assign them any rights to the Running R?"

The anger that flashed across her face was like red lightning in a thunderhead. "No. And if he had, I would've burned the will, dug up his coffin, and thrown his damn bones in the river."

19

K agán hummed while standing at the kitchen counter with her back to the door. Late afternoon sun filtering through the window gave her raven hair a coppery glow as her right elbow sawed back and forth.

Before I had a chance to say hello, she whipped around, her fingers clutching the ivory handle of a blade the shape of a half-moon. Blood dripped from it.

"Whoa!" escaped my lips before I registered a slab of meat on the cutting board. "What kind of knife is that?"

"An ulu. We use it for everything. Filleting salmon. Gutting seals. Skinning walrus. Cutting a child's hair."

I could see all those things, including Wilbur Pillsbury laid out on a frozen field. "Did you bring that from home?"

"It belonged to my mother and hers before her."

"Your mother doesn't need it anymore?"

"She's dead."

"Sorry for your loss."

"Why do you say that? You didn't know her."

"No, but I sure felt the loss when my mom died."

"Were you by her side when she made the journey?"

I shook my head. The truth was, I got the news of her death toward the end of my first tour. The counselors at Walter Reed took lots of notes when they learned I'd re-upped for another tour instead of taking emergency leave to go home for her funeral.

"I was with mine and it made a difference," she said.

"How so?"

Kagán didn't answer but said instead, "Death is only a part of the journey."

"But sometimes that journey gets driven by someone else."

"You mean, Wilbur Pillsbury's."

"That's what I want to talk to you about."

"You suspect me of killing him?" Her grip on the ulu tightened.

I pulled the deerskin pouch from my pocket. "The Numu healer and dancer who lives with my family said you'd know what to do with it."

Kagán took it without putting down the ulu. "She thinks I need medicine?"

"Girl Born in Snow can see things in dreamworld. I think she knows you can too. If she's right, I want your help to see who killed Wilbur Pillsbury and why. I'd also like you to see what Stuart Kinsey is planning to do next."

"How come?"

"He threatened my wife and children."

Kagán slipped the pouch into a pocket and turned back to the counter. She finished slicing steaks from the slab of beef, wrapped them in brown butcher paper, and placed them in the refrigerator. When she turned around, I couldn't see where she put the ulu.

"We'll go for a ride now," she said.

"Where?"

"To where you can see the things you wish to see."

I followed her out of the kitchen. She stopped in the entranceway long enough to take a wool jacket from one of the upturned deer hoof hooks. It was embroidered with red and black animal figures: a thunderbird, bear, wolf, and killer whale. After slipping on the jacket, we walked to the corral.

"Yours is the buckskin," Kagán said.

"Yes, Wovoka. Which horse do you ride?"

"The buckskin with you."

"I'll get his saddle."

"We don't need one."

I retrieved a bridle from the trailer, opened the gate to the corral, and called him over.

"Attaboy," I said as I put it on him.

Grabbing a handful of mane, I swung aboard and reached down for Kagán. Her hand was cool to the touch as it gripped mine and she swung up behind me effortlessly.

"Across the river," she said.

I tapped my heels against Wovoka's sides and steered him toward the ford. Kagán rode with her arms at her sides, but when we started into the water, she clasped them around my waist and didn't let go even after we reached the other side.

"Go, boy," I said when we were back on the road. He broke into a trot and then a canter.

It wasn't even dusk yet, but already the air had the chill of the coming night. The burned-out hulk of the camper came into view. As I started to rein Wovoka toward it, Kagán's voice brushed my ear.

"There's nothing there anymore. Not even Wilbur's spirit. Keep going."

"All the way to the Broken Wing?"

"I'll show you."

After a mile, Kagán clucked her tongue and Wovoka immediately turned onto a trail so faint I might've missed spotting it even in broad daylight.

The Tlingit woman resumed humming as we crossed a field dotted with sage, junipers, and patches of snow. Hills rose on the far side and the trail climbed them. The scrub gave way to pinyon pines that grew thicker and taller the higher we went.

"I should've brought a flashlight for the ride back," I said.

"Sister moon will be out soon and show us the way," she said.

"Only if the clouds lift."

"They will."

When we reached the top, Kagán said, "Here."

She slid off the back before I had time to rein to a stop and began arranging rocks to make a fire circle. Gathering fresh fallen branches still green with pine needles, she assembled them into a thick carpet around it.

I left Wovoka to graze and rustled up dry wood. A handful of tinder, a struck match, a few blows of breath, and a curl of smoke turned into a flame.

Kagán sat cross-legged next to the fire and beckoned me to sit down.

"There," she said, pointing to the valley below that was becoming more visible as the clouds lifted. "See the color on it?"

"That's alpenglow."

"No, it's truth."

In the light of the fire, I could see the tattoo bands on her face had designs.

"Do all Tlingit women tattoo their faces?"

"Some, not all. It depends on the clan and the times they live in."

"Do you mind me asking what yours signify?"

"Yes, because that means you're not Tlingit. If you were, you'd know."

"When I first moved to Harney County, November—Girl Born in Snow—took pity on me and began to teach me Numu ways and their language. Later, when I asked her why she was doing it, she reminded me she'd raised my wife after her mother died when she was five years old and had seen in dreamworld that one day we'd fall in love. She didn't want to waste all the time raising Gemma only to have her go off and marry an uneducated savage."

Kagán smiled. She even gave a murmur of a laugh.

"Fine. I will tell you. My tattoos represent important events in my life and tell others what my lineage and clan is."

"You mean, when you were born, became a woman, got married, had children?"

"Yes, but not the last two. I've done neither."

"And your lineage. You told me you were from the wolf moiety and thunderbird clan."

"You remember. Some Tlingit women also do it to show their status within the clan. Others as a form of beauty. Like White women use makeup and jewelry."

"I've wondered if your nose piercing is walrus or mammoth."

"Walrus."

"Is there a story behind how you got it?"

"Mm, but not one I'm going to tell you."

"A secret, huh?"

"Secrets lose their power when they're told."

"But you do have some secrets you're going to tell me, right? It's why we're here."

"Mm."

"You said you told Wilbur Pillsbury the story of the ancients who came to Thunder Valley. Did you ever bring him up here?"

She shook her head and then poured the contents of the deerskin pouch into her palm and blew it into the fire. The pinch of plants November had picked, dried, and ground with a stone pestle ignited when they reached the flames. The smoke wafted toward us. I recognized sage, willow, and a flowering evergreen called desert sweet. I had pen and ink drawings of all three in my sketchbook.

Kagán breathed in the pungent scent and motioned for me to do the same. When she let it out, words followed.

"Thunder Valley is sacred ground. It's where the ancient People of the Tides lived and died, where their clan houses and totem poles crumbled and returned to Mother Earth."

She cupped some smoke, brought it to her face, and rubbed it into her tattooed skin.

"Where we sit now, Thunderbird once perched. He took pity on the ancients for they were only human, and he gave them life to live again as a plant that grows, the river that flows, and the wind that blows."

Turning away from the fire, she stared at me. Her eyes shone over the walrus ivory piercing. "Thunderbird took their story of confusing vengeance with justice back to my people so we could learn from it. But not all of us did, myself included. Vengeance is what brought me here."

"To the home of the father you never knew," I said. "Adam Railsback."

Kagán's head cocked. "Girl Born in Snow's medicine is powerful indeed to let you see that. Or do you read Tlingit women's tattoos after all?" She touched the bottom band.

"I didn't know it until I spoke to Jo today."

"And what did she say that made you see it?"

"She told me about the kind of man her husband was. How he fathered other children in Idaho. A son and daughter. How he often traveled to Alaska to hunt. The slight curl in your hair is one of the first things I noticed about you. It's the same as Cass's. You both share similar features. I assume his father had black hair and brown eyes too while Aiden gets his fair hair and blue eyes from Jo."

Kagán's brown eyes narrowed. "And did my White father rape the Idaho children's mother as he did mine?"

"I don't know."

She returned her gaze to the flames. "My mother was not even sixteen when Adam Railsback came to our village. He'd hired some men from another clan as trackers to help him hunt for wolf and grizzly bear. G̲ooch and xóots in our language.

"The clansmen were not honorable Tlingit because they brought a White man like him to our village in exchange for money and whiskey. They helped him kill and skin a she-wolf and bear that shared the forest with us. They pretended not to see when he took my mother into the woods and raped her.

"He was gone when my clan awoke in the morning and discovered what he'd done, but they didn't go seek justice or wreak vengeance. They remembered Thunderbird's lesson and accepted what had happened and didn't turn their backs on my mother."

Kagán blew another pinch of November's medicine into the fire. It sparked when touched by flame.

"But my mother was never able to lose her shame for what Adam Railsback had done to her. He robbed her of her childhood and chance to chart her own destiny. He never paid for the injustice he'd committed.

"I made her a promise when she lay dying in our clan house. Though she could never receive justice for what Adam Railsback had done, I could avenge her and sister wolf and brother bear too. I would find where he lived, no matter how long it took, no matter how far away it was, and kill him with her own ulu. I'd leave him laying naked outside his house like he'd done to her and I'd bring spirit wolf and spirit bear back their skins so they'd no longer be cold."

I felt a shiver. The first evening stars glimmered in the dusking sky. A pale moon rose and began to brighten. The fire started to dwindle. I added another piece of wood.

"But when you finally arrived at the Running R," I said, "you discovered Adam Railsback was already dead, killed by his own son."

"Yes. Just as my father had robbed my mother of her innocence, my half-brother robbed me of my vengeance."

"Yet still you stayed. Why didn't you take the wolf and bearskins from the living room floor and go home?"

"Because one evening I came up here." She patted the carpet of pine branches we sat upon. "I lit a fire like we have done and asked Thunderbird what I should do. He told me I'd confused vengeance and justice the same as the ancients had. But then he placed his powerful wing around me.

"'Remember, daughter, you are People of the Tides,'" he said. "'You are Shangukeidí—of the Thunderbird clan. It is the mother who determines a child's clan, not the father. Sometimes justice and vengeance can be one and the same. Only you can decide how it should be delivered and when.'"

"And have you found a way to do that?"

"Yes."

"What is it?"

Silver flashed as Kagán drew the ulu from her wool jacket with the embroidered animal figures and slashed an *X* across the view of the Running R.

"That is the price Adam Railsback must pay for what he did."

20

Kagán slid off the back of Wovoka after we forded back across the river and the lights from the house drew close. I rode to the corral and was putting him in when KT came out of the stable.

"Looks like you took a swim." He pointed his hand-rolled at Wovoka's wet legs and my own. "Best bring him on in so I can take a sack to him. Sun down, moon up, gonna freeze if it ain't already."

I led the buckskin in and tied him to a post while KT grabbed a couple of empty burlap sacks and proceeded to rub him down.

"Get his blood pumpin'," he said. "Need sumpin' yourself, got a bottle'll warm you up."

"Thanks, but I'm good with a hot shower and a change of clothes. I'm planning on spending the night."

"Still investigatin', huh? I take it you crost the river to take your own look-see of the camper case I missed sumpin'."

KT was as nonchalant as they came, but beneath that pulled-down brim of his pinch crown hat were the eyes of a hawk.

"Didn't need to look at it since you already had. No, I rode over there with Kagán."

"You don' say."

"She wanted me to see the view of Thunder Valley the way she sees it. How her people's ancient ones saw it when they came here. At least according to legend."

"What sorta legend?"

I told him a short version without a mention of vengeance and justice.

"Sounds like a Lost Tribes of Israel sorta deal."

"In a way. The group of ancients that came were like one of the ten tribes that never made it back home."

His eyes stayed on Wovoka as he rubbed him down. "What else she tell you?"

"About her life in Alaska. Her clan, her family, and so on."

"Adam Railsback was big on Alaska. Went up there to hunt. Moose, caribou, bear, wolf, you name it, he kilt it."

I wondered if KT had put two and two together too. "You ever been to Alaska?"

"No reason to. No beeves. Least none I heard about."

"Do you hunt?"

"Only when I been hungry. Deer. Elk. If you don' eat it, what's the point?"

"Speaking of eating ..."

"Sorry. I been keepin' you from supper. Don' worry about Wovoka here. I got him."

The hot water was plenty and the shower felt good. Restorative too. I changed and went downstairs to look for something to eat. Jo and Cass were finishing up at the dining table.

"I apologize, we didn't wait for you," Jo said. "I was already preparing supper when Kagán returned from her walk."

"No apologies needed and no reason you should've waited.

Keeping irregular hours goes with what I'm doing." I chinned at the empty chairs. "Where's Aiden?"

"Portland. He drove up this morning for a meeting with the project's consultants. Architects, engineers, contractors. Those sort of folks."

"Does that include the outfit Wilbur Pillsbury worked for?"

"Most likely. I imagine they'll be sending down a replacement."

Cass was staring at me, his lips in an angry grimace as if he'd bitten into a piece of steak that was off.

Before I could ask him what was wrong, Jo said, "Oh, I almost forgot. You got a phone call. Chief Deputy Nelson asked that you call him back as soon as possible. He said he tried you on your radio but couldn't reach you."

The last part prompted Cass's stare to turn into a glare.

"He say what it was about?"

"No, just to return his call."

"All right if I use your phone?"

"Of course, don't be silly. I'll ask Kagán to prepare a plate for you."

At that, Cass angrily pushed away from the table, the chair legs scraping the floor.

I ignored him and went to the living room. Orville answered on the second ring. "We have a development. Are you free to speak?"

"Go ahead."

"We have located the owner of the Double Ought, Mr. Nils Sandberg."

"Where is he?"

"Doc's."

"What?"

"After we issued the alert for Sandberg's pickup, a state trooper found it. He was on patrol and spotted a vehicle below a logging road off the main highway. He went to investigate. Apparently, Sandberg turned off the highway and onto the road, lost control of his vehicle, and went over the side. The pickup smashed head-on into a tree. Sandberg was not wearing a seat belt. He sustained fatal injuries to his head and chest."

"You said 'apparently.'"

"Nothing is official yet. The trooper is still working on the accident report. I sent Deputy Wakefield from our office to assist and also examine the site and vehicle."

"Did Doc retrieve the body himself?"

"Negative. Burns Fire Department did. Mr. Sandberg is next in line for Doc."

"Meaning nothing's official yet."

"The wrecked vehicle and the dead driver are incontrovertible facts. What is not is the cause of the wreck or the cause of death. Considering how many times Sandberg must have driven back and forth between his ranch and Burns over the years in all kinds of weather, what are the odds he made a wrong turn?"

"Something that would take your computer to calculate."

"Exactly."

"What about Kinsey's rig? Any line on that?"

"Not as of yet."

"What does Pudge have to say about this?"

"A reverse of one of his homilies. We are in a hole and so we need to keep digging."

"He there?"

"The sheriff returned to No Mountain. Something to do with Gemma and Nagah having to fly home later than expected."

"I'll give him a call. In the meantime, I have a line on Adam Railsback's other family. Their last known whereabouts was Sun Valley, Idaho."

I gave Orville their names.

"Soon as you find out anything let me know. I can take a run out there. It'll be easier for me to talk to them than you or Pudge because I won't need to hassle with asking permission from local law enforcement and deal with all the interagency bullshit."

We signed off and I walked back to the dining room. It was empty, but I could hear voices on the other side of the door that led to the kitchen. One was Cass's and he sounded even more heated than he'd acted at dinner. The other reminded me of a wolf snarling a warning at an intruder to stay clear of her young.

"Everything okay in here?" I said as I opened the door.

Cass wheeled around. "You! I thought I could trust you. I thought you were on my side. And then you go do this."

"Do what?"

"Don't play dumb. I saw you. Kagán didn't go for a walk. You sweet-talked her into going with you. On your horse. Riding double. Bareback. You ... You ... Piece of shit."

And then I saw it. Saw what Kagán and I both knew. Saw what Cass didn't know. Saw what he wanted but it could never be.

"Whatever you're thinking, you got it wrong," I said.

Kagán shook her head at me, warning me off from telling him the truth.

"Do I?" Cass's fists were clenching, unclenching, and clenching again. He was rising on the balls of his feet. "I saw you take her. I saw you come back. Hours later. In the dark."

"What you saw was me going back to take another look at the murder site. That's right, murder. Doc ruled it. Someone killed Pillsbury with a knife to make it look like an animal did."

"And you take Kagán there on what, some kind of date?" Cass's shoulders turned slightly. He was readying to let go with a roundhouse.

"One of your neighbors is also dead. Nils Sandberg. Chief Deputy Nelson thinks it was made to look like he ran off the road in his pickup and hit a tree."

"You're lying," Cass said.

"I'm not."

"Oh yeah, and why would anyone want to kill Nils?"

"Kinsey was staying at the Double Ought. Sandberg over-heard his goons laughing about Pillsbury not being able to spill his guts anymore. Sandberg told me about it when I stopped by earlier to see if Kinsey and those two had blown up the camper. They're cleaning up after themselves."

"That doesn't make sense. Nils would've sold to Kinsey. He's been trying to get out of ranching for years."

"So he told me. Now, it looks like Kinsey can pick up the Double Ought for nothing."

"That still doesn't excuse what you did with Kagán—"

"What I did was what I've being doing since the start. Helping Sheriff Warbler catch a killer. That's it. Nothing more. Are we clear on that?"

"I ... I ..."

"Are we clear?"

Cass glanced at Kagán. "Sorry, I ... uh, I ... aw, hell with it." He rushed out.

"He doesn't know," I said.

"Mm," Kagán said.

"How long has he been trying, you know, go out with you?"

"Since I got here."

"You need to tell him."

"I've told him I'm not interested. I've shown him I'm not. Many times. A woman doesn't need to say why."

"But in this case, it's—"

"My decision. Not his. Not yours. Mine!"

Kagán was speaking, but I could hear Gemma's voice. What I'd want to hear Hattie say when she grew up.

"You're right," I said.

"Do you really think who killed Wilbur also killed the Double Ought rancher?"

"Tell you the truth, I'm not sure of anything anymore."

Kagán left and I found the plate she'd prepared for me and ate my dinner standing up while looking out the window as stars salted the sky and river below. When I finished, I went back to the living room and called home.

Pudge answered.

"Does this mean Gemma's not back?" I said.

"Yep. She and Nagah walked into a real mess at the C Bar C. Thought all they were going to be doing was vaccinating a small herd but found half of 'em were already infected. They're trying to save the ones they can so the family doesn't lose everything, beef prices being what they are. Gemma said they're hoping to fly home later tonight."

"Orville filled me in on Nils Sandberg. He said there's still no sign of Stuart Kinsey's Suburban. Sure would like to know where he and his goons were when Nils died."

"Kinsey's in Portland."

"How do you know that?"

"Because Bust'em drove him there in that fancy new rig of his right after they left our little dust-up."

"He what?"

"The little brown-noser radioed on the way to say he was filing a report on me for drawing my piece. He did it so Kinsey who was sitting next to him could hear him be the tough guy. He also said he and Kinsey were going to have supper with the state AG and I was gonna be topic number one. You? Topic number two."

"Riding with Bust'em gave Kinsey an iron-clad alibi for Nils Sandberg's apparent accident," I said.

"Yep."

"But no sign of the two goons?"

"Not yet, but something tells me they're gonna have alibis too."

"So does Aiden Railsback. He drove up to Portland for a meeting with their engineering consultants."

"Seems like everyone's in Portland but you and me."

"Kinsey's playing us," I said.

"Tell me something I don't know."

"Well, I wish you'd tell me something. I'm operating in the dark here."

"Okay, here you go. Orville's friend at the FBI sent over a report this afternoon. It was an investigation into Kinsey when he was suspected of running a Ponzi scheme down in Florida."

"What did it say?"

"That the Feds had turned one of Kinsey's business partners, but he went missing the day before he was supposed to testify against him. Word is he was fed to the gators."

"Any proof?"

"No one was willing to ask the gators for it. He wasn't the only one. A couple who said they'd been swindled by Kinsey's scheme and were making a stink—they're the ones who first brought it to the Feds' attention—went missing too."

"Gators again?"

"Either that or buried deep in the swamp that was supposed to be a sunny beachfront lot they put all their retirement savings up for."

"Has the FBI been any help ID'ing Laurel and Hardy?"

"They say they're working on it. We are too. Orville's going over to the Double Ought first thing in the morning with his bag of tricks to see what he can turn up."

"Sounds like it's shaping up to be a busy day."

"That it is, son. That it is."

21

I climbed into bed, clicked off the light, and listened to the old house creak and the cattle in the pasture low. All families had secrets, but the more time I spent at the Running R, the more I realized the cemetery out back wasn't the only place that held skeletons. The different ways it could go wrong if Kagán didn't tell Cass they shared the same blood got me tossing and turning.

A fitful sleep finally came, complete with troubled dreams. A drunken and depressed Ernest Hemingway was ranting about plane crashes while rifling through his gun cabinet trying to decide between a W.C. Scott & Son side-by-side or a double-barreled Boss to blast the airplane buzzing his house on the Big Wood River out of the sky.

The dream abruptly switched to inside the plane. Gemma was behind the stick and I was in the passenger seat. Suddenly, there was a loud bang and the plane began to plummet and we were spiraling down and down as the side of a snowy mountain came spiraling up and up. I shouted just before we hit the ground and woke in a tangle of sheets.

It had been a long time since I'd had that particular nightmare, a nightmare that was all too real because it had been real, a plane crash that had left us fighting not only for our lives, but for Hattie's who was born beside the wreckage on the mountain.

My heart was pounding and so was my head when two booms ejected me out of bed. A third and a fourth explosion rocked the stairs as I ran down with my boots in one hand and jacket in the other.

The front door swung open as I reached for the knob.

"Plane crash!" KT shouted. "It flew over us and kept on goin'. Looks like it went down at the Broken Wing."

I yanked on my boots and stepped outside. As Wovoka and the horses in the corral snorted and stomped their hooves and bashed against the rails, a red cloud rose in the night sky.

Cass came thumping down the stairs. "What the hell?"

"Plane went down next door," KT said.

I was no longer listening, but running for my pickup with my jaws clenched to hold back the scream that was trying to erupt. Gemma! Was my nightmare a harbinger? Had she talked Nagah into flying over the Running R on their way home to buzz me a "Goodnight" the same as she had him waggle the wings when she left?

Hunching over the wheel, I floored it, taking the road down from the house as if it were a bobsled run. Someone was in the cab with me yelling, "No, no, no." Another shouting, "Please, please, please."

The highway came up fast and I don't know how my rig managed not to overshoot it or roll when I made the turn. The red stain kept growing bigger as I neared the turnoff to the Broken Wing. By the time I was barreling up the ranch road, yellow and black merged with crimson. Even with the windows rolled up, I could smell the stink of burning flesh. Not all of it was cow or horse.

I shot across the bridge and slammed to a stop. The scene

out front of the burning ranch house reminded me of a Vietnam village after a bombing run. Instead of hooches, the house, stable, and barn were in flames. A bunch of cows had taken a direct hit. I pictured dead and dying water buffalo. As men ran around throwing water on the flames, gunfire rang.

Zeb Calhoun was standing in the middle of the bedlam with his Winchester pointed at the sky. A steady stream of brass shone in the firelight as he worked the lever and shot round after round. His twin lay crumpled beside his boots. Jeb's eyes were open and fixed, smoke curled from his singed ZZ Top beard. Both legs were stumps.

"The plane," I shouted at Zeb. "Where is it? The fuselage. The wreckage. The people inside it."

He lowered his rifle and looked at me, his face contorted by rage and confusion.

"The plane that crashed into the house," I said. "Where is it?"

He pointed his Winchester at the sky. "Out there somewhere. Dropped its bombs and kept on flying."

"Bombs?"

"I was awake when it come, sitting on the porch smoking my pipe. Wife don't like it inside. Heard the engine. Didn't see no running lights. Engine grew louder. Next thing I know I'm flying myself. Blown clean outta my rocker."

He shook the rifle at the sky. "Sumbitch dropped sticks of dynamite on us. One landed on the roof. Another on the barn. Killed my stock. Killed my brother too."

I glanced at Jeb. He would've bled out in minutes without tourniquets. I'd seen it too often in 'Nam.

Headlights stabbed the darkness as pickups roared across the bridge. Cass and KT were in the lead vehicle. They jumped out, fired up a gas generator riding in the bed of their rig, attached it to a pump they placed next to the river, and began spraying the house with a hose. Other Running R hands joined the bucket brigade line that ran from the river to the barn.

Zeb looked down at his brother's corpse. "There's no turning the other cheek now."

I asked him who he thought did it.

"The outfit tried to buy us out. The ones in bed with his lot." He chinned at Cass Railsback.

"Cass has been against the deal from the start. Still is as far as I know."

"Mebbe so, but his mother and little brother ain't and blood's thicker than water."

The makeshift fire hose and bucket brigade began making a dent in the flames. I went to my rig and radioed the sheriff's office in Burns. Orville had already gone home for the night and I asked dispatch to alert him to the situation.

"Patch me through to Sheriff Warbler," I said. "I'll tell him myself."

Gemma answered the phone. Her voice was full of sleep, but she was wide awake by the time I finished telling her what happened.

"Oh no. How many dead, how many injured?"

"One KIA that I know of. Not sure about the WIA."

"I'll go wake Pudge."

The radio's hum and crackle was broken by a roar. "What the Sam Hill!"

The old lawman repeated it after I filled him in. "I don't give a gol'durn damn who's got an alibi. I'm gonna ask the judge for arrest warrants for Kinsey and every last one of 'em. First things first, we got to tend to the wounded and investigate the scene."

I told him I'd already called dispatch to relay the information to Orville. "I'm sure ambulances and fire trucks are en route."

"And I'll be right behind them," he said.

"You know what this means. First the murder at the Running R, then the Double Ought's owner dies, and now this at the Broken Wing. It isn't a simple fight over land anymore."

"Nope. The bad guys are waging a multifront war to try to spread us thin. Saw it when I was in the Pacific. Damn near worked."

"Don't forget they threatened to bring it to No Mountain."

"I haven't," he growled. "Son, I got to free up this line so I can call the state police. Let the FBI know too. Maybe that plane came from Idaho or Washington State. That'd make it intrastate and that'll get the Feds' attention. I'll see you in Thunder Valley."

"Roger that."

Within the hour, multiple sirens split the cold night air and the flashing lights of arriving Harney County sheriff's vehicles, Burns City fire trucks, and ambulances soon out-glowed the flames at the Broken Wing. As the professionals went to work, I rejoined Zeb Calhoun. He and KT were standing vigil over Jeb's body.

"I knew it was gonna come to something, but I didn't reckon on this," Zeb said. "Attacking a man's house? Trying to kill his wife and children too? It don't get no lower."

"Why did you say the plane was dropping sticks of dynamite?" I said.

"Because of this. I found it on the ground over there where I got blown."

He pulled a red stick from his barn coat pocket. The fuse had a blackened end and was half as long as it should've been. "Looks like it went out on the way down."

"You need to hand that over to the sheriff's department. They can run it through the lab for fingerprints and maybe find out where it was sold and to who."

The long beard waggled. "The only person I aim to hand it

over to is the man who dropped it. And when I give it back, I'm gonna make sure the fuse is good and lit when I ram it down his throat."

"But it's evidence that might be able to nail who ordered this done. The man who dropped it is surely working for someone. Someone who will hire someone else to do it again."

"You know how it is, podner," KT said to Zeb. "You gotta cut off the snake's head make sure you don' git bit agin."

As Zeb was thinking on it, Orville zoomed up in his dragster-looking wheelchair. His eyes went from the dead man on the ground to the red stick. "I presume the perpetrator pitched that from the airplane along with the ones that did detonate."

"What makes you think that?" Zeb said.

"The crater in the middle of the dead and injured livestock has the earmarks of a dynamite blast. I can test that stick and improve our chances exponentially of tracing it to the perpe-trators."

Zeb mulled it over and then held out the dynamite stick. "Do your thing, Deputy. That still don't mean I ain't gonna get another and do what I said when I get hold of who killed my brother."

He turned to KT. "I'd be obliged if you took care of the wounded stock for me. I'd do it myself, but my family—"

"Say no mo', podner. I'll git 'er done."

Zeb went to his wife and newly widowed sister-in-law who were holding each other up as children clung to their legs. He put his arms around them and started singing a hymn, his voice a surprisingly rich baritone.

As the women's sopranos joined in, KT walked among the wounded cows and horses, the echo of his pistol shots providing counterpoint to the mournful verses of "Nearer, My God, to Thee" that rose to the heavens like the smoke from the dyna-mited ranch.

22

———

Dawn was an hour gone when I pulled into Ketchum, the town that provided services and housing for the people who worked at Sun Valley Lodge and operated the ski lifts. Unlike the fiery red that stained Thunder Valley's sky several hours before, lavender was quickly becoming a bright blue over the snowcapped Smoky Mountains. It imbued Ernest Hemingway's home with surely more peace and beauty than he'd felt himself before putting a shotgun to his head.

I parked in front of the Sunny Up Café, got out, and stretched my legs. I'd driven there straight from the Broken Wing after a meeting with Pudge. When the old lawman arrived at the ranch, the fire was mostly out and the wounded were being evacuated. In addition to Jeb Calhoun, a hired hand died after a jagged board sent hurtling by the blast speared his chest.

The sheriff huddled with Orville and me and made assignments. Orville would supervise the crime scene investigation and lab work on the stick of dynamite. I was to keep on narrowing down the list of possible suspects in Wilbur Pillsbury's death, which was more than likely the same list for the two men killed in the bombing and murder of Nils Sandberg.

While Pudge thought Adam Railsback's Idaho family members were improbable candidates for any of the killings, he asked me to go talk to them in order to cross them off the list.

"Got to do our due diligence, which is a lawyer's hundred-dollar-an-hour way of saying eliminate the longshots," he said.

Pudge added he'd continue trying to block interference from Regional Sheriff Buster Burton, the state attorney general, and any other higher-ups Stuart Kinsey managed to persuade. The way he pronounced it would lead anyone to think he'd said bribe.

I sat down at the café's counter and ordered a cup of coffee along with the breakfast special. As the short-order cook set to work frying up eggs, hash browns, and sausage links, I took another look at Orville's handwritten note.

It listed Connie Long's home and work addresses and another home address for her daughter, Pauline. Both lived in Ketchum. Orville had jotted two question marks next to the son's name, Ernest. The chief deputy said he'd been unable to find anything about him, but give him time and he would.

The waitress brought my order. As she put the plate down, I said, "Thank you, Connie."

Her smile was worn and her kitchen sink dye job needed touching up. Nicotine stained her fingers and her eyes looked like they were used to frequent drops to get the red out.

"Do I know you, handsome?" she said. "You're not a regular here."

"Your name tag."

"Oh, right. Sometimes I have to look at it to remind me what it is myself."

"Working long shifts can tire anybody out. Don't I know it."

"You don't look so worse for wear."

"Couple days off does wonders, you know."

"I wouldn't. I'm six on, one off, except Thanksgiving through

New Year's. Then it's seven and none. Busiest time of the year around here." Connie Long took a swipe at the counter with a rag. "You're not from Ketchum, are you?"

"No, Oregon. Ever been?"

"Never have, never will. Don't like anything about it."

"How come?"

"Long story. A long, sad story."

"I had one of those too. It always dogged me until I learned the only way to forget it was to tell it. If you want, I'm a good listener. Say, over a drink after you get off?"

Connie had a smoker's laugh. "Aren't you the smooth one."

"Sorry, meant no offense."

"I bet."

She moved down the counter and took an order. I finished eating and drained the coffee cup. I was fishing in my wallet when Connie came back and placed the bill down.

"Five," she said.

I fished out a ten.

"No, five tonight. It's when I get off. There's a place down the street called the Sun Also Sets. If you're not just playing games, I'll see you there."

"Looking forward to it."

Outside, I checked Orville's note again. Pauline Long's address had an apartment number to go with it. A visitor's center was right across the street and a red-cheeked woman wearing a white ski hat and purple down vest gave me directions to Pauline's street a short stroll away.

I knocked on the apartment door and a young man with bleary eyes, scruffy beard, and tousled blond hair answered. He was wearing sweatpants, a Black Sabbath T-shirt, and looked like he'd been in bed thirty seconds ago.

"Ernest?" I said.

"Who's that?" he said.

"Pauline's brother."

"Didn't know she had one."

"Is she here?"

"What do you want with her?"

"It's a private matter."

"Hey, dude, any matter with Pauline matters to me. Dig?"

"Are you her husband?"

He snorted. "MYOB, dude."

When he started to shut the door, I straight-armed it. "Business is why I'm here, but since you're not Pauline's brother or married to her, then I can't discuss it with you. Legally or financially."

"What are you, some kind of bullshit bill collector?"

"Other way around," I said.

"Huh?"

"Know what the opposite of collecting is?"

"Uh ..."

"Distributing." When his expression remained blank, I said, "Giving."

"Like as in money?"

I gave him the smile again. "If Pauline's not here, do you know when she'll return?"

"After work."

"Which is at the ...?"

"Roundhouse. Top of Bald Mountain."

"Thanks."

"Hey, dude, be sure to tell her I helped you out. You know, me helping you helps her, right? Okay?"

He asked for a response again, but I let it bounce off my back.

The snow on the face of Bald Mountain sparkled like cut diamonds as I rode the chairlift to the restaurant perched 7,700 feet up. As the building came into view, I started counting all the windows but soon lost track. The door to the restaurant had a closed sign on it printed in lettering that looked German. I tried the knob anyway. It was unlocked. The dining room was the shape of an octagon and had a timber pole ceiling. Every table had a mountain view.

"Sorry, we don't offer breakfast," a woman called from across the room. "We start seating for lunch at eleven. You're welcome to come back then."

"I was hoping to speak with Pauline Long," I said.

"That's me. I'm the restaurant manager. How can I help you?"

She was a younger version of her mother, but without the world-weariness. If I squinted, I could see some of Cass Railsback's features too: the dark eyes, the black hair with a swirl in it.

"I'm an old friend of your brother's. I lost track of him and was hoping to get back in touch," I said.

"You served with Ernest?"

The answer was a fifty-fifty chance—military or prison. I went with my gut.

"I did. Wound up doing three tours."

"And afterward?"

"A tour at Walter Reed. It took—"

"You don't have to tell me," she said quickly. "Ernest struggled too."

"They didn't train us for that."

She nodded. "So, you're trying to get back in touch with Ernest because—"

"It's what they counsel you to do. Reprocessing, they call it. Reexperiencing. Go back and revisit the bad stuff and express remorse if you need to. Even though it's going on ten years since I mustered out, I do it from time to time when, well, I need to."

"I wish Ernest had learned that. He never got over the war.

Never properly healed up here." Pauline touched the side of her head.

"And now?" I said.

"I don't know. Mom and I, we haven't heard from him for quite some time. He just stopped coming home. No calls, no letters. Nothing."

"And your dad?"

"What about him?"

"Might have he heard from Ernest?"

Her sigh was deep and pained, and made me feel like shit for lying to her. "Our dad's been out of the picture for a long time."

"Sorry," I said. "Sorry, to have bothered you."

"Wait. If you find Ernest, tell him we miss him. Mom and me. We still love him. We want him to come home. Whatever happened over there, he was only doing what the generals ordered him to do."

I got back on the lift and kept my eyes closed and my face aimed at the sun as I rode down the mountain, hoping the rays would burn away the guilt that had settled in my heart, hoping the whoops and hollers of the skiers schussing below would drown out the sounds of the men in my squad who still talked to me from the grave. We were only doing what we'd been ordered to do, but the orders had come from more than generals.

The day was still young and I debated whether or not I should take Pauline's answer as the final one and drive back to Harney County, but once again I heard a voice from a long-dead squad member. It was DJ's, my radioman. He was explaining why he and the other men all got matching tiger tattoos during a leave in Saigon.

"The big cat reminds us that curiosity eventually kills him," he drawled, "but it ain't till the tenth time that it kills him for good."

I rubbed the tiger tat on my bicep that I'd gotten right after they did. I still wanted to know if Connie Long or her son had anything to do with the trouble in Thunder Valley.

With hours to kill before five o'clock, I went to Ernest Hemingway's grave in the Ketchum cemetery to see if he had any insights to share. His final resting place was beneath a cold granite slab with his name and dates engraved in it that was flanked by two spruce trees. Visitors had left bottles of cheap booze on the marker.

An older woman walking past with an unleashed sporting dog running point paused. The dog stopped when she did and held his position.

"Are you going to take one or leave one?" she said.

"Excuse me?" I said.

"It's an either-or proposition for most people who come."

"Their bad taste or bad manners?"

She gave an approving smile. "You should go to the memorial his friends built for him on Trail Creek Road. It's not far from the lodge."

"Why?"

"Because you appear to be in need of answers for whatever it is troubling you."

She began walking again and so did her dog. I decided she must be Mary Hemingway, Ernest's widow who still lived in the house on the Big Hole River where he'd killed himself. She was the one who found him and I wondered if they still talked like I did with my dead.

It was a short drive to the Hemingway Memorial. Clear, cold water ran through an aqueduct made of cut stone. The sculpture of a bearded head sat atop a bronze column. It was the writing on the plaque that I realized the woman had wanted me to see. Hemingway had written it as an epithet for a friend killed in a hunting accident.

I read his words out loud: *"Best of all he loved the fall. The leaves yellow on the cottonwoods. Leaves floating on the trout streams. And above the hills, the high blue windless skies. Now he will be a part of them forever."*

They were good words. True words. And it was good to hear my own voice saying them.

I walked back to my pickup saying the words again and then drove to the Sun Also Sets to wait for Connie Long and tell her the truth about why I was really there and ask her about Adam Railsback and her missing son.

23

I'd been driving all night after leaving Ketchum with only an hour or so break, but I was wide awake now. A cloud of black smoke rose a half mile away and scarred the early morning sky. It was coming from the vicinity of the Warbler ranch.

The pickup didn't even have time to clatter when I flew over the cattleguard. Twin rooster tails of gravel shot up as I sped up the drive. The smoke was wafting from a blaze out front of the house. Nagah was feeding sticks of greasewood to the flames as November swayed and sang.

I slammed on the brakes and watched them for a couple of minutes to give my pulse time to slow before getting out. Gemma met me on the front porch.

"What gives?" I said.

"Pudge," she said. "He overdid it by going to the Broken Wing fire and got a fever. I warned him to slow down, but you know him."

"Did you take him to the hospital?"

"No, he's here. I insisted he stay in bed this morning. November's singing a healing song and Nagah is offering prayers to Mu naa'a for help." Mu naa'a, or Wolf, was the Numu word for Creator.

"I'll dance and pray too if it'd help any," I said.

She touched my cheek. "I'm glad you're home."

"I wish it were for good, but we still have a ways to go before we can prove a case."

"Pudge told me he's narrowed down who the prime suspect is."

"That just got more complicated. Turns out there's plenty of people with a stake in whether or not the development project goes through who might've killed Pillsbury."

"Does that include the family in Idaho?"

The story Connie Long told me at the bar in Ketchum was still fresh in my mind, but so was Kagán's.

"They're not the only ones I need to talk to Pudge about."

"But not right now. If he gets any more run-down, he'll get a chest infection and you know what that means."

Gemma said it matter-of-factly like any doctor would, but it was her father she was talking about and I knew no amount of medical training and professional distance was soothing her pain. It was etched in her face and trapped in her eyes.

I pulled her close. "Don't worry. Orville and I'll double down and pick up the slack while Pudge mends."

"You can start by reading a fax Orville sent. I've been holding off letting Pudge know about it."

"Deal," I said. "Just as soon as I get a cup of coffee. Make that a pot."

The tray to the fax machine in Pudge's office was overflowing with sheets of paper. I picked up the stack, eyed the couch, but quickly nixed stretching out on it to read. After going more than twenty-four hours without sleep, my eyes wouldn't've stayed open a minute.

Taking a seat at his desk, I read the top page. It was stamped

"Confidential" and a few words had been blacked out, but not the title: *Stuart Robert Kinsey—A Summary of Official Records and Field Reports*. The FBI had compiled it.

The first section was comprised of photocopies of his birth certificate, driver's license, passport, and a mugshot. The bio listed his father as the owner of a suburban New Jersey real estate agency and his mother a realtor. Kinsey was an only child. He attended public schools, earned decent grades, played on the basketball team in high school, and was a member of the math club.

He lived at home while attending college at nearby Montclair State University and worked for his parents' agency on weekends and during summers putting up for sale signs, mowing lawns at new listings, and hosting open houses.

Kinsey's first brush with the law occurred during the summer after his junior year. Three complaints were filed with the National Association of Realtors that he'd been soliciting bribes at open houses in exchange for guaranteeing the prospective buyers their offers would be accepted. He denied it, saying it was a simple misunderstanding. A month later, a pair of undercover cops pretending to be a married couple at an open house arrested him when he pitched his scam.

Kinsey was taken to jail and booked, but his father's lawyer cited entrapment and got the charges dismissed. It didn't stop him. Having gotten a taste of easy money, the twenty-year-old promptly dropped out of college, moved to Manhattan, and took a job at a boiler room enterprise hawking penny stocks. After two years mastering high-pressure sales tactics, he quit and opened his own boiler room pumping and dumping real estate investment trusts and bundled high-risk mortgages.

Within three years Kinsey had a penthouse apartment on the Upper East Side, spent his evenings at Studio 54, and jetted down to Miami for weekends. The Security Exchange Commission finally caught up to him and charged him with twelve counts of fraud. The IRS also went after him for tax evasion and the FBI launched an investigation into his alleged ties to a money laundering scheme run through a casino in the Dominican Republic.

Denied bail as a flight risk, Kinsey was jailed in the Manhattan Detention Complex's south tower, better known as the Tombs, for seven months while the cases against him played out. His parents mortgaged their house and used all their savings to help pay his legal bills. He was eventually offered a plea deal for time served along with a hefty fine. Kinsey took it and hired a car to pick him up out front of the Tombs and went straight to La Guardia where he boarded a flight to Miami. He never went back to New Jersey and never thanked his parents who'd bankrupted themselves getting him sprung.

The final summary provided more details on the Ponzi scheme in Florida that Kinsey was suspected of masterminding but never charged with. It included the name of the missing business partner who was going to provide testimony to the FBI and a description of the retired school teachers who disappeared after claiming they'd lost their life savings in Kinsey's scam.

The last page was a photocopy of an old clipping from the *Paterson Times* about the murders of two New Jersey cops. Their names were circled and Orville had written a note in the margin: "The same undercover officers who arrested SK for soliciting bribes."

That gave me a bigger jolt than the coffee. I picked up the phone and called Orville.

"I'm back in No Mountain and just read the report on Stuart Kinsey," I said. "By my count, that's five murders he's associated with."

"Associated being the operative word there," the young chief deputy said. "He has never been charged for any."

"Kind of like your 'apparently' regarding Nils Sandberg driving his pickup into a tree."

"Actually, that has gone from apparently to proven. I have a summary of Doc's postmortem in front of me. Mr. Sandberg died from blunt force trauma to the front of his skull at least an hour before his vehicle went off the road and struck the tree. Doc was able to determine it by comparing the timing of blood coagulation and bruising with the pickup's dashboard clock that stopped as a result of the impact."

"Meaning he was probably murdered at the Double Ought and his body driven there and put behind the wheel. The killer either pushed Sandberg's rig with his own or jammed the accelerator down."

"Affirmative on the first scenario. Scratches on the Ford's back bumper appear quite fresh. There was neither dirt nor rust in them."

"But I bet there are matching scratches on the front bumper of the black Suburban Kinsey's goons drive."

"That will be difficult to prove."

"How so?"

"Multnomah County Sheriff's just faxed a response to my statewide alert regarding the Suburban. It was reported stolen to authorities in Portland last night and then discovered early this morning in flames at an abandoned lumber mill. So much for fingerprints and scratches."

"Who filed the stolen car report, Kinsey or one of his thugs?"

"Regional Sheriff Buster Burton did. He was with Stuart Kinsey when Kinsey took a call from his driver reporting the vehicle had been stolen."

"Pudge said Kinsey has an alibi for everything. He wasn't

kidding. Now, we're going to learn Laurel and Hardy have been in Portland this whole time too."

"I do have some new information about them."

"From your friend at the FBI?"

"Actually, from the New Jersey State Police, specifically its Special Investigations Unit."

"They know Laurel and Hardy?"

"Yes, but by their real names."

"Which are?"

"Give me twenty minutes and I will tell you in person. I was on my way out the door to meet with Sheriff Warbler when you called."

"Wait a minute. You can't talk to him. Pudge is home in bed. He's got a fever."

"That may be true, but the sheriff is not asleep. He called me on his two-way radio and ordered me to come down immediately."

I pictured the old lawman pulling the blankets over his head and whispering in his walkie-talkie so Gemma wouldn't hear.

"If Gemma finds out he's been radioing you, there'll be hell to pay," I said.

"I have no choice. He is my superior officer."

"Okay, I'll explain it for you. See you in twenty."

"Explain what?" Gemma said.

I swiveled in the chair. She had a fresh pot of coffee in her hand.

"That was Orville. Pudge radioed him to come down."

"I knew I should've taken his two-way from the nightstand."

"Remember what I said earlier about work being good medicine for Pudge?"

"I do, but I'm glad it's you and not me who's going to try to sell that to November."

24

The pyre of greasewood had become a cone of embers and ash by the time the chief deputy crossed the cattleguard and muscled his wheelchair up the front steps. I let Orville in and we found Pudge sitting up in bed. His flannel nightshirt didn't have the gold star pinned to it, but the badge was within reach. So was his .45. The short-brim Stetson hung on the bedpost.

"Tell me about Kinsey's hired guns," the old lawman said before coughing into a handkerchief, which he quickly hid from view.

Orville started with his call to the Montclair Police Department after reading the old newspaper article about the shooting deaths of their two undercover officers. He told the cop who answered that the officers had once arrested Stuart Kinsey and now he was operating in Harney County and there'd been a murder. Orville was promptly transferred to a detective in the Cold Cases Unit at the Special Investigations Section of the New Jersey State Police.

The handkerchief came out again. "The detective got a name?"

"Joe Wojcik. He's been with the unit ten years."

"And the murdered cops are his case?"

"It and dozens more, but this one is special because the victims were law enforcement."

"Are Kinsey and Laurel and Hardy named in the cold case file?"

"Yes, but I did not call them that. I said we did not know their names and gave him descriptions."

"He knew them?"

"Affirmative."

Hardy's real name was Vincent "Vinnie" Valante and Laurel's Henry "Smiles" Wax. Both grew up on the tough streets of Paterson, New Jersey. They graduated from a neighborhood street gang to petty theft to felonies to organized crime. Both served time in juvenile hall and prison.

When Orville asked Detective Wojcik how the three hooked up, he answered that Paterson and Montclair were worlds apart in terms of money and class but only ten miles by car.

Valante was already in the Montclair jail for boosting a car when Kinsey was brought in for soliciting bribes. The two were put in the same cell. After his father arranged for his release, Kinsey told the Paterson hood that if he ever needed anything, to look him up.

Valante didn't forget during the two-year stretch he did at the state pen in Rahway for grand theft auto. When he got out, he tracked down Kinsey. His timing was perfect. Kinsey was launching his own boiler room and needed someone to collect payments and make sure whiners kept their mouths shut.

It was a perfect fit. Valante had spent his time in Rahway pumping iron in the yard and serving as a cell block enforcer. He also had a boyhood friend with a special talent for keeping patsies in line, Henry Wax. Kinsey hired Vinnie and Smiles and they'd been with him ever since.

"Were the two undercover cops killed before or after they went to work for him?" Pudge said.

"It was right around the same time," Orville said. "The two officers were shot while sitting in an unmarked car not long after Valante was released from prison."

"The gunman got them both before either one could return fire?"

"There were two shooters. One on each side of the vehicle. They fired multiple rounds."

"Laurel plus Hardy equals two," I said.

"That is Detective Wojcik's summation as well," Orville said. "He also shared with me a psychiatric evaluation of Henry Wax that was made when he was incarcerated at a mental facility for juvenile delinquents. He had been arrested for assault and battery of a senior citizen. Wax was sixteen at the time. The psychiatrist who evaluated him wrote that he exhibited all the classic symptoms of a sociopath bordering on psychopathy. He lacked any remorse and had extreme antisocial tendencies."

Pudge asked Orville why no one had ever been charged with the killings of the two undercover cops.

"The local police found no evidence at the scene and had no witnesses. It ultimately became a cold case and turned over to Detective Wojcik. He looked back through all the cases the two undercover officers had worked together, including Stuart Kinsey's. He interviewed Kinsey as a matter of course, but it did not raise any red flags at the time."

"What finally did?" Pudge said.

"When the detective discovered by chance that Valante was working for Kinsey and the two had been in jail in Montclair at the same time. He brought them both in for questioning. He also brought in Wax after he learned he was working for Kinsey too. None of the three confessed or implicated the others despite what Detective Wojcik described as undergoing a Jersey-style interrogation."

"Meaning using a large telephone book and a set of jumper cables attached to a car battery," Pudge said. "But Wojcik still suspects them."

"Affirmative. He believes Valante and Wax killed the two police officers as a kind of loyalty test. Kinsey either ordered them to do it or they came up with the idea on their own to prove themselves."

"Or maybe they just did it for kicks," I said. "The sociopathic thing."

Pudge nodded and then coughed. "Dangerous for all three should one of them turn."

"Detective Wojcik said he offered each immunity, but no one took it."

"What else does the Special Investigations Section handle besides cold cases?"

"Major crimes including homicide and kidnapping, organized crime, and, more recently, criminal activities associated with gambling. New Jersey voters approved legalizing casinos two years ago and the first opened in Atlantic City last year. Two more are scheduled to open this year."

"Makes for a shorter commute for the East Coast mobs who control them in Vegas," the old lawman said.

"Didn't the FBI look into Kinsey's possible connection to a money laundering scheme involving casinos in the Caribbean?" I said.

"Yes, in the Dominican Republic to be precise," Orville said. "But they were never able to gather enough evidence to prove a case. I asked Detective Wojcik if he was aware of that and did he think Kinsey might have a similar connection to the casino in Atlantic City."

"What'd he say?"

"The casino is so new it is too soon to tell what, if any, criminal activities might be going on there. But then he added something interesting."

Orville looked at Pudge and me.

"Well, go on, son. What?" the sheriff said.

"New Jersey is not the only state that legalized gambling recently. The detective pointed out the Seminole Indians in Florida operate a high-stakes bingo hall and are moving toward adding other games of chance."

"And Kinsey lived in Miami and was making money off his Ponzi scheme that needed laundering."

Orville nodded. "When I pointed that out to Detective Wojcik, he said, and I quote, 'And now Kinsey's got a development scheme going in your state that will need laundering one day. Don't you got a lot of Indians living in Oregon too?'"

Pudge started coughing uncontrollably. The bedroom door swung open and Gemma rushed in followed by November.

"That's it. Party's over," Gemma said. "Out. Now!"

Orville and I did as ordered despite Pudge's protests. As November was closing the door behind us, she fixed her stare on me.

"If Pudge goes to meet his wife in the spirit world today, he will have to tell her it was men's pigheadedness that killed him, not the cancer."

The chief deputy and I regrouped in Pudge's office. The coffeepot was still on the desk, but its contents were lukewarm at best. I poured myself a cup anyway and asked him what he thought.

"Everything points to Kinsey, Valante, and Wax, but we still do not have any hard evidence. Anything we do have is speculative as well as circumstantial."

"'What's past is prologue,'" I said.

"*The Tempest.* Now you are reading and quoting William Shakespeare along with your favorite poet."

"It's something we used to say in 'Nam. The French had fought there for ten years and lost. We should've listened to Shakespeare. Would've saved a lot of GI lives."

Orville stared down at the stack of faxed pages I'd been reading. "We will have to keep pushing to build our case. We are bound to get a break sooner or later."

"Anything come up with the stick of dynamite?"

"All we have learned so far is the name of the manufacturer. It is a very common brand and sold throughout the state. The only fingerprints on it were Zeb Calhoun's from when he picked it up and put it in his pocket. The person who lit and dropped it from the plane must have been wearing gloves."

"What about ID'ing the plane or at least where it took off from and landed?"

The young deputy held up his hands and flashed his fingers over and over. "There are hundreds and hundreds of airfields in the state. I contacted my friend at the FBI and told him what happened and asked if there was anything they could do. I reminded him that Thunder Valley was less than two hours from the Idaho border by air."

"Crossing state lines. That would make it federal. What did he say?"

"He told me they would look into it and relay any information he could about air traffic at the time in question. He did not come right out and say it, but I believe the military deploys advance radar technology to track private planes on a regular basis to support Drug Enforcement Administration activities."

"That radar will have to be pretty fancy. KT told me the plane flew very low over the Running R and without any lights. It's a wonder it didn't smack into the mountains surrounding Thunder Valley."

"The pilot must have exceptional skills to navigate in the dark while opening the window, lighting a fuse, dropping the dynamite, and hitting a bull's-eye. That rules out Vincent Valante and Henry Wax. There is nothing in their records that show either has pilot experience."

"But someone else does. Or at least did."

"Who?"

"Ernest Long. Adam Railsback's son from another mother. The one in Idaho."

"Did you talk to him?"

"No, only his sister and mother. His sister said they hadn't seen or talked to him for years, but his mother had a different story."

"How so?"

I saw myself sitting at a corner table in the Sun Also Sets with Connie Long. I waited until she was halfway through her first cocktail before I told her the truth about why I was there. She started to throw the drink in my face, but reversed course and downed it in a single gulp.

"Story of my life," she said. "I'll never be free from Adam Railsback. Even dead, he still continues to break my heart every day."

I hid my surprise that it was almost word for word the same sentiment Jo Railsback had expressed. I signaled the bartender for another round.

"I've already spoken with Pauline and know she had nothing to do with the killings in Thunder Valley," I said. "The same as I know you couldn't have either."

"What makes you so sure?" she said.

"You can fake a lot of things in life, but not surprise when hearing about a murder. Especially more than one."

The cocktail waitress delivered Connie's drink. She clutched it with both hands and raised it to her lips.

"Pauline told me about Ernest," I said. "Turns out we share some things in common. Vietnam. Combat. Combat fatigue. Your daughter says you haven't seen him in a while."

"I blame all that on Adam too," she said. "Ernest was always trying to prove himself to his father by living up to his namesake, the great Ernest Hemingway. But when Adam left us, Ernest blamed himself and tried to prove his worth even harder. It's why he learned how to fly at sixteen, why he became a crop duster pilot, why he enlisted in the army and learned how to fly helicopters."

"He flew choppers in Vietnam?"

Connie guzzled the new cocktail. Ice cubes clinked against her teeth. "Not the big jolly green ones. The little ones with all the guns on them."

"So, he was Air Cavalry. I was in the same division, First Cav, but on the ground."

I didn't add that the guys flying the attack choppers were called Headhunters. No wonder he suffered combat fatigue. Like my war, his was nonstop action from the get-go.

"What do you think Ernest is doing now?" I said.

"The last time I talked to him was right after Adam's death. He called home and we talked for an hour. He was very angry. Said someone killed his father and they shouldn't get away with it. I told him it had been ruled an accident, but he didn't believe it." She downed the dregs of the cocktail. "And you know what? Neither did I."

After I finished telling Orville that, he stared at the stack of faxed papers long and hard before looking up.

"We need to find Ernest Long and find out where he was the night the Broken Wing was bombed."

25

Blackpowder Smith was ringing up a customer in the dry goods portion of his establishment when I came in. "Why, howdy there, young fella. I'll be right with you."

He carried the customer's boxes out to her car, tipped his black hat with the rattlesnake skin band, and returned.

"I sure do miss your son when he's in school. Or should I say my back does. Johnny's turned out to be the best box boy I ever had. Even runs the cash register when I get busy in the saloon. Knows every price without having to look at the sticker."

"He's got a head for figures, all right," I said.

"And then some. Better be saving your pay for college. That boy's Harvard material."

"Hope he doesn't go that far away."

"Clip a bird's wings, it'll stick around 'cause it ain't got a choice. Let it fly free, you give it a reason to want to fly back."

"Gemma gave me your message that you heard from your grapevine."

"Sure did. Need to wet my whistle while I tell it."

We moved to the saloon and he ducked behind the bar and poured me a glass of water. "Your usual," he said.

Then he poured his usual from the whiskey bottle. He held up his glass. "Here's mud in their eyes 'cause we're going need it to be there to keep 'em from seeing what they'll be aiming at. Namely, us."

"Sounds like you know what happened at the Broken Wing and Double Ought."

"News travels fast around here, especially the bad kind. Then there's the absolute rotten kind. News you smell before you hear it. The grapevine says Bust'em Burton convinced the AG to order Pudge's immediate dismissal despite the fact he was duly elected by Harney County voters."

"He didn't mention it when I was at the ranch just now."

"Cuz Pudge don't know about it yet. It's rotten news, but fresh as morning dew. Word is his hand-picked replacement is driving to Burns as I drink." He raised the glass and took a slug.

"Who is it?"

"The chief deputy sheriff over in Coos County. When Pudge hears, it's going make him sicker than he already is. Them two got history. Bad history."

"But Orville's already the chief deputy here."

"AG is naming the Coos County deputy interim sheriff so he'll be above Orville and have the authority to fire him if he has a notion, which he will cuz Bust'em will tell him to. If that ain't bad enough, I heard even more."

"What could be worse?"

"My neighbors, the folks working in the other buildings? The dress shop, barber, fix-it man, tooth doctor. Each and every one got a certified letter offering to buy 'em out, lock, stock, and barrel."

"Stuart Kinsey sent it."

"Thunder Valley Inc. is on the letterhead, but they're one and the same, ain't they?"

"Kinsey's trying a squeeze play to get you to close up and sell him your liquor license, but he doesn't know who really owns those buildings."

A grin appeared above the white billy goat beard. "That's for me to know and him to find out."

"You're not worried your tenants will tell him?"

"They know better. It was part of the deal when I leased the buildings to 'em, why I've never raised their rents. Most been here long as me when I struck it rich way back when prospecting and used some of the gold I found to buy No Mountain to keep a dying town alive."

"Kinsey will learn about it eventually."

"If he does, then I'll tell him what I told your Laurel and Hardy boys. Get the hell out!"

"You need to be careful, Blackpowder." I gave him the short version of their history. "These guys don't believe the law applies."

"Don't fret, young fella. I took precautions. Got more than my sawed-off within easy reach. I normally log my rack time upstairs, but now I'm doing it down here."

"In the bunkroom?"

Blackpowder maintained a set of cots in a converted storeroom for customers who adhered to his policy of handing over their car keys and agreeing to sleep it off before he'd serve them another round.

"That or standing up right here," he said. "I been known to sleep with one hand on a gun and one eye open plenty of times."

"This group will come after you with more than guns," I said.

"I heard what they did to the Broken Wing, but you got to remember my dry goods store sells more than canned beans and soda pop. I stock whatever a rancher might need, from tools to horseshoes to this." He reached behind the bar and held up a stick of dynamite. "I'll be damned if I'm going bring a rock to a bomb fight."

"Okay, Blackpowder, but watch your back."

"That's why I got eyes on both sides of my head."

His cackle followed me out.

I swung by the old lineman's shack to check the answering machine before returning to Thunder Valley. The little red light on it was flashing like a fire truck's.

One caller asked if hunting out of season was really against the law. Another was from a driver who'd struck a pronghorn at the Hart Mountain Refuge and wondered if it would be okay to have it for supper, and, if so, what was the best way to cook it. Two back-to-back messages were from neighbors feuding over a noisy rooster. One demanded I get off my lazy ass and come arrest both the neighbor and his damn chicken, and the other demanded I get off my lazy ass and come give his rooster the same level of federal protection I gave to the damn pigeons.

The caller on the final message sounded as if he had a bad cold. He didn't provide a name but said he'd stopped by the Malheur Refuge and found the visitors center had been vandalized and the nearby pond was full of shotgunned birds.

I jumped in my pickup and sped south. US Fish and Wildlife Service rangers had a good reason they were issued .357 magnum revolvers, and the boosted firepower wasn't only for stopping a charging grizzly. I'd had run-ins with rifle-toting drunks using refuge signs for target practice and showdowns with commercial poachers armed with machine guns. Catching an offender in the act made me deaf to excuses and I never hesitated to slap the cuffs on a violent criminal and haul him off to jail.

The stubble in the fields alongside the two-lane was crowned with rime that sparkled like a tiara on one of Hattie's dolls and the causeway over the Narrows was slippery. I didn't slow down until the turn onto Sodhouse Lane. Even though I doubted whoever was sick enough to slaughter sitting ducks and destroy a public building was still at the refuge, I didn't want to risk sliding off the road and missing a chance to intercept them.

The visitors parking lot was empty. I parked in it to save a couple of minutes rather than taking the service road around to the back. I grabbed the pump shotgun from the rack and left the .30-30.

A footpath wound through a stand of trees before forking. One branch led to the visitors center, which was closed for the season. The other went to Marshall Pond. Choosing birds over a building was an easy decision.

The pond looked like a glazed jelly donut that someone had squeezed too hard. The frosted shoreline was splattered with pools of blood as were the carcasses of snow geese and tundra swans that floated in the open water. I cursed loudly to try and drown out the high-pitched squawks of wounded waterfowl and the pathetic flapping of shot-shredded wings.

Shouldering the 12 gauge, I aimed and fired, pumped in a new round, and aimed and fired, pausing only to reload when the magazine was empty. I didn't stop until there was no more movement and no more cries. My heart was pounding in my ears and the taste of bile and anger stung my mouth.

"You're out by my count," a voice called from behind me.

I wheeled around.

Vincent Valante and Henry Wax stood side by side. They both wore heavy wool black overcoats that reached their knees. Valante had on a black knit watch cap pulled down tight. He was holding an automatic at his side. Wax wore a black knit ski cap pointed at the top like an elf's. The barrel of the pump shotgun he was bearing at port arms blocked the left corner of his fixed grin.

"Detective Joe Wojcik said to say hello," I said. "So, hello Vinnie and Smiles."

"Big deal, you know our names," Valante said.

"Yeah, but I still picture you as Laurel and Hardy."

"Who's them?"

"Comedians. Went from silent pictures to the talkies."

"Funny guy, huh?"

"They were," I said. "Hilarious."

"I meant you." He flapped his double chin at Wax. "Isn't he, Smiles? Funny."

Wax's grin stayed put as he nodded.

"Wojcik said he finally came up with an eyewitness to the Montclair undercover cops' shooting. A lady walking her dog. The dog died years ago, but the lady's memory is as sharp as the blade that carved up Wilbur Pillsbury."

"You hearing this, Smiles? Guy's like a walking talking history book."

"Here's another chapter," I said. "Kinsey's business partner that was going to rat him out, the one you fed to the alligators? Someone finally got hold of that old gator and slit him open. There was still a hand inside him. FBI's got it now running the prints."

"Now you're switching to comic books."

"I got one more for you, Vinnie. The black Suburban you lit on fire? It didn't burn up all the way. They're matching paint scrapes on the front bumper to Nils Sandberg's pickup."

"Your mouth is running but not your brain. Not too smart, is he, Smiles?"

"Nils overheard you two talking about Pillsbury no longer able to spill his guts about what he found on the Running R that would kill the deal. Heard Smiles here finally open his mouth. Laughing like a hyena about it."

Wax's grin finally twitched and his eyes narrowed. His grip on the shotgun tightened. He didn't say anything, but even an amateur poker player could read all the tells.

"You done? Because you're about to be done for good," Valante said.

Wax swung the shotgun so the barrel was level with me.

"See the box on the tree behind me?" I said. "The hole in the center? There's a movie camera inside filming everything."

"You're lying."

"Scout's honor."

"So what? Soon as we take care of you, we take care of it. No camera. No film." Valante's Oliver Hardy toothbrush mustache hunched like an inching caterpillar as he chuckled.

"Doesn't use film," I said. "It's beaming live right now to thousands of birdwatchers across the world not to mention the Fish and Wildlife Service."

"Now you're being pathetic. Take what's coming to you like a man."

"What, you were in solitary confinement between '69 and '72? Didn't watch all the landings on the moon? Neil Armstrong, Buzz Aldrin. One small step. One giant leap. Beaming it back to earth for everyone to see on TV in the comfort of their family room. Walter Cronkite doing the play-by-play. How do you think they got those pictures back? Same as right here."

The toothbrush mustache went flatline. Wax's grin stayed fixed, but the shotgun's barrel was suddenly pointing at the ground. Both men lowered their chins to hide their faces.

"Drop the shotty," Valante said. "Unbuckle your holster and kick the piece into the pond. Do it."

I let the 12 gauge go. It was empty anyway. As I undid my holster, I thought about the last time I did that. It was for Zeb and Jeb Calhoun. I could see Jeb's body, the stumps that were all that was left of his legs. I kicked myself for not having driven up the service road where I would've seen Valante and Wax's vehicle stashed behind an outbuilding and gotten the drop on them instead of the other way around. I kicked the holster, but not too hard.

"Now, turn around and start walking real slow," Valante said. "That's right. Walk straight toward the field."

I took a look at their feet. They were both wearing street shoes, not boots. They wouldn't last a minute chasing me across snowy, icy stubble if I could duck their first shots.

"Don't forget you're on candid camera, boys," I said and took off running.

The roar of a shotgun filled my ears, but not my backside with lead because Wax had blasted the box with the hole in it instead. I was running zigzags by the time Valante raised his automatic and started firing. Slugs whizzed by me.

I ran like I used to through the jungle, ran full-out like I did back in school for the track team, ran to circle back to my rig and get the Winchester to stop them from trying to finish me off when they discovered the box didn't hold a camera but a nest that was used every spring by a pair of wood ducks.

As I ran, I thought about Wilbur Pillsbury lying in the snow. Whoever killed him and jumped from snow patch to snow patch sweeping away their tracks certainly hadn't been two big-city thugs who didn't know what kind of footwear to bring to the High Lonesome.

The realization that there was more than one killer on the loose in Harney County made me run even faster.

26

The gunfire was only an echo by the time I cut back through the field. Valante and Wax were louts, but they were also street-smart. They'd figured out what I was up to and beat feet back to their vehicle in a race to intercept me in the parking lot.

A final obstacle remained between me and it. The pond was fed by a canal that brought in fresh water from the Blitzen River. In a month it'd be iced over and I'd be able to skate across. Now, I'd either have to wade through freezing water or find the two-by-four I'd placed across it two springs ago to keep fawns from drowning when they followed their mothers to greener pastures.

Cattails, sedges, and big sagebrush crowded the bank and hid the narrow bridge from view. I bulldozed my way through the thick wall of vegetation a couple of times, only to come up empty. The third time worked, but a bridge for a twenty-pound fawn looked like a tightrope made of dental floss.

Speed was my best chance. I flattened some brush for a running start, took a deep breath, and then bolted while keeping my eyes focused on the far bank. The two-by-four bounced with every step and threatened to buck me off. Bowing wood groaned, icy water splashed, and a startled rough-legged hawk shrieked.

I kept on going, hoping that if the two-by-four sank, either momentum would carry me across or I'd learn if I could walk on water.

I never found out.

When my boots reached dry land, I crashed through the wall of brush and stormed across the parking lot. The roar of a vehicle announced Valante and Wax were coming, and coming fast.

I pulled the Winchester from the pickup's gun rack, laid the barrel across the hood, and aimed at the service road. Hitting the front tires wouldn't slow them down, but a couple through the windshield might.

Their new rental was identical to the last, a Suburban the same color as their knit caps, overcoats, and street shoes. It bounced down the potholed service road. Wax was driving while Valante aimed his automatic out the passenger window.

They tried to kill me once; they'd try again. Gun or driver? Gun or driver? Valante's size made the choice for me. He was the bigger target so I fired at him first, then levered in a second round and shot at the fixed grin leering behind the wheel.

Tires squealed and the Suburban swerved as it flew past my rig, screeched into a four-wheel skid, and came to a stop facing me. The windshield now spidered by two .30-30 slugs obstructed my view of the driver and passenger. I couldn't tell if they were sitting upright or slumped over with holes between their eyes.

Running to the other side of the pickup to keep steel between us, I jacked in another round and shot out the front left tire and then the right.

The Suburban sagged, but the engine still huffed like a bull speckled with banderillas and slowed by a picador's lance. It was gathering strength and resolve to give a final charge. I fired at the front grill and twin funnels of steam rose from the punctured radiator.

"Get out with your hands clasped behind your heads or the next one hits the gas tank," I yelled.

The passenger door opened and Valante stumbled out. Blood streamed from what remained of his left ear. He looked at me with dazed eyes.

"On your knees," I said.

He did so slowly, painfully.

"Come on out, Wax," I said. "I'm not counting to three."

"He won't," Valante wheezed.

"Is he dead or paralyzed?"

"You're a cold fish."

"If it's not one or the other, he soon will be."

"Smiles don't know how to give up. He don't think he's got to."

"Then I'll shoot him where he sits."

"That'd be murder."

"No, it'd be resisting arrest."

"I'll tell the cops you didn't give him a chance."

"Who says you'll still be talking?"

Wax finally opened the door. Cuts from flying safety glass peppered his fixed grin, but he'd been even luckier than Valante. The only bullet hole I could see was the one in the pointed top of his elf-like knit cap.

"Hands behind your head and lie face down," I said.

He took his time doing it.

Valante said, "How you going cuff the both of us?"

"One at a time." I lobbed my handcuffs to him. "Get up and put them on Smiles. Hands behind his back. Make them good and tight. Do it."

"This is a waste of time. Mr. Kinsey, he'll spring us in a minute. You? You'll be the one rotting in jail."

"Cuff him or I'll shoot your other ear off."

Once Wax was handcuffed, I tossed a second pair to Valante and had him cuff one of his wrists. I grabbed a coil of rope from the back of the pickup and followed my rifle right up to him. Kicking him in the kneecap without saying a word to drop him to the ground, I had both his wrists cuffed behind his back before he had time to cry out.

I looped the rope through their cuffed wrists, yanked them to their feet, and marched them to the pickup.

"Get in the back. Down on your bellies. Now!"

"We can't ride back here," Valante said. "We'll freeze to death."

"Serve you right for bringing big-city clothes to the country. Now get in."

When they were on their stomachs, I quickly knotted the rope looped through their cuffs to the bed's tie-down anchors.

"Word of advice? Don't talk. You'll likely bite your tongues off."

I got in and fired the ignition. If my cargo ignored the advice and chose to swear at every pothole I hit, I didn't notice. I was too busy radioing the sheriff's office and asking Orville to ready a cell.

27

Orville Nelson was flanked by Deputy Wakefield and another heavily armed deputy waiting out front of the sheriff's office.

"Where are your prisoners?" he said.

I hooked a thumb at the pickup's bed. He pushed on the arms of his wheelchair to look over the side panel at the two prostrate thugs whose overcoats and knit caps were dusted with frost.

"Are they dead or alive?"

"Like fish sticks, but they'll thaw."

Orville ordered the two deputies to unload Valante and Wax. "Use extreme caution. Both are killers."

The cold had stopped Valante's wounded ear from bleeding. He mumbled through blue lips as they slid him out. "I want to make my call."

"After you are booked and processed," Orville said. "Then you can call your lawyer."

"I got rights, you freakin' cripple."

"Yes, you have the right to remain silent. I advise you to do so immediately before you slip on the ice and knock your teeth out."

That earned a grin from me. It grew even bigger as Deputy Wakefield and his partner frog-marched Valante and Wax inside.

"How were you able to apprehend them?" Orville said as he spun his chair around to follow them.

"With a little luck and a lot of know-how about the lay of the land at the Malheur Refuge. How's Pudge?"

"Madder than the proverbial hornet. Regional Sheriff Burton called him at home to tell him the attorney general had approved his immediate dismissal."

"I'm surprised I didn't hear Pudge swearing when I drove through No Mountain just now."

"I presume Gemma and November hogtied him like you did your prisoners; otherwise he would be here. Sheriff Warbler is bound and determined to fight it."

As the deputies took Valante and Wax upstairs to the cells, I trailed Orville down the hall to his office. He rolled behind his desk, his expression turning glum.

"While I was awaiting your arrival, I received a call from Sheriff Burton too. He told me he and the Coos County chief deputy sheriff will be arriving shortly. Burton appointed him interim sheriff and I am to obey his every command."

"Do you know him?"

"Only by reputation, which, I must say, is not without tarnish."

Orville stared at his desk. "I am very conflicted. On one hand, I swore an oath of loyalty to my badge. On the other, I owe everything to Sheriff Warbler. He hired and trained me. When my injury disqualified me from joining the FBI, he made me a deputy and then his chief deputy. I also feel sad and mad about his illness. Cancer is so unfair."

"Hang in there and see if things don't settle down. Bust'em may have landed the first punch, but he hasn't knocked Pudge out yet. Cancer hasn't either."

"There is another pressing concern."

"What?"

"Once Sheriff Burton discovers Vincent Valante and Henry Wax are upstairs, I am confident he will continue to curry favor with Stuart Kinsey by releasing them immediately."

"But Harney County sheriff's didn't arrest them; I did. I got them cold on two federal beefs, not to mention attempted murder. Fish and Wildlife and Harney County have a long-standing agreement on mutual assistance. I've jailed offenders here before."

"That may be true, but now they are being held in a county jail that is no longer under Sheriff Warbler's purview."

"Typical Bust'em. The only justice he knows is justifying doing whatever it takes to get ahead."

"I am also sure he is going to block our investigation into Wilbur Pillsbury's death, starting with ordering me to hand over all of the field notes and reports we took from the camper so he can give them to Stuart Kinsey."

"But I thought you've been making copies."

"I have, and I discovered something very curious. Pillsbury devised a numerical cipher to map locations at the Running R."

"Cipher like a secret code?"

"Yes."

"Were you able to crack it?"

"It was hardly on the order of what the Navajo code talkers did during World War II, but, yes. It is based on longitude and latitude resolution down to the sixth decimal point with an obfuscating multiplier added to it."

"Meaning?"

"Pillsbury used his surveying equipment to map the

Running R down to the centimeter. That is the equivalent of the width of a Cheerio. I know this because it is my son's favorite cereal."

"At one hundred and fifty thousand acres, that's a lot of Cheerios. Why was he being so exact?"

"He was an engineer, so it was in his nature."

"And why create a secret code?"

"I believe he added the multiplier to conceal the true position of specific locations. Not the house or the barn or the river, but sites within undeveloped portions of the property."

"Which ones?"

"I am still compiling a list and inputting them on my own set of digital topographical maps. Once I complete that, I will examine them to see if there is a pattern or if they share certain qualities that can help explain why he was shielding them."

"From who?"

"I am not sure. He must have found something or some things on the ranch that he was not ready to share with Thunder Valley Inc. or the permitting agencies. Perhaps both."

"If that's true, it sounds like he didn't trust Stuart Kinsey either. Or maybe he found something valuable like a gold vein or a reservoir of oil."

"Or the opposite," Orville said. "Something that could halt the project. Habitat for an endangered species. A midden of archaeological or paleontological significance. A sacred Native American site. Maybe he was going to make Kinsey pay to know what and where it was."

"Pudge would be proud of the way you're thinking that no one's above suspicion. Were you able to trace Pillsbury's steps by following his log entries for the days and nights leading up to his death?"

"I am still working on that, but should have something soon."

"I've got something too. Things have been moving so fast, I didn't have a chance to tell you earlier. When I went back to check out the camper before it was blown up, I discovered the keys were missing. They weren't in the back when I searched it nor in the ignition or cab. They weren't in Pillsbury's pockets either, only that broken compass."

"What do you think happened to them?"

"Pillsbury was murdered elsewhere and his killer drove him there and dumped him. There was melted snow on the driver's side floor. The killer either tossed the keys or stuck them in his pocket out of habit. He could still have them."

"That would be a smoking gun."

"If we're lucky."

"I agree with the theory that Pillsbury was killed elsewhere. Have you spoken to Doc yet?"

"I'm going there next. When you have a map of Pillsbury's movements, let me know. Likewise with the secret locations."

"Affirmative. But before you go, take a look at this."

Orville opened a folder and pulled out a shiny sheet of fax paper. It was a headshot of a man who looked vaguely familiar. I took a harder look and then understood why. He shared similar features with Cass Railsback and Pauline Long.

"It's Ernest Long," I said.

"Yes. I was able to search the US Army Air First Cavalry database. He had enlisted under his own name."

"Were you able to find anything more recent about him? Like his whereabouts, what he's been doing?"

"Negative. After his discharge from the army, he moved around a lot, but the trail went cold a year ago."

"A year ago? That was the last time he talked to his mother. The same time his father was shot and killed by Aiden Railsback."

"You can keep that copy. I have another."

I pocketed it, told Orville I'd check in with him later, and headed for the front door. Before I reached it, Sheriff Burton stepped out of Pudge's office to block my path. A man wearing a Coos County Sheriff's Department uniform stood behind him. He had a flattop glistening with Butch wax and a nose that had been broken more than once.

"Hold it right here," Burton said to me. "I was just giving Interim Sheriff Jackson explicit instructions that you are prohibited from ever entering these offices, but here you are."

"Doing my job," I said. "I arrested two men on federal code violations at the Malheur Refuge and brought them here per our mutual assistance agreement."

"Don't play games with me. I know exactly what you did. Namely, wrongfully detaining two individuals."

"They're killers, Bust'em. New Jersey State Police likes them for two deaths in Jersey and the Feds for another three in Florida. They're prime for Nils Sandberg's death. That makes six. It would've been seven if I hadn't stopped them from killing me."

He ran a finger over his brush mustache. "Do you have physical evidence of that? Eyewitnesses?" When I didn't answer, he scoffed. "Precisely what I thought. That is exactly why I have ordered their release."

"You have no right. They're my arrests. Federal arrests."

"Doesn't matter. This is my jail. Do you read me? Mine."

Burton raised his finger like a gun and poked me in the chest.

"I've never forgotten that time you sucker-punched me. I've also never forgotten all the times you sided with Warbler against me."

His poke was even harder this time. "Your temporary deputization by Warbler is hereby terminated. I order you to stop investigating Wilbur Pillsbury's death immediately."

He poked again. "Furthermore, I order you to cease

harassing Stuart Kinsey and interfering with Thunder Valley Inc.'s operations. Violate my orders and I'll have you arrested."

When I didn't respond, Burton tried imitating a drill instructor's voice. "Do I make myself clear?"

"As ditch water."

His mustache twitched. "I'm filing a disciplinary report with the Fish and Wildlife director and demanding he order Liz Bloom to terminate your employment immediately."

"Good luck with that, Bust'em. Liz has backbone to spare while the only one you know is the bottom end of Stuart Kinsey's you're so busy kissing."

"That's gross insubordination. I'm going to have you up on charges."

"Whose, yours? I don't work for you, and pity the poor people who don't have a choice."

I turned to the new interim sheriff. "You're hitching your wagon to the wrong horse, Jackson. Ask Bust'em why he never eats in a restaurant when he comes to Burns. The people here don't forget his weaselly ways when he wore the Harney County star. They season his order with spit. Side with him and you'd better know how to cook."

I took my time walking out and drove around the corner to the county coroner's office.

Doc was in the autopsy room studying a set of X-rays when I pushed through the swinging doors.

"Got a sec? I need your help."

"That's something new," he grumbled. "Anybody comes in here without my invitation is beyond speaking."

"I suppose you heard Bust'em fired Pudge and installed a lackey."

"Gossip is as unavoidable as death and taxes."

"Now he's released Stuart Kinsey's goons I arrested and told me to quit looking into Pillsbury's murder."

"Sheriff Burton's judgment has always been suspect, but believing you're going to oblige him is a real topper." He set down the X-rays. "You said you needed my help."

I filled him in on my run-in with Valante and Wax. "I accused them of killing Pillsbury even though I don't think they did."

"Why not?"

"Their choice of footwear for starters. They're big-city boys. They don't know how to ride a horse, much less cover their tracks. I think we're dealing with two sets of killers here. One who did Pillsbury and one who beat Nils Sandberg to death and then tried to make it look like an accident by pushing his pickup off the road."

He gave a mocking shake of the head. "And did one of the two killers also bomb the Broken Wing and kill Jeb Calhoun or do you think there's a third killer too? Maybe even a fourth."

"Still working on that."

"But you do think Vincent Valante and Henry Wax killed Sandberg."

"Without a doubt. They had means, motive, and opportunity. They were staying at his place with Kinsey. I think the old-timer overheard something he shouldn't have and the pair was cleaning up on their boss's orders. I told them we know Sandberg was killed by a blow to the head before he was put in his truck and pushed off the road and we have paint scrapings from the Suburban they lit on fire in Portland."

"If there are multiple sets of vehicle evidence, no one has told me, much less sent them here for analysis."

"I said it to see what they'd do."

"Which was?"

"Shoot at me."

"It appears they aren't very good aims because here you stand."

"What I need is information on Pillsbury's murder. It's the key to everything, including Sandberg's death and the bombing at the Broken Wing."

"Pudge and Orville have a copy of my findings. It includes time of death and the manner."

"Were you able to tell if he was dead before being carved up?"

"The exact timing of the sequence of events has been challenging to quantify, but the state and aging of tissue damage suggest that the first wounds were inflicted hours before the fatal one. Given the precision of the amputation of the ears, I surmise it was done by a scalpel or a straight razor. Additional wounds were inflicted post-death."

"To make it appear to be a wild animal attack," I said. "That's been my theory all along."

"The problem with the theoretical is, it remains that until proven."

"The nonfatal wounds were likely the result of torture, right?"

"Yes. What I can't answer is, why."

"To get information."

"About what?"

"Orville discovered Pillsbury was using a code of sorts to conceal the exact locations of places."

Doc rubbed his chin. "I presume Chief Deputy Nelson deciphered the code." When I nodded, he said, "And I also presume he is creating his own map of these locations using his computer."

"As well as using the dates of the entries in Pillsbury's logbooks to track his movements prior to his murder. With all that, we might be able to locate where he was tortured and killed before being transported to where his body was found."

"I may be able to help narrow that down some."

"How's that?"

"I was about to write it up as an addendum to my post-mortem after examining the compass you found in his pocket and talking to a professor of geology at the university in Eugene."

"But the compass was broken."

"Yes, the crystal was cracked and the housing dented, but the magnetic needle inside was only partially damaged. The professor told me it was likely still weakly attracted to the earth's magnetic field and was pointed roughly toward the last direction it was facing before it broke."

"Which was where?"

"Southwest of where we found Pillsbury's corpse."

"Southwest? But that'd put Pillsbury back on the other side of the river before the bridge washed out."

"Indeed it would."

28

———

The road up to Running R's ranch house took me back to the beginning. Solve Wilbur Pillsbury's murder, I said to the hanging spurred *R* as I passed beneath it, and the rest of the killings would fall into place.

I pulled to a stop behind my horse trailer, half expecting KT to amble out of the stable, a hand-rolled clenched in the corner of his mouth and a laconic "Howdy, podner" drawled through a cloud of tobacco smoke.

But he didn't appear. Nor did he when I walked up to the corral's rails and gave Wovoka an attaboy. The buckskin stallion nickered and shook his black mane as if to say he was more than ready for me to solve the crime so he could get home to Sarah.

Heated voices coming from the stable's open sliding door drew me toward it. Cass and Aiden were inside jawing angrily. Elbows were cocked and fists balled.

"Afternoon," I said.

Cass's head swiveled. "I told you you're not welcome here. Get your horse and go."

"That's the first thing we've agreed on in a long time, big brother," Aiden said.

"Tell me who killed Pillsbury and I'll be happy to oblige."

"Screw you," Cass said.

"That's another thing we agree on," Aiden said. "Screw you, Nick Drake."

I took out the faxed photo of Ernest Long and showed it to Cass.

"Ever seen him before?"

He looked at it before shaking his head. "Nope. Never. Who is he, a suspect?"

I didn't answer, but held the photo up to Aiden. "What about you, recognize him?"

Aiden gave it a passing glance. "Uh, no."

"Take a closer look," I said.

He groaned before doing so. "Uh, can't say I do. Satisfied?"

"He's your half-brother from Idaho, Ernest Long."

"What the hell?" Cass said. "Give me that."

I showed him the photo again.

"You got to admit there's a family resemblance," I said. "He's got your hair and coloring, the same as you do your father's. His father."

Aiden hooted. "Dear old Dad. Glad I got Mother's good looks."

Cass shot his fair-haired brother a glare and then trained it on me. "Why are you showing us this?"

"Because he might've had something to do with killing Wilbur Pillsbury and bombing the Broken Wing."

"Why would he do that?"

"Good question. What do you think, Aiden?"

"Why are you asking me?"

"Because you've met him before."

"No way."

"No, two uhs. You hesitated twice. You recognized Ernest from the photograph. That proves you've seen him before."

"I tell you I haven't. I don't know him."

"Sure you do. Like you knew all about your father's other family in Idaho. You said bastards, plural. You knew there were two kids. A boy and a girl."

"That doesn't prove I met him."

"I went to Sun Valley. I talked to your half-sister, Pauline. Talked to her mother too. Connie said Ernest was convinced his father's death was no accident when he learned you shot and killed him."

I waved the photo in front of Aiden's face. "I think he came here looking for you to avenge his father's death. An eye for an eye. You had to convince him it was an accident. To get him to buy it, you told him you were wracked with guilt and would find a way to make it up to him."

"You are so full of shit."

"Is that what made you go looking for Stuart Kinsey? Find a way to keep your half-brother from killing you?"

"How many times do I have to say it, I don't know this guy. I don't know what you're talking about."

"Ernest worshiped his father, but I can't say the same about you, can I? Did you really fumble the rifle he handed you and put a round in his heart?"

"Is all this true?" Cass shouted at him.

"Of course not. Sheriff Warbler ruled it an accident. Who are you going to believe? The sheriff and me or the guy who wound up marrying the girl you always dreamed about?"

Cass raised his fist at Aiden's chin. "You're trying to pay off this bastard from Idaho because you killed Dad?"

"Can't you see? He's making it all up. He's not even supposed to be here. The old sheriff, Warbler? He's gone. They fired his fat ass."

"Who did?"

"Stuart. Well, he had it done. And this dumbshit game

warden? He's no longer deputized. We don't have to answer his bullshit questions. Don't have to help him at all. We can kick him off our property right now."

"How do you know all this?"

"Stuart called me a little while ago. Don't you get it? We're in the big leagues now. Stuart's a heavy hitter. So are his partners, Burt Symes, Jeffrey Parker, and the rest. They eat little guys like the fat-ass sheriff and glorified dog catcher here for lunch."

Aiden took a deep breath. His chest swelled. "Don't get distracted, big brother. What we're trying to do, what we've been doing all along. Nothing's changed. It's still save the Running R, save us from bankruptcy, and make a shitload of money while we're doing it."

Cass shook his head. "By giving Dad's bastard a piece of the ranch?"

"I'd never do that. Trust me. I'm not going to let you and Mother down. I promise."

"We'll see," Cass said.

He stalked out, leaving only his silhouette in the doorway before the sun swallowed it whole.

"Where's Ernest now?" I said.

Aiden scowled. "I told you, I don't know what you're talking about."

"You're lying. You know where he is."

"Why do you care about this, anyway? It's not your problem. Warbler's out. So are you. Go back to No Mountain and leave us alone."

"Not a chance."

"How come?"

"Because of Pillsbury. Because of Nils Sandberg. Jeb Calhoun too."

"What do you really want, money? A piece of the action from Thunder Valley Inc.? Name your price."

"I want to know where Ernest Long is?"

"How should I know?"

"Because you offered him something and he's not going to forget it. He's been waiting a year for it. Where is he?"

"I don't know."

"Stop lying. Tell me where he is."

"You're crazy."

"Yeah, I was at one time. But you know who still is? Ernest. You have no idea of what you're dealing with, who you're up against. Once he decides you're playing him, look out."

"Get off my property or I'll shoot you for trespassing."

"Like you did your father?"

"You bet. I'll shoot you right in the heart and it won't be an accident."

"You can try," I said.

Aiden huffed, but then followed his big brother out of the stable and his silhouette was gobbled up by the sun too.

I went to the house. Kagán was in the living room sitting cross-legged on the wolfskin.

"Did you find what you're looking for?" she said.

"Some, not all. Did Aiden and Cass just come in here?"

The Tlingit ran her palm across the wolfskin. "No."

"What about Mrs. Railsback? Is she here?"

Her black hair swished. "I'm all alone."

"Do you know where she went?"

"Riding. Like she does most afternoons."

"Any place special?"

"You'd have to ask KT."

"He'd know?"

"He usually goes with her."

"I see."

"Do you really?"

I squatted beside the skin of the female wolf Adam Railsback had killed. Wolves were beautiful creatures, but also capable of extreme violence. Like humans. I ran my fingers over the fur. It felt soft and coarse at the same time. "Like life," I mumbled.

"What?" Kagán said.

"You asked me if I see. I'm not sure I'm seeing anything—anything that counts, that is."

"You didn't find what you were looking for after you went to the Broken Wing the night it was bombed?"

"I found more questions than answers. I went to Idaho right after that and spoke with your half-sister, Pauline Long. Her mother too."

"What's Pauline like?"

"Nice. Hardworking. Worries about her mother. Worries about her brother too. Ernest."

"My third half-brother?"

"Yes."

"What's he like?"

"I didn't meet him, but he could be dangerous. He was a soldier in Vietnam like I was. Suffered combat fatigue like me too."

"But you're still a warrior."

"I'm a wildlife ranger," I said. "There's a difference."

"Wild animals are sacred to my people. They provide us sustenance and clan identity. Their spirits are our guides as we journey through life. We worship animals. We protect them. Tlingit are warriors because of them." Kagán traced a dark line of fur. "You are a warrior because of the animals you protect."

"Do you want to see what your half-brother looks like?"

"If you believe it matters." She studied the photo. "He looks like Cass."

"You've never seen him?"

"No, I've never been to Idaho."

"I think he's here in Oregon. Close by. Real close."
"Then perhaps I'll meet him and can ask him."
"What?"
"Did his father rape his mother like he did mine."

29

J o Railsback was on the front porch reaching for the door when I opened it.

"Oh, you're back," she said and then noticed the duffle bag in my hand. "Does this mean you know who killed Wilbur or are you giving up?"

"No on both accounts."

"Is Sheriff Warbler still investigating the murder?"

"Not officially. Stuart Kinsey had him fired."

"Why on earth would he do that?"

"You'll have to ask Kinsey."

"I will, but why are you leaving?"

"I need to get back home."

"Because you miss your wife and children?"

"Of course, but what I really need is some sleep. I drove straight to Sun Valley after the Broken Wing bombing and then back again."

"Did you talk to the Longs?"

"The mother and daughter. They don't know anything about Wilbur Pillsbury."

"And the son?"

"They haven't seen or heard from him since he learned of his father's death."

I set my duffle bag down and showed her the photo. "This is Ernest. It was taken several years ago."

"My God, he looks like Adam. Cass too. Why are you showing this to me?"

"I believe he's here in Harney County. Have you seen him?"

"No, and if I had, I'm sure I'd remember. I mean, look at him." She frowned. "Is he here because of what happened to my husband?"

"His mother said he didn't believe his father's death was an accident. I think he came here, threatened Aiden with retribution, and your son promised to pay him as a form of penance. Most likely give him land or money or both."

"Did you show this to Aiden?"

"Yes, and Cass too."

"Did they recognize him?"

"Cass didn't, but Aiden did."

"Is this man dangerous?"

"Very."

"Adam, Adam, Adam," Jo cried out. "What have you brought down on our family? My family."

She rushed upstairs.

I hoisted the duffle bag and headed for my pickup. Two horses were hitched to a rail. One was KT's buckskin and the other the bay mare that Jo had ridden when we forded the river to reach Pillsbury's camper and body. That seemed like weeks ago.

The head wrangler was unbuckling the billet strap on the bay's saddle.

"Comin' 'n goin' are you, podner?" KT said.

"Been doing it so much I've forgotten what it's like to see the inside of my eyelids."

"Done that plenty myself. Goes with cowboyin'."

"You and Mrs. Railsback have a nice ride?"

"Best part of the job is ridin' just to be ridin'. Not movin' the beeves or chasin' a stray, but enjoyin' the sunshine. Everythin' smellin' fresh. Hearin' that ole river talkin'. Yep, t'were real pleasant."

"Can I show you something?"

KT gave the photo a close look.

"I didn' know better, I'd say t'were Cass, but Cass never were in the army and this fella here is wearin' a uniform."

"It's Ernest Long. Adam Railsback's son with another woman. The family lives in Idaho."

"Nope."

"It's Ernest, all right. Chief Deputy Nelson got the photo from the US Army."

"I meant, nope, he ain't in Idaho. He's here in Harney County. Leastways last time I saw him."

"Where, when?"

"Right here on the Runnin' R. Out on the landin' strip. He flew Mr. Kinsey in along with those two money men. The ones over for supper you met. T'were the beginnin' of fall they was here afore."

"Who else saw him?"

"Lemme recollect. Aiden for sure. I drove him out to the strip to pick up Kinsey and the other two."

"Was Cass with you?"

"Nope, t'were only Aiden and me. We brung 'em back to the house and they went in fer coffee and I went back to my chores and then Aiden drove 'em round the ranch hisself and then back to the strip and away they flew."

"Did the pilot tour the ranch with them?"

"Nope. Stayed with the plane the whole time. High-wing Cessna. Single-prop four-seater."

"What about Jo? Did she see Ernest?"

"Nope. Didn't go to the strip, not when I were pickin' 'em up and Aiden takin' 'em back."

As I mulled that over, KT finished unsaddling the bay and then unsaddled the buckskin. He carried both saddles into the stable and came back with a pair of curry combs.

"Don' mind me sayin', but you look poleaxed." He began rubbing down the bay, starting at the neck, a comb in each hand. "Gotta admit, I feel a mite poleaxed too. It ain't coincidentallied that Adam Railsback's son from Idaho winds up on the Runnin' R, is it?"

I told him why Ernest came looking for Aiden when he learned of his father's death.

"Aiden must've gotten Ernest a job flying Kinsey as a way to pay penance for killing his father," I said.

"Makes sense. But there's always that one heifer gits it in her thick skull to go left at the fork when all the other beeves go right. Know what I'm sayin'?"

I thought about Stuart Kinsey's history of cons, how he was bent on gaming the system, how that took always being a couple of moves ahead.

"It could've been the other way around, I suppose. Maybe Kinsey found Ernest first and put him into play as a way to pressure Aiden into giving up more of the Running R."

KT rubbed down the mare's shoulders, moving both combs in a circular fashion. "Chicken 'n egg sorta deal, what come first, huh?"

"I suppose."

"Well, one thin's fer sure. T'weren't no chicken that flew o'er the ranch the other night and t'weren't no eggs dropped on the Broken Wing neither."

"No, that was a trained pilot who knew what he was doing."

"Flyin' or blowin' up stuff?"

"Both."

First Air Cavalry pilots weren't only trained to fly, but also how to destroy their choppers with whatever was at hand to keep them out of enemy hands if forced to crash land. Tossing in a grenade or two usually did the trick, but sometimes they had to get creative, like trying to ignite the bird's kerosene-based jet fuel, which had a higher flash point than gasoline.

Air Cav pilots were also trained how to evade the enemy after a crash landing. How to cover their tracks. How to look for sign. How to figure out how to get back home without being captured or killed.

It was the kind of training that would lead a killer to think about sweeping away his footprints from patches of snow and going back later to blow up a camper to destroy any evidence he may have left behind.

I'd received explosives and evasion training too. My squad and I had blown up gun emplacements, booby traps, spider holes, and tunnels, including a section of the miles-long Cú Chi tunnel system the VC used as an underground base during Tet. We'd also taken out bridges, from ones no wider than two thick culms of bamboo lashed together to spans strong enough to bear the weight of a light tank.

Maybe that's what Ernest Long had done. He tortured and killed Wilbur Pillsbury for some reason on this side of the river, then took out the split log bridge after he drove across it in the camper to buy himself time while he looked for a place to dump the body.

"The night the bridge collapsed," I said, "did anyone see or hear it go down?"

KT stopped swirling the twin curry combs. "I didn'. Don' believe nobody else did neither. T'were the middle of the night."

"Cass told me it was overdue for repairing or replacing, but funds being in short supply, well, it got put off."

"T'weren't in that bad a shape. Nothin' some new rope wouldn' put right. See, the bridge were made of split logs and anchored to both sides of the river. Held fast by big ole rope used fer moorin' ships. Hawsers, they call 'em. Ends was tied round big old boulders on the bank take dynamite to move."

"What happened?"

"T'were stormin' for a while and it take a day or two for all that rain 'n snowmelt comin' down the little streams to reach the big river and raise her up. I reckon the hawsers holdin' her fast musta snapped or knots loosened up so she slipped the boulders and away she went."

"Being made of wood, it didn't sink, did it?"

"Nope. Got busted up some on the rocks downriver. When the water went down, lot of it washed up on the bank."

"How far downriver?"

"Mile, mile 'n change."

"Is that at the end of the ranch?"

"Nope. Ranch goes on two bends past."

"Is down there like this up here? Fields, sage scrub, forest, meadows."

"Yep, though ain't much in the way of buildings like here outside a lineman's shack. Been there since way back when."

"When I first moved to Harney County, I lived in a lineman's shack. Did so until I got married and moved to the Warbler ranch. Mine was used by railroad linemen keeping the track clear during the winter. A lumber company built the line to bring logs to their mill in Hines. The shack's now my office."

"That a fact? Well, this one were used by cowboys when they was out patrollin' the boundary line. Give 'em a dry place to bed down with a little woodstove to keep 'em from freezin' their peckers off in winter."

"I'd like to see it."

"Well, yer welcome to. Stay the night, you want. Need to cut some wood so you don't—"

"Freeze nothing off."

KT chuckled.

"I'll saddle Wovoka."

"You can drive your rig there, you want. Road's rough but doable. Pillsbury, he drove up and down it two, three times. Mebbe more."

"What for?"

"Doin' whatever Pillsbury done. Surveyin'. Diggin'. Writin' his reports. T'weren't many corners of the Runnin' R he didn' git to. God rest his soul."

"Is the road the same one that goes down to where the bridge used to be?"

"Yup. Keeps on goin' past it and the ford. Keep the river on your left and look for a big ole hill black as coal and shape of a cone. Shack's betwixt it and the river. Can't miss her."

30

———

ovoka whinnied his disappointment when I left without him. The road to where the bridge used to be was clear of snow and the ruts weren't too deep, but it turned rougher past the ford. I slowed after a mile and began searching the riverbank. Fifteen minutes later I spotted a raft of split logs, half in, half out of the water.

Climbing aboard confirmed it was the remains of the bridge. Large cleats bolted to both ends of the outside logs had hawsers fastened to them with clinch knots. The ends disappeared into the river.

I grabbed one and began hauling it in. The current pulled the thick rope taut like a big trout fighting a hook. When I had more of it than the river did, the current let go and the remainder of the hawser whipped back and landed at my feet. The rope hadn't frayed and snapped; it'd been sliced clean. I retrieved the hawser cleated across from it. That one had been cut too.

After taking some photos for evidence, I resumed driving. The river thrummed as it sawed through the valley floor, occasionally gonging and crashing like cymbals as it banged into boulders and bashed against logjams.

A stream crossed the road. It wasn't too wide and didn't look too deep, but I stopped and got out to check before proceeding. The water was crystal clear and the rays of the late afternoon soon cast diamonds upon the surface. The singing of red-winged blackbirds and song sparrows lured me upstream.

Silver and green spots the color of old dimes and pennies glimmered in a pool. A pair of trout huddled in the lee of a round rock. Their fins moved slowly as if trapped in a bowl of gelatin and their gills had lost their pink and were quivering instead of flapping. Unless there was a deep pond somewhere farther upstream they could retreat to when the ice came or make their way down to the main stem of the river, their future was no brighter than the sections of the Running R destined to be bulldozed and paved over.

Sage scrub gave way to pinyon and ponderosa pines. Something that was shades lighter than the bark was moving between two trunks. It froze. So did I. A bobcat stared back at me. But something was off. Its ear tufts were too long. So were its legs. Its tail was too short and the tip all black. The fur was more gray than buff. I couldn't see any spots.

"A lynx," I said without saying it out loud so as not to spook the creature.

I'd lived in Oregon ten years and it was my first.

Slowly, I raised the camera and brought the viewfinder to my eye. Twisting the zoom ring on the telephoto lens first and then the focus ring, I breathed in, held it, and clicked the shutter. The big cat tensed. I clicked again. It bolted. I clicked again, unsure if I'd captured any of the images, knowing I'd have to wait to get the film developed to find out.

As I returned to my pickup, I ran through what I knew about lynxes. It wasn't much. They'd migrated to Oregon from Canada and were trapped for their fur up until fifty years ago. Sightings of them were rare at best ever since the Roaring Twenties.

Seeing one put a spring in my step and got me thinking luck was going my way. I might even spot a wolf.

"G̱ooch," I said, trying to mimic Kagán's pronunciation of wolf in Tlingit. "G̱ooch naa," I said, reciting the name of her moiety.

The light was dimming as the road took a long, sweeping S-turn paralleling back-to-back bends in the river. A big black cinder cone dusted with snow that reminded me of Vinnie Valante's and Smiles Wax's overcoats lying in the back of my pickup loomed ahead. It signaled that the Cascadian chain of volcanic peaks 150 miles to the west wasn't that far away as the lava flowed.

I spotted the lineman's shack near the river. A path led to it, but I drove past before stopping. Pocketing a flashlight and grabbing my Winchester, I circled around the back to stay out of the line of fire from the door and small window beside it.

No smoke came from the stovepipe. The rear wall was cold to the touch when I palmed the clapboard siding. I pounded my fist on it, fired a round in the air, and then ran around to the front and kicked open the door.

The only greeting I got was the scurry of tiny feet and the glow of BB-sized eyes reflecting the beam of my flashlight. The eyes blinked off as the mouse scampered away. Stepping just inside the doorway, I took off my muddy boots and began searching the shack in my socks.

The interior walls were sided with lath that had been lightly plastered. They were darkened by smoke from a woodstove that stood in the middle. Areas closest to the ceiling were marred by drooping water stains, one the shape of South America, another the Indian subcontinent. Metal-framed bunk beds with sagging mattresses and no blankets lined a windowless wall.

Two ladderback chairs faced each other across a wooden table scarred from cigarette burns. A kerosene lantern with a smoke-streaked glass chimney was positioned in the middle. A battered wooden crate with "Blitz Weinhard Beer" stamped on the side and "From the West's Oldest Brewery" lettered beneath it had been shoved in the corner.

I checked for signs of recent use. A cast-iron fry pan hanging on a post was clean. The coffeepot on top of the woodstove was empty. So was a tin water bucket. I pushed down on the mattress on the bottom bunk. The springs creaked loudly and a cloud of dust rose. It was the same for the top one.

The table didn't have any dust on it. Nor did the chairs. I picked one up and examined it. The seat was worn smooth from years of jeans sliding on top. The legs were wobbly. The bottom couple of inches of the front legs were scratched as if nicked by spurs. The back creaked. I put it down and checked the other chair. It was in a little better shape, but not by much.

KT said Wilbur Pillsbury had driven up and down the road, and although he may have come inside and sat down at the table, that didn't mean he'd ever slept there. Why would he when he had a nice, clean, comfortable camper equipped with its own bed? If his killer had dragged him inside and tortured him, why weren't there any signs of a struggle or bloodstains?

"A dead end," I said to the mouse and went to put my boots back on.

Something pricked the sole of my foot before I reached them. I ran my hand across the bottom of my sock, felt a splinter, and brought it up for a look.

It wasn't a sliver of wood, but a fresh pine needle. A needle like those on an ersatz broom used to sweep footprints from patches of snow leading from a faceless and disemboweled body.

I yanked on my boots and ran outside, circling the shack in

ever-widening rings, examining the ground for footprints and drag marks. I searched nearby pines for freshly broken branches used to make a broom.

Zilch. Nothing. Nada.

The light was going out of the sky when I finally gave up. Returning to the shack to close the door, I gave it one last sweep with my flashlight. Beady eyes shone back and then the mouse scampered toward the wooden beer crate and disappeared behind it.

Why was a mouse in a place with no food on the shelves, no crumbs on the floor?

I yanked the crate aside and exposed a hole no bigger than a half dollar at the base of the wall. Dropping to my knees, I aimed the flashlight's beam. The glow from the mouse's eyes quickly blinked off as it fled between the shack's inner and outer walls from a nest made of shimmering strips of bloodstained blue nylon.

I kicked the hole to enlarge it and tore away the lath. The corner of something mottled and rubbery peeked out of the nest. I plucked it out and held it up.

It wasn't a piece of cheese the mouse had stashed. It was the lobe of an ear. Wilbur Pillsbury's ear.

31

First light was an hour shy and I was running on fumes when I rolled across the cattleguard and drove straight to the corral. Sarah whinnied the loudest to welcome the buckskin stallion home as I led Wovoka out of the trailer and turned him loose.

Following clouds of cold breath to the back door, I let myself in. November was sitting in the kitchen, the blue flame beneath the kettle the only light in the room.

"A watched pot never boils," I said.

"But an angry man does," she said.

"What did you see in dreamworld?"

"A mild man pleading for his life. An angry man take it and dance across the snow. He flew like Thunderbird, but rained fire not water. Buildings were burning."

"The Broken Wing," I said. "He dropped dynamite on it from an airplane."

"No," she said, her rheumy eyes clearing as they flashed. "It was No Mountain. It was here."

"When will it happen?"

"When the angry man's fury becomes too much to bear."

"For him or for us?"

November didn't answer, but the hiss of the gas flame and roil of the water couldn't drown out my own fury rising at the thought of someone coming to harm my family and town.

"How's Pudge?" I finally said.

"The spirit world beckons. Whether he chooses to go now or later is up to him."

"Is he well enough to hear what I learned in Idaho and Thunder Valley, what's going to happen next?"

"If it will help him choose to go later. Gemma is not ready to say goodbye. Hattie and Johnny also."

"Nor me. What about you?"

November took a deep breath. "Because I have lived in the brown world so many more years than him, I always thought I would go first and welcome him along with his wife and ancestors."

"Is that what you believe the spirit world to be?"

The old healer tsked. "The spirit world is everything and everywhere. It has no beginning, no end. My husband and daughter, Shoots While Running and Gentle Wind, are there. When I want to speak with them, all I need do is think the words and open my own ears to hear theirs. I will do the same with Pudge."

A smile crossed her lips. "Of course, he will have much to say."

"Well, he's not gone yet. There's a lot we need to do right here and now."

"Yes," she said. "Would you like coffee?"

"It's all I've been living on for days. If I cut myself shaving, I'd bleed black."

November placed the tip of her finger between my eyes. "Then rest, my son. When you awake, you will be restored."

"But I need to talk to Pudge now. I put lots in motion and they're not going to stop moving while I sleep."

"You can only defeat the angry man when you are calm in spirit and strong of mind. Go. Rest."

I was too tired to argue and headed for the bedroom. Gemma was still asleep even though life on the ranch always started by dawn. I undressed and slid into bed. If I woke her, I didn't know. I was seeing the inside of my eyelids as soon as my head hit the pillow.

The trouble was, the images playing on them were anything but peaceful.

Wilbur Pillsbury wearing his blue nylon parka was tied to a wobbly ladderback chair as Ernest Long sharpened a pearl-handle straight razor on a leather strop while Stuart Kinsey, Vinnie Valante, and Smiles Wax dressed in matching straw hats and red-striped vests stood behind him singing "By the Light of the Silvery Moon."

A huge mouse with a writhing snake for a tail crouched on its haunches and sank its yellow incisors into a human ear. A raven flew in, snatched a nose off the floor, and flew back out. A pair of lips lying on the floor wailed.

Thump, thump, thumping grew louder as Jeb Calhoun walked in circles on stumps. Nils Sandberg banged his head over and over. A bay mare carrying Jo Railsback and KT galloped across a split log bridge. Cass and Kagán danced on top of a towering totem pole crowned by a screaming Thunderbird.

The cacophony grew noisier. I tried silencing it by sticking my fingers in my ears but couldn't find them. I tried to call out but couldn't speak because I had no tongue. I tried opening my eyes but the sockets were empty.

As hands grabbed to hold me down while they cut away the rest of my face, I thrashed.

"Shh, shh, shh," whispered the mouse.

"It's only a dream, dream, dream," chanted the raven.

"It's okay, okay, okay," purred the lynx.

"I'll protect you, you, you," howled the wolf.

The wolf! I wanted to see her. Feel her soft but coarse fur. Hear her tail twitching. I sat up and opened my eyes. Gemma was sitting on the edge of the bed with her hands on my shoulders, her lips pressed to my ears.

"It's okay," she whispered. "It's only a dream."

I shook my head to clear the horrors from it and asked what time it was.

"A little after nine."

"Is Pudge awake?"

"Yes."

I kissed her, swung out of bed, and jumped in the shower and then into my clothes.

"Out of the army a decade and you still take combat showers," she said.

"Unless we're sharing one. Then it's long and slow even after the hot water runs out."

Gemma laughed. "Sounds like the bad dream you were having was like all dreams and melted away when you woke up."

"Not this one. It was too real and will become so unless we stop Kinsey and his killers. Why I need to talk to Pudge."

"He's waiting for you."

"In his bedroom?"

"No, his office. And he's wearing his badge and uniform, Bust'em be damned."

"Good, because nothing short of Pudge being Pudge will do."

My stomach was still sour from living on coffee. I ignored the pot November had left on the dining table and grabbed a piece of fry bread from the woven basket. Pudge wasn't only in uniform; his .45 was strapped on too.

"I've been on the phone with Orville while you were

catching forty," he said. "He gave me the broad brush on your visit to his house last night, but go ahead and paint the rest of the numbers. Only way we're gonna see our way through this is if we see the whole picture."

I started with my visit to the lineman's shack at the Running R and described in detail how I discovered the mouse nest and ear. When I stopped off at the ranch to collect Wovoka and the trailer, I lit out without saying a word to anyone.

"Since Bust'em banned me from the sheriff's office, I drove straight to Orville's house and asked his wife to call him. She made up an excuse and told him to come home right away. When he arrived, I told him how I discovered the split log bridge had been cut loose and what was inside the shack. I gave him the evidence and rolls of film."

Then I worked backward and described the reactions I got showing Ernest Long's photo to the folks at the Running R.

"You believe Jo and Cass have never seen him?" Pudge said.

"They could see Ernest's resemblance to Adam Railsback when I pointed it out, but they hadn't met him. Aiden knew him, all right, but he flat-out lied and said he didn't. KT? He not only remembered him, but described the plane he was flying when he brought Kinsey and two of his so-called investors to the Running R. It was a Cessna high-wing."

The sheriff coughed into a handkerchief he kept balled in his fist and then asked if it was the same plane used to bomb the Broken Wing.

"I don't have any evidence to prove it, but it's more than likely. Since it was a high-wing, all it'd take is open the window, bank the plane to get a visual, light the fuse, and drop the stick."

"Be a lot easier as a two-man job. Ernest being the pilot and a passenger playing bombardier," Pudge said.

"And I know who'd be the first in line to enlist. Smiles Wax."

"We need to find out who owns that plane and where it was

the night of the bombing. Could be Kinsey leased it. If that's the case, the pilot would've had to log every mile he flew as part of the contract."

"Orville's already doing that."

"When I was on the phone with him, he said you were betwixt and between if Aiden introduced Ernest to Stuart Kinsey to get him a job or the other way round. Kinsey using Ernest to play Aiden for a sucker."

"It's only a theory, but it fits with Kinsey's history of running scams. If he did find Ernest first, then that would be what they call a long con."

"Been reading up on swindles, have you?"

"Orville must've because that's what he said when I ran the what-ifs by him. You know, what if Kinsey starting thinking of targeting Oregon because of all the California money flowing into it. What if while doing his homework he learned about Sunriver's success and discovered Thunder Valley was ripe for the picking. What if he spotted an opening at the Running R when he found out they were facing bankruptcy. What if he came across the news that Aiden killed his father. What if he learned Adam had another family in Idaho and roped in Ernest to use as a human weapon."

"That's a helluva lot of what-ifs."

"I've had a helluva lot of time behind the wheel thinking about it while driving back and forth to the Running R and Sun Valley."

"Stuart Kinsey's a con artist. Leastways he always has been. This deal in Thunder Valley, you think it's all a con or is he really trying to develop it?"

"Not a hundred percent sure. Both come with risks. Scamming has a faster payoff, but developing isn't against the law. Either way, I think he's trying to get his hands on as much property in Thunder Valley as he can for free. You know what Mark

Twain said. 'Buy land. They're not making any more of it.' For Kinsey, stealing it is even better."

"But the background checks on his financial partners came back clean. The banker and Texas oilman are who they say they are."

"Who better to target for a con than folks with deep pockets? Kinsey hooks Symes and Parker on the idea of it becoming the next Sunriver and reels them in by taking them on a couple of site visits and meetings with architects. As long as they keep writing checks, Kinsey will keep stringing them along. If they pull out, he still has the land he conned the Railsbacks to sign over."

"Him being a leopard and can't change his spots and all." Pudge coughed. "You're pretty sure Ernest is our killer."

"For Jeb Calhoun and the cowboy who died in the bombing at the Broken Wing, no one else flies a plane."

"But why bomb it? To scare the Calhouns into selling for pennies on the dollar?"

"They were never going to sell, and Zeb won't ever now. It's sacred ground, anointed with the blood of his twin brother. No, I think Kinsey ordered it done to apply additional pressure on the Railsbacks to sign over even more land to him."

"What about Wilbur Pillsbury, Ernest kill him too?"

"Yeah."

"But torturing and cutting a man to pieces? Where'd he get that idea?"

"There were plenty of stories making the rounds in 'Nam of GIs captured in the field being tortured. Maybe Ernest had a buddy who was. Or maybe he was on the ground and saw what South Vietnamese soldiers did to guerrillas and villagers they were trying to get intel from."

"Makes me think Kinsey's been playing Ernest too. Setting him up to be the fall guy for all this."

"I still like Valante and Wax for Nils Sandberg's murder. Cleaning up for Kinsey. Not that they're above torturing someone if he ordered them to. But they wouldn't've bothered to put Pillsbury in the camper and drive across the river to dump him."

"You got an answer why Ernest did?"

"Part of it is guesswork, but it goes something like this. Ernest got what he wanted from Pillsbury. He killed him, put him in his camper, cleaned up the shack, and was going to drive it onto the Broken Wing's side of the fence to throw off suspicion. It was snowing and on the way there, he ran off the road and into the field. When he couldn't get the engine restarted, he pocketed the key, dragged Pillsbury's body out, and tried to make it look like an animal did it."

"I recollect you thought he'd stashed a horse to make a getaway."

"I was wrong about that. Another case of target fixation. The killer danced his way into the woods and brushed away his tracks, all right, but instead of continuing upriver like I thought, he walked back downriver, crossed the split log bridge, and then cut it loose to buy time."

"Son, if all this proves true, that's some mighty fine police work you've done. Like I've said before, you're a natural at this. Still wish you'd considering putting it to work sheriffing people instead of critters."

"You know I prefer working outdoors."

"But now you got a family. Who better than you to protect them from the bad guys? Other Harney County families too. They need a man like you. Deserve it."

It was an old argument and I let it go.

"The one question I don't have an answer for is what Pillsbury knew or have that Kinsey wanted so bad he ordered Ernest to torture him for it."

"Only way to find that out is to ask them," Pudge said.

"Unless Orville can figure it out from the coded map Pillsbury created."

"Even if he does, we're still gonna have to take them down. And that means doing it on our own. We can't ask that Coos County clown sitting at my desk for help because he'll tell Bust'em and Bust'em will warn Kinsey. I told Orville he also has to be careful what he says to his contact at the FBI. The Feds invented CYA."

The old sheriff grimaced as he shifted painfully. "I read Orville's report about Pillsbury. He sure doesn't strike me as the kind of man who can take a punch, much less let his ear get sliced off before giving up the goods."

"Agreed, but maybe he didn't know what he really had."

"I don't know about that. If he went to the trouble to create some kind of secret code, he must've had more than a notion what it was."

I tore off pieces of the fry bread and began chewing them one by one.

"Sorry," I said, realizing Pudge was watching me eat. "Want one?"

He waved it off. "No, but it got me thinking."

"That you're getting your appetite back?"

"Not me, but Ernest. Maybe he got hungrier as time went on working for Kinsey and figured out he was being played. He decided one piece of fry bread wasn't enough. He wanted the whole batch and Pillsbury gave him the recipe—his secret code. Pillsbury told him what it leads to, but Ernest killed him to keep him from telling anyone else. Now the tables were turned so all the fry bread was on his side."

"Kinsey finds that out, Ernest's a dead man."

"True, but Kinsey probably still thinks he's a shell shocked patsy. Ernest continued to play dumb after he got the info out of

Pillsbury. He told Kinsey Pillsbury didn't give him nothing. Then he went out and bombed the Broken Wing to show he was still willing to take orders and could be trusted."

"Right now, it doesn't matter if Ernest is playing a double-cross. It also doesn't matter if Kinsey is running a scam or doing a development deal for real. He needs Blackpowder's liquor license as another marker he can show Symes and Parker to keep them pouring in money. He needs to get rid of you and me because he knows we can't be bought like Bust'em. He already tried once by sending Vinnie Valante and Smiles Wax down to the Malheur."

"Now you think he's coming after us here?"

"I'm not the only one. November told me she saw in dream-world an angry man flying like Thunderbird and dropping fire on No Mountain and the ranch."

Pudge's shoulders stiffened. "She did, did she? Well, if I've learned anything living under the same roof as that old medicine woman all these years, it's that she sees tomorrow while I keep seeing yesterdays. It's time I open my eyes to today, starting with protecting hearth and home."

"Roger that," I said.

"I'll give Blackpowder a call so he can alert his neighbors and rustle up some ranchers to come in and defend the town. Meanwhile, there's work to be done right here to make Kinsey and his gang think twice about trespassing."

"After we do that, we need to put up the best defense there is."

"Got that right. Offense."

"Fight fire with fire," I said.

"And plenty of lead," the old lawman said.

32

A long, black V of tundra swans winged over the High Lonesome as ribbons of purples and grays striped the dusky sky. The block-long row of false-fronted buildings that lined Main Street was even darker with the exception of one. The front window of Blackpowder Smith's saloon had a cheery glow and the Open sign was lit.

Pudge and I sat in our pickups thirty yards deep in the desert scrub at the entrance to town. Orville's rig, joined by four driven by local ranchers, was similarly parked at the opposite end.

As the last of the swans passed overhead, Mars, Jupiter, Saturn, and Venus shone in a celestial parade. The planetary alignment was believed to be a good omen by stargazers, modern and ancient alike. I wished it would prove true tonight.

Minutes passed. An hour. Then two. Finally, headlights swept the darkness on the two-lane coming down from Burns. I raised my binoculars and counted three Suburbans in tight formation driving fast.

"Three rigs. Three minutes out," I said over the radio to Pudge and the others.

"Everybody get ready, but nobody moves until I say so," the old lawman said.

"You're the boss, but don't forget who's the bait," Blackpowder Smith cackled.

"Orville, any news from your buddy tracking air traffic?" Pudge asked.

"Negative. But if Ernest Long is flying at extremely low altitude, it will be very difficult, if not impossible, to detect him by radar."

"Then we do it the old-fashioned way. Everybody, clean the wax out of your ears."

The caravan approaching town suddenly slowed. My hands tightened on the wheel as my foot itched to slam the gas pedal to the floor.

"Come on, come on," I said. "Keep coming."

The brake lights on the lead vehicle suddenly flashed red as the Suburban came to a halt. The two others screeched to a stop right behind.

"They smell a trap," Pudge whispered over the radio. "Everybody hold. Don't flush 'em."

"I'm going need more cheese," Blackpowder said.

"Hang on, Black. I'll think of something," Pudge said.

"Too late. Already done it."

Music started blaring, but it wasn't coming from someone breaking radio silence by accidentally hitting the volume knob on their pickup's AM. Blackpowder's solution for adding more bait to the trap was punching the buttons on the saloon's jukebox and cranking up the volume.

I wasn't the only one who could see a bar full of folks drinking and dancing. The lead Suburban's brake lights flicked off and the rig moved forward. The two behind followed like ducklings.

As soon as the last vehicle passed in front of us, Pudge barked into his mike. "Go! Go!"

The old lawman and I hit the gas at the same time and shot through the scrub side by side, cranking our wheels onto the blacktop in sync slicker than a pair of ice skaters rounding the rink.

We hit our headlights as we roared down Main Street. Pudge also flicked on his light bar and siren. The flashing red gave the block of false-fronted buildings a hellish hue. Orville's light bar added more scarlet as he and his posse blocked off the other end.

The Suburbans slammed to a halt. After a couple of minutes, the driver's door on the middle vehicle swung open. Smiles Wax got out and opened the rear passenger door. Stuart Kinsey stepped out without so much as a glance back at Pudge and me. He walked to the front door of the saloon. Smiles opened it and followed him inside. The jukebox went silent.

Vinnie Valante got out and took up position in front of the door holding his automatic at his side, daring us to challenge him.

"Got to admit, Kinsey has stones," Pudge said.

"What do you want to do?" I said.

"Find out what cards he's holding."

The old lawman squared his short-brim Stetson, hitched his gun belt, and strode toward Blackpowder's. I grabbed the Winchester and fast-stepped to back his play.

"Get out of my way," Pudge growled at Valante.

The bandage on what was left of the heavyset gangster's ear moved back and forth. "You got no authority. You don't got shit."

Pudge spit in his eye. As Valante reflexively raised his hand to wipe his face, the old lawman's .45 came out of the holster faster than I'd ever seen him draw it. He stabbed it against Valante's gut.

"Wrong. I got this."

I wheeled around and swept the Winchester across the Suburbans. The first and third held four men each. All were pointing guns through open windows.

"Look before you leap," I said and tipped my head toward the posse's pickups.

Ranchers were standing in the beds. All were shouldering rifles aimed at the gunmen. Orville was out of his rig and wheeling toward us one-handed. The short-barreled riot gun that normally rode in a scabbard behind him was clutched in the other and pointed at Valante.

"I have him, Sheriff," the chief deputy said.

Pudge pushed past the thug and entered the saloon. Blackpowder was standing behind the bar, his sawed-off double barrel leveled at Stuart Kinsey and Smiles Wax.

"Why, howdy there, Sheriff. You too, young fella. Mr. Kinsey here was just explaining the birds and bees to me."

"That a fact," the old lawman said.

"Yep. Says he drove all the way down here to tell me his offer for my liquor license himself seeing I didn't take kindly hearing it the other day from this grinning gunsel and his chubby pal."

Kinsey gave a mock bow. "As I said, Mr. Smith, the error was mine. Business should always be conducted up close and personal. I believe the number I presented to you is more than generous."

The old codger hooted. "What's generous is me not filling you full of buckshot coming into my establishment in the dead of night with a gang of armed desperados."

"A man in my position must take measures to secure his personal safety while traveling in a land with inadequate law enforcement." He turned to Pudge. "Wouldn't you agree?"

"You look out front, you'll see we don't lack for law here in

No Mountain," the sheriff said. "And we most certainly intend to enforce it."

Kinsey sighed. "The only thing I see is a terminally ill man still trying to cling to his glory days by wearing a badge and uniform that he's no longer fit or entitled to wear."

"What I'm entitled to is the same as anyone living in Harney County. Protecting my family from swindlers and killers. Now, I'm gonna start asking questions and you're gonna start answering."

"Be my guest." Kinsey's sleek smile showed capped teeth.

"Where's Ernest Long?"

"I don't believe I've had the pleasure."

"Don't shit a shitter, Kinsey. You know him. You found him in Idaho, wound him up, and turned him loose on the Railsbacks."

"If you say so."

"I do."

"Saying and proving aren't the same thing."

"But you know what is? Ordering a killing done and doing it yourself. Both go down the same way. Murder. And they get the same penalty too. A concrete cell if you're lucky. A wooden box if you're not."

Pudge clicked his cheek. "You ordered Valante and Wax to kill Nils Sandberg and likewise Ernest Long to kill Wilbur Pillsbury. Then they're the two men who died at the Broken Wing when you had him drop dynamite on it."

Wax's fixed grin hadn't moved, but his right shoulder drooped as if readying to grab for the gun in his shoulder holster.

I aimed the Winchester at him. "I haven't forgotten about all the birds you killed at the pond. That's a federal law you broke. Trying to kill me? That's my own."

"You have a very active imagination," Kinsey said to Pudge.

"What I got is an active investigation of four dead men in my county who deserve justice. That makes them my business."

"Regional Sheriff Burton would beg to differ, I'm sure. If something were to happen to me or my associates, it will be you facing justice."

"I don't need a badge to tell me which direction the sun rises in Harney County. Your hands are dirty for all those killings. Same as their dirty for trying to con the Railsbacks and your walking checkbooks, Symes and Parker."

Kinsey's eyes narrowed. "I already warned you I'll do whatever it takes to protect my reputation. Did you forget what a lawsuit will cost you? Your ranch. Your family. Everything."

"But you forgot something. Even a con artist can be conned. All you got to do is con him into believing he's the smartest man in the room. That's what Ernest Long did to you. He told you Pillsbury never gave up what he'd discovered. But he did and so Ernest killed him. Now he's got the secret, not you."

"You have no idea what you're talking about."

"You think you're the only huckster ever come to Harney? Right behind the first wagon train that rolled in here in the 1800s was one carrying a charlatan selling snake oil."

"You're living in a fantasy world."

"I'll grant you Harney's mighty special. Spiritual? Ask the Paiutes who've lived here ten thousand years. Magical? Every damn day of the week. But fantasy? Nah. We're down to earth. What is, is. What ain't, ain't. Ernest not only has Pillsbury's secret, he's got you by the short and curlies."

Kinsey's blink was a millisecond, but it was still a blink.

"There's two ways to play this," Pudge said. "One is, you surrender and we drive you and your gang over to Klamath County. That's out of Bust'em's territory and his say isn't worth a bucket of warm spit there. They believe in justice the same way I do."

"And the second way?" Kinsey said.

"You and Wax go for your guns and then we drive your bodies to Klamath."

"I see." Kinsey glanced at his gold wristwatch. "I believe there's also a third way."

"Trying to buy me off? Save your breath."

"This." Kinsey crouched and put his hands over his ears.

A blast rocked the building and the saloon's front window exploded as a fireball brighter than the flashing red lights outside lit up the night sky.

33

———

The floor bucked like a bronco and knocked Blackpowder backward. As he stumbled, he pulled the sawed-off's trigger. Smiles Wax ducked the blast while drawing his semiautomatic and got off a shot at the old saloonkeeper who slumped behind the bar. Then the killer shifted his aim and shot Pudge. The sheriff let out an oomph and fired his gun while falling.

I took a bead on Wax but saw he was wearing a new smile— the one drilled in his fixed grin by Pudge's .45. As he collapsed, I swung the Winchester at Stuart Kinsey, but he'd jumped through the empty window frame as soon as Blackpowder had fired.

The right side of Pudge's uniform was already dark with blood when I got to him.

"Just a scratch," he wheezed. "Go after Kinsey."

"He's not going anywhere. I got to apply pressure here."

I grabbed his hands, placed his palms against his side, then put mine over his and pressed.

He pushed mine away. "I got terminal cancer. You think I'm worried about a gunshot? Go get Kinsey. That's an order, son."

"Yes, sir."

I picked up the Winchester and ducked out the missing window while the ranchers and Kinsey's hired gunslingers were trading shots. A gunman swung his gun at me and fired. He missed, but I didn't, and what was left of his forehead turned as red as the flames burning the dynamited building next door.

The explosion had rocked Orville's wheelchair, forcing him to drop the riot gun he'd been holding on Valante to keep from tipping over. The Oliver Hardy lookalike had been thrown backward against the wall, but was now raising his automatic at the chief deputy.

"Freakin' cripple," he sneered.

The bang of the gun was loud and seemed to freeze time, but then it sped up as Valante yelped and Orville hit the button that fired a second round from the concealed 9mm attached to his chair. A bullet for each knee. Valante's toothbrush mustache spread as he screamed in pain and sat down hard.

"Who is the cripple now?" Orville said as he rolled up and cuffed the thug.

"Pudge, Blackpowder. Both down inside," I yelled. "I'm going after Kinsey."

"Ernest Long is circling for another bomb drop," he yelled back.

"He flies low enough, I'll say hello." And brandished my rifle at the sky.

I looked up Main Street, knowing Kinsey would run away from gunfire. Pudge's pickup roared to life. The tires squealed as it U-turned and sped north on the two-lane. I ran to my rig to give chase, but the whine of an airplane stopped me.

The glow from the burning building illuminated a high-wing Cessna. It was coming in low. I started shooting at it, but ducked when a building down the block blew. Glass and boards went flying. More flames licked the sky.

The plane went into a steep climb and executed a turn to come around for another run. I braced myself and readied to fire. That's when I heard its engine echo.

Only it wasn't an echo. It was a second plane chasing the high-wing.

The light from the burning buildings illuminated both planes as they pulled up in tandem and roared past. The second one was Gemma's, and, as we'd planned, Nagah was flying and she was shooting.

Either Ernest decided he didn't need to convince Kinsey he was still a patsy and risk his life getting shot out of the sky while dropping more dynamite or he'd figured out it was him making a getaway in Pudge's pickup. He aimed the Cessna north and flew after it.

I dove into the front seat of my rig and radioed Gemma. "Don't follow him, I know where he's going. Circle back and land as close as you can. Pudge's been shot. Need to get him to the hospital ASAP."

The ranchers had gotten the upper hand on the hired gunslingers. Any that were still alive were being trussed up like calves by cowboys who were old hands at tie-down roping. I climbed through the missing window into Blackpowder's.

Orville was leaning over Pudge and pressing on his side.

"How's he doing?" I said.

The chief deputy frowned.

"I'm fine," the old lawman huffed. "Kinsey dead?"

"Drove off in your pickup. Ernest is flying after him."

"Well, hell, son, what are you standing here for? Go get 'em."

A moan and a cuss sounded from behind the bar. Boots scraped and bones creaked and Blackpowder pulled himself upright.

"You hit?" I said.

"Winged is all, but this'll help."

The old codger pulled a bottle of whiskey from behind the bar and guzzled. Then he looked at the floor where Smiles Wax was staring sightlessly at the ceiling.

"That's one mess I'll be happy to mop up."

"Gemma's landing," I said to Pudge. "We need to get you to her plane."

"It will be faster if he rides," Orville said.

I hoisted the sheriff and sat him on the chief deputy's lap. Orville held him fast while I wheeled them up the street.

Nagah had already turned the plane around when we got to it. Gemma was standing beside the door. "Put him in the back seat. We'll fly straight to the ER."

The old sheriff broke free of Orville's encircling arms and grabbed my shirtfront. "Where's Kinsey and Long going?"

"The Running R," I said.

"Then that's where we're going."

Gemma put her hands on her hips. "No way. You need surgery or you'll bleed out."

"You're a doctor and the plane's got a first aid kit. Patch me up while we fly."

"But I'm a horse doctor."

"And a damn good one. Come on, time's a-wasting. Let's go."

Gemma threw up her hands. "Stubborn old fool." She shot me a look. "And you're no better."

"Yeah, but what I said about this being good medicine? November said it too."

Orville took my arm. "Here. Take this." He handed me a large sheet of folded paper.

"What is it?"

"It is my preliminary mapping of the locations on the ranch that Pillsbury obfuscated with his secret code."

"Did you make any sense of them?"

"Not beyond identifying where they are. I am still working on what they are, but perhaps you can find out."

"I'll try. You'll get the firefighting going here?"

"Affirmative. With luck, we can stop the flames from consuming any more buildings."

Once Pudge was loaded, Gemma got straight to work cleaning and dressing the gunshot. I climbed into the seat next to Nagah. He chanted a prayer in Numu as he worked the rudder pedals, pushed the throttle, and pulled back the yoke.

In seconds, the plane was airborne and hurtling toward a showdown in Thunder Valley.

34

The planets were still parading in a line, but even those celestial radiances didn't make landing on a dirt strip for the first time any easier. Nagah had followed the two-lane up from No Mountain and counted off roads leading to the ranches on the riverside. When he found the right one, he banked, circled, and came back to make his approach.

"You got this," Gemma said.

"I know," he said, "but everyone should brace in case of cows."

As he started the descent, I watched the needle on the altimeter plummet like a floor indicator on an old-fashioned elevator with a snapped cable.

"Now!" I shouted into the radio's mike.

Drivers waiting on the four sides of the landing strip turned on their headlights. They helped more than Mars and Venus and all the rest.

The plane's wheels hit the ground, bounced once, twice, and kept on rolling. Nagah taxied to the end where a man with a slouch hat and ZZ Top beard waited beside his pickup.

"Welcome back to the Broken Wing," Zeb Calhoun said.

"Thanks for answering your radio and arranging the welcoming party," I said.

"You got my attention when you said you knew who killed Jeb, may he rest in peace."

I helped Pudge down. Gemma climbed out right behind him.

"Good evening, Zebadiah," she said. "Remember me?"

"How could I forget? You saved half our cow-calf pairs back in '74." He nodded at Pudge. "Sheriff, whatever you need, you got. I only ask to be part of it."

"You already are," he said.

Nagah joined us. Zeb sized him up. "That was some fancy flying in the dead of night. You're old Tuhudda Will's grandson, aren't you? He show you the way?"

"As always," Nagah said.

Pudge was holding his side, but his meaty palm couldn't conceal the bloody shirt and the bulge of the wound dressing beneath it. Zeb registered it, but didn't comment.

"Here's what we got," the old sheriff said. "The man who dropped dynamite on your spread did the same to No Mountain a bit ago. He flew to Thunder Valley and landed next door. Another man's there too. He's the one behind all the killings."

"Stuart Kinsey," I said.

"Damn carpetbagger," Zeb said. "It's all about the money, ain't it? Taking our land."

"That's right," Pudge said. "But it gets a might complicated."

"How's that?"

"The pilot is Adam Railsback's son, but Jo isn't his mother."

"You don't say? That means he's at the Running R, but she sure didn't invite him."

I nodded. "Likewise Kinsey."

"You landing here instead of there means you're fixing to be uninvited guests too." Zeb scratched his considerable beard.

"Saddling up and riding over there likely get most of us shot. Old Great Grandpappy Railsback built on the high ground for a reason. I know for a fact they got everything round it wired with flood lights. Pick us off at night easy as in daytime, they want."

"We're planning on taking a different approach," I said.

"Drop dynamite on 'em like they done us?"

"A bit more subtle considering there are innocent people inside."

We explained our plan. Zeb did a lot of beard-scratching as he listened and then called a man over.

"Saddle four horses for our friends. Everybody else, check your irons for full loads and wait in your rigs for me."

Pudge, Gemma, Nagah, and I mounted up and rode into the dark following the trail that I'd taken from the Broken Wing to the Running R the night of the big storm. When we reached a fork, I reined to a stop.

"This is where we part company. The Running R's landing strip is that way. After you disable Ernest's plane so nobody can make a getaway, there's a dirt road that'll take you straight to the stable. Zeb and his men will block the ranch's entrance at the two-lane to make sure Bust'em and any flunkeys he brings with him don't get in and no one gets out. See you in one hour."

"Don't be late," Gemma said and blew a kiss.

Nagah and I cut back to the Calhouns' bridge, crossed the river, and rode through the woods where Zeb and Jeb had gotten the drop on me. The planets were still lighting the way as we jumped the fence between the two ranches and found the trail that led back to the river and the ford I'd seen but hadn't crossed.

When we reached it, I held up. "It's fast water, but looked doable when I first spotted it. Horses won't need to swim. Just trust them."

"I will trust Grandfather more," Nagah said.

I urged my horse forward. He balked at first, but after some tongue clucking and a pat on the withers and an attaboy, he stepped in, held his head high, and kept on stepping.

Nagah's mare whinnied and started crow hopping. It was a surefire way of getting knocked off her feet, but then the young Paiute started singing to her. The tune was calmer than the rushing water and she quieted down and followed my horse.

When we reached the other side, we paused to give them time to settle.

"The ranch house is up the hill," I whispered. "We can ride most of the way."

"I can see it in here." Nagah tapped his heart.

I checked my field watch. "Ten minutes. Let's go."

The horses made short work of the climb up from the river. We dismounted and hitched them to a tree and continued on foot.

The lights were on at the rear of the house as well as in the bedrooms upstairs. Either my eyes were playing tricks on me or a full-grown she-wolf really was standing in the window of Kagán's room. We quickly crossed the backyard and pressed ourselves against the wall.

"Hold, hold, hold," I whispered.

A gunshot split the silence. Footsteps sounded in the house. Voices shouted. Someone was yelling out front. Someone started pounding on the heavy front door.

I reached for the back door, opened it, and stepped into the kitchen. Nagah did too. I held up my fist.

"Who's out there? What's going on?" a voice I didn't recognize shouted from inside the house.

"It's KT," the wrangler called from outside. "Got me some intruders. Shot one."

More voices sounded. The heavy front door opened. As it

did, I pushed the door to the darkened dining room open a crack. It was empty. Nagah and I slipped inside.

Ernest Long was in the entryway holding a gun. KT was holding one too. Gemma was holding up Pudge between the pair. The dressing on the wound in his side was missing and the bullet hole oozed fresh blood.

"Who the hell are they?" Ernest said.

"The sheriff and his daughter," KT said, holstering his six-shooter. "They was skulkin' outside the stable. He went for his gun and I drew mine. T'were fair 'n square. No backshootin'. Got him in the side there."

Jo cried out from the living room. "This is madness!"

"Now we got us a party," Ernest crowed. "Bring them in here."

"You should've kept dropping dynamite," Stuart Kinsey said as they entered. "We wouldn't have such a mess if you'd followed my instructions."

"Shut up!" Ernest said.

Pudge was shoved onto the couch. He let out an oomph louder than he had at Blackpowder's saloon.

Gemma said, "Get your hands off me."

Ernest laughed as he pushed her down next to him.

I gripped my sidearm and burst in. Nagah was right behind me shouldering the Winchester.

Jo, Aiden, and Cass were tied to chairs. The brothers were both gagged. Kinsey stood with his back to the fireplace, a silver automatic in his hand. KT's eyes were blank slates when they met mine.

At the sound of our entrance, Ernest Long leapt behind Jo and put a straight razor against her throat. I kept my gun aimed at him while Nagah covered Kinsey.

"Who the hell are you?" Ernest said.

"The law," I said.

"I thought he was the sheriff?"

"I'm a different kind."

"Drop your gun or I'll slit her throat."

"Then you'll go down for another murder. Drop the razor."

"No, you drop your gun. I'm warning you."

"I was warned by worse in Vietnam."

"You were in 'Nam?"

I nodded. "Sergeant Nick Drake. First Cav."

"I was there too. Air First Cav. Warrant Officer Ernest Long."

"A Headhunter," I said.

"Roger that, Sarge."

"I met your mom, Connie," I said, softening my tone. "Sister too. Pauline. They're worried about you. They said you didn't leave the war behind."

"Well, they shouldn't be. They should be thanking me. I'm doing this for them. Get us what my father would've given us if these people hadn't killed him and stolen it."

He held the straight razor closer to Jo's neck.

"Your father's shooting was an accident," Pudge said.

"No, it wasn't. You're in on it too."

KT was watching under the brim of his pinch crown hat. He took the cloth bag of tobacco out of his shirt pocket, sprinkled some into a paper, and rolled himself a smoke. Cass was trying to yell through the gag. He bucked the chair he was tied to. Aiden was dazed. Blood trickled from the side of his head where he'd been pistol-whipped.

I said to Ernest, "You want what's on the map Pillsbury gave you, don't you?"

"How do you know about that?"

"Did he tell you what's there? Why Stuart Kinsey's so hell-bent on stealing this land from the Railsbacks? Kinsey's playing you for a sucker, tricking you into doing all his dirty work for him."

"That's a damn lie," Kinsey said. "I don't know what he's talking about, Ernest. I swear. I'm trying to build a resort here. I'm paying you a very generous salary, and don't forget the percentage of the profits I promised you."

"You're running a scam like you've always done ever since Montclair," I said. "Scamming the Railsbacks, scamming Symes and Parker, and scamming Ernest here too."

"Don't listen to him," Kinsey said to Ernest. "He's lying. We have nothing to worry about. I have Regional Sheriff Burton in my pocket. He's our free ticket out of here. You'll see."

"Bust'em," Pudge spat. "You just admitted he's in cahoots with you. We all heard it. He's going down and he's going down hard. You're going to jail too. Vinnie Valante's already there. Smiles Wax? He's in hell."

I turned back to Ernest. "Did Pillsbury tell you why he mapped all those locations? What's in them?"

"What if he did?"

"Then you'll know for sure Kinsey's lying to you. What did Pillsbury say?"

"Treasure. Treasure without measure. Those were his exact words." Ernest's eyes grew shiny and wide. "Like, like, veins of gold as wide as rivers. Silver ones too. Opals big as fists. Diamonds the size of boulders."

"See? Kinsey's been using you from the start to help him scam your half-brothers out of their land so he can keep all that treasure for himself."

"They're not my brothers!" Ernest yelled.

"Yeah, they are."

"And I'm your sister," Kagán said. She entered from the dining room wearing the wolfskin as a cape. Her face tattoos and ivory piercing gleamed.

Ernest recoiled. "Who are you?"

"Kagán. Your father raped my mother when he was in Alaska. Did he rape yours too?"

Cass went from trying to yell through his gag to gagging on it. He went limp and stopped bucking.

Jo drew in her breath sharply and expelled it in a long, mournful cry. "Adam, Adam. What have you done to us?"

"My father ... my father was an honorable man!" Ernest screamed. "She ... she's the whore." He pressed the straight razor and a line of blood glistened on Jo's neck.

KT had the hand-rolled between his lips and struck a wooden match with his left thumbnail. As it flared, he drew his six-shooter and fired once, twice. It was back in the holster before Ernest Long hit the floor with a bullet between his eyes and Stuart Kinsey crashed backward into the fireplace with one in his heart.

The cowboy's bowed legs carried him across the floor in two strides as he picked up the straight razor that had clattered to the floor and cut the ties around Jo's wrists. He pulled her upright and she buried her face in his chest.

"It's okay, Jo," he said as he rubbed her back. "Ever'thin's gonna be Jake now."

He looked at me. "Sorry 'bout your plan, podner, but a man's only got so much patience. And, well, devil's right hand, you know."

35

When dawn broke, the skies over Thunder Valley were free of clouds. Black turned to gray to purple to red to orange to blue. Birds greeted the big yellow sun with song and the smell of coffee brewing wafted from the Running R's kitchen.

Pudge was lying on the couch, a throw blanket pulled up to his ashen chin, a fresh dressing on the bullet hole made by Smiles Wax.

"We can't wait any longer," Gemma was telling him. "We need to get you to the hospital."

"Give Orville and Wakefield another minute," he said and stifled a cough. "They need to wrap this up and I got to make sure they do it right so when Bust'em tries to go after them, we can turn it back on him and prove he's as guilty as Kinsey."

The two deputies had arrived earlier to investigate the deaths of Ernest Long and Stuart Kinsey and finalize the four murder cases. After taking statements and loading the bodies into his rig, Orville came back inside to say they were finished. I beckoned him to the table to take a look at the map he'd made of Wilbur Pillsbury's coded locations.

"Can you make any sense of it?"

"I previously compared it with USGS topographical maps and ones from the Forest Service, but I still need to cross-check it with old land survey maps," he said. "I will do that using my computer when I return to the office."

"But what's your gut tell you?"

"It appears they correspond to random land features."

"Such as?"

"The river. Bends in it. Hills. Cinder cones. Those sort of things."

"Not veins of gold or heaps of diamonds?"

"From what you told me, it sounds as if Ernest Long was unable to discern that Pillsbury was speaking metaphorically when he called it a treasure without measure."

Nagah and Kagán came in from the kitchen where they'd been talking for hours. The Tlingit woman carried a cup of broth to Pudge while Nagah handed me one filled with coffee. He looked at the map with the spots Orville had marked. Then he closed his eyes, opened them, and looked again.

"Kagán," he said softly. "Have you seen this?"

"What is it?" she said.

"It's a map of the ranch," I said. "The marked spots are locations that Wilbur Pillsbury concealed from Stuart Kinsey using a secret code."

Like Nagah had done, Kagán looked at the map, closed her eyes, then looked again. She traced the locations with her fingertip, moving from one spot to the next without lifting it.

"Oh my," Orville said. "I never thought of that." He handed her a pencil.

She connected the dots and shaded in the outline. The shape was as plain as day.

"Shangukeidí," she said and bowed her head.

"Thunderbird," Nagah said.

"A treasure without measure," I said to Kagán. "You told Pillsbury about the legend. He must've found something at each spot while doing his surveying that proved the ancient Tlingit were here. Remnants of a totem, a clan house, a firepit, old tools. He realized it was worth more to your people than any resort that could ever be built on top of them."

"They were placed to pay homage to Shangukeidí for teaching them the lesson about vengeance and justice," she said. "All these years later, it proved true again. Vengeance didn't bring down Stuart Kinsey and Ernest Long. Justice for Wilbur Pillsbury and the others did."

"Do you want to see Thunderbird from the air?" Nagah said.

"I'd love that," she said.

"Take the high-wing," Gemma said. "I loosened the ignition wire, but it's easy to fix. I'll fly Pudge to the ER in our plane."

Kagán was still wearing the wolfskin as a cape. She said something to Nagah in Tlingit. He rolled up the bearskin. KT gave them a ride to the high-wing and then came back and took Pudge, Gemma, and me to the Broken Wing's airstrip.

"You think the Running R will make it?" I said to him as we shook hands.

"Cowboyin's hard. So's ranchin'. But hard work ain't no reason to quit," he said. "See you round, podner."

We took off and caught up to the high-wing circling over Thunder Valley. Gemma banked the plane so we could see the ground. The cinder cone near the linesman's shack where Pillsbury was murdered came into view. It was the shape of Thunderbird's beaked head. The spirit bird's wings spread the breadth of the valley and the body tapered to a tail that was right over the ranch house at the Running R.

"Look," Gemma said. "Nagah has turned the plane around. He and Kagán are flying north."

"Where does he think he's going?" I said.

"Where he's been headed all along. He told me he had a vision the day Tuhudda died. When the North Star and the Light from the north meet, they'll join together to help all Native people find their way."

Nagah waggled the plane's wings and soon it was but a silver speck in the sky.

Pudge was riding in the back seat and had been quiet the whole time. As we gave one last look at Thunderbird and turned south for Burns, he finally spoke.

"Take me home. I'm not going to the hospital."

"You have to," Gemma said. "You've lost too much blood. You need a transfusion. You probably have an infection too. You need surgery, antibiotics. A human doctor, not a horse doctor. You'll mend; you'll see."

"No, I see things pretty clearly," the old lawman said, his weakened voice rising to compete with the drone of the plane's engine. "The only thing I need is to go home. See my grandkids. See November. See your mother. She's been waiting on me a long time and I don't aim to make her wait another month or so while I get weaker and sicker and end up in the same place."

"But—"

He leaned forward and put his hand on her shoulder. "The doctor in Bend told me the other day what I've known all along. Take me home, darling."

We flew the rest of the way in silence as the sun shone brighter and the late fall landscape couldn't make up its mind if it was winter or spring.

When we landed, Hattie and Johnny came running to greet us. Pudge found the strength to take them both by the hand and walk to the house as if nothing was wrong. He was telling them some kind of tall tale, because Hattie was giggling and Johnny laughing. Gemma walked beside them, smiling through her tears.

I busied myself tying down the plane and putting the chocks against the wheels. It gave me time to try to come to grips with what was happening, what Kagán had signaled when she came to Harney County, and what November had confirmed: The only constant in life is change. It was true with the weather. It was true with the seasons. And it was true with humans too.

I had seen a lot of men die in my lifetime. Both in Vietnam and in Harney County. Some while standing beside me, some by my hand. It never got easier, not even with the evil ones who deserved it. I'd mourned my mother's and father's deaths the only way I knew how at the time. I'd mourned the deaths of the men in my squad by trying to join them through drug use. I'd mourned Tuhudda's in the spiritual way of his people. But when it came time to mourn Pudge's, I wasn't sure how I would do it. All I knew was, it would hurt.

By the time I got to the house, November was sitting in a rocker placed in front of Pudge's office. The door was closed. She was rocking and humming and her eyes were open, but what she was seeing wasn't me or anything inside the house.

Gemma was sitting on our bed thumbing through a family photo album, tears glistening in her eyes, a lump in her throat. "It goes by too fast," she said. "It goes by too fast."

I sat down and put my arm around her. When she paused at a snapshot of Pudge with Hattie, Johnny, and her, I said, "But, see, the love goes on forever."

Day turned into evening. November kept rocking. I made supper, and as we ate, Gemma and I told the kids what was happening. Tears turned into remember whens and then we all went to bed, lulled to sleep by the sound of the rockers creaking.

In the morning when the first beams of light found their way through our bedroom window and danced on the quilt, silence woke me. It woke Gemma too. The chair had stopped rocking.

"All is well," November said. "Pudge has made the journey.

Henrietta welcomed him home. Tuhudda did too. He is with his ancestors, his friends, the soldiers he served with in the war. He is there. He is everywhere."

November put her arms out for Gemma as I opened the door to the office and closed it behind me. The old lawman was seated at his desk, his head resting on his chest as if he'd fallen asleep doing the paperwork he'd always detested.

Pudge's short-brim Stetson was hanging on the back of the chair, his holstered .45 too. He'd unpinned his seven-point gold star and placed it on the desk. Next to it was a handwritten note.

Son,

Ten years ago you came to Harney County looking for salvation. The people, the land, the wildlife, Gemma, November, and the kids helped you find it. Now, it's time you helped them. Election for sheriff is coming up in a year. I've been doing some polling since I got the cancer and knew running wasn't in the cards for me. Everyone agrees you're the right man for the job. Orville said he's never wanted it, rather stick with computers and forensics and such.

These past few days sealed the deal on my thinking. You were like a dog on a bone working this case. Wouldn't let go no matter how often and hard you got kicked. Look how it turned out. The good guys won.

I know what you're thinking. You like working alone. You had your fill leading men in Vietnam and blame yourself for how it turned out. True, not everyone's cut out to lead, but you are. I know it. You answered the call once. It's time you answered it again. Harney County needs you.

Here's all you need to know about sheriffing. This badge? You got to want it to wear it. You got to earn it to keep it.

Ask your heart and you'll know what to do. Ask Gemma, although I already know what her answer will be.

Pudge

I put the letter and badge in the top drawer and went out. Gemma and November were still embracing.

I hugged them both and then said, "Let's go for a ride."

"I'd like that," Gemma said.

"I will take care of Pudge," November said.

We went to the stable and saddled Wovoka and Sarah. We didn't need to ask each other where we were going. The buckskin stallion and sorrel mare knew too. They climbed the trail behind the ranch to the rise with its 360-degree view.

As we sat the horses and admired the wide open spaces, I questioned if I could give all that up. To trade the freedom of working outdoors on my own for the politics and paperwork that came with sheriffing. To ride a desk instead of Wovoka. To have to deal with courts and judges and reporters. To answer to the state attorney general and a regional sheriff too.

I pictured Bust'em Burton. But it won't be you.

"Who 'won't be you'?" Gemma said.

"What?" I said.

"You were talking out loud."

"I was? Just thinking to myself is all."

"About what Pudge asked you to do. Run for sheriff. Make sure Bust'em doesn't get away with what he did."

"Pudge told you?"

"He's my father; he didn't need to say it. But there's a bigger reason for running than Bust'em."

"What?"

"All that." Gemma swept her hand across the horizon. "So, what's it going to be, yes or no?"

I looked down at the ranch. Hattie and Johnny were walking toward the stable to do their morning chores before breakfast and school. Up the gravel drive and across the cattleguard, the road led to the two-lane north to Burns and Thunder Valley.

I could see No Mountain. Like old teeth, two of the false-front buildings on Main Street were blackened stumps, but teams of townspeople and ranchers were busy clearing debris. The rebuilding had begun. Just past town was the old lineman's shack with his crooked stovepipe that had been my first home in Harney County. Beyond it, Malheur Lake shimmered.

To the southeast, the last remaining leaves on the aspen trees streaked the canyons climbing Steens Mountain in copper and gold. Splashes of purple still showed in the sea of sagebrush that lapped at its base. A herd of pronghorn grazed on an island of tall grass while a northern harrier hovered above. The big blue sky went on and on.

The old sheriff had loved those things. Lived for them. Fought for them. Died for them. He was as much a part of the High Lonesome as they were and always would be.

It was a good reason, a true reason, to say yes.

ABOUT THE AUTHOR

Dwight Holing is the award-winning author of twenty books, including two bestselling mystery series: the Nick Drake Novels and the Jack McCoul Capers.

His Nick Drake mysteries have won the Silver Falchion Award for Best Western, the CLUE Award for Best Mystery & Suspense, and the Laramie Award for Best Novel with Western, First Nations, and Americana Themes. His short fiction was awarded the Arts & Letters Prize for Fiction.

Dwight Holing is a member of Mystery Writers of America, Western Writers of America, and Sisters in Crime where he serves on the board of directors of its Capital Crimes chapter. He lives beside a coastal river in California with his wife and two dogs who'd rather swim than walk.

ACKNOWLEDGMENTS

I'm indebted to many people who helped in the creation of *The Thunder Head*. As always, my family provided support throughout the research and writing process.

I'm especially grateful to my advance reader team who read early drafts and gave me very helpful feedback. They include Gene Ammerman, Jeffrey Miller, Kenneth Mitchell, John Onoda, Haris Orkin, and Leslie Wood.

Thank you Emma Moylan for proofreading and copyediting. Kudos to design artist-extraordinaire Rob Williams for designing and creating the cover.

I offer my respect to the Central Council of the Tlingit and Haida Indian Tribes of Alaska. The Central Council's mission is to preserve the Tribes' sovereignty, enhance economic and cultural resources, and promote self-sufficiency and self-governance for its citizens.

I also offer respect to the Burns Paiute Indian Tribe of Oregon, and the Klamath Tribes, whose mission is to protect, preserve and enhance the spiritual, cultural and physical values and resources of the Klamath, Modoc and Yahooskin Peoples by maintaining the customs and heritage of their ancestors.

Any errors, regrettably, are my own.

GET A FREE BOOK

Thank you for reading *The Thunder Head*. Reviews are the lifeblood of books so please leave one on the retailer's site.

If you belong to a book club, consider encouraging your fellow members to choose *The Thunder Head* or any of the other Nick Drake mysteries for discussion. Contact Dwight Holing directly if you'd like him to join your club's meeting in person or via Zoom to talk about the book, the series, and his writing process. His contact information is on his website where you can subscribe to his free newsletter where he posts information about the crime fiction world plus upcoming book tours and events.

Sign up for his newsletter to get a free book and be the first to learn about the next Nick Drake Mystery as well as receive news about crime fiction and special deals.

Visit dwightholing.com/free-book. You can unsubscribe at any time.

ALSO BY DWIGHT HOLING

The Nick Drake Novels

The Sorrow Hand (Book 1)

The Pity Heart (Book 2)

The Shaming Eyes (Book 3)

The Whisper Soul (Book 4)

The Nowhere Bones (Book 5)

The Forever Feet (Book 6)

The Demon Skin (Book 7)

The Broken Blood (Book 8)

The Thunder Head (Book 9)

The Yellow Hair (Book 10)

The Jack McCoul Capers

A Boatload (Book 1)

Bad Karma (Book 2)

Baby Blue (Book 3)

Shake City (Book 4)

Novels

Hard Blue Empty: A Mystery

Short Story Collections

California Works

Over Our Heads Under Our Feet